In memory of the incomparable John D. Shea

"Let the future tell the truth, and evaluate each one according to his work and accomplishments. The present is theirs; the future, for which I have really worked, is mine."

Nikola Tesla

"And the fourth angel poured out his bowl on the sun, and it was given power to scorch the people with fire. And the people were scorched with intense heat, and they cursed the name of God, who had authority over these plagues, yet they did not repent and give Him glory..."

Revelations 16:8 - 9

Contents

Prologue 7

God's country 12

One of nature's great mysteries 18

Aye aye, commander 21

For emergencies only 27

Konnichiwa! 34

The magnitude of your impending good fortune 40

Freedom for the pike means death for the minnows ... 46

A Handful of Dust 56

Watch where you put your hands 65

Tanto nomini nullum par elogium 75

Bingo! 83

A gift from a grateful nation 91

Sometimes the quickest path is through the mud 106

A nice day for an apocalypse 121

Atlas Shrugged 136

No harm, no foul 148

Time will tell 159

Smoking up with Peter the Great 166

It's Snowing in Cambodia! 182

Vacation is over 190

No going back 194

Oh captain, my captain! 200

Oblivion on an empty stomach 210

Deeper, deeper 218

The future is bright 225

Epilogue 232

Prologue

Peenemünde, Germany. October, 1942

The intemperate jangle of the telephone disturbs the man from his silent world of trigonometric calculations and parabolic functions. He contemplates the device with distaste as it rings a second time. No good could come of this. Reluctantly, he picks up the receiver and holds it to his ear.

"Schafer."

An unfamiliar female voice responds. "Captain Schafer? This is Stephanie, from Director Herzog's office. The Director would like to have a word with you. Now. Could you come to his office?"

"The Director? Of course. Shall I inform Colonel…"

"There is no need. Come at once." Her voice is calm, poised, mellifluous.

"Of course."

"Heil Hitler."

Thankfully, he has not yet replaced the receiver in its hook. "Heil Hitler," he murmurs, quickly.

He gazes out the window in the newly reclaimed silence. The scudding gray Baltic skies are already darkening, though it is not yet five o' clock. In the distance, a lighthouse blinks its warning light out toward roaring, tumultuous waves. Absentmindedly he touches the lone framed photograph that rests on his desk: a blonde woman, possessed of an uncertain smile, heavy with child. He rises from his chair and straightens the collar of his uniform as best he can by the vague reflection cast in the window. He places a notebook and pen into his briefcase, and exits the office.

It is a lengthy walk to the Director's office, entailing two flights of stairs. People mostly pass one another in silence, the only sound the gentle slap of patent leather shoes on the tiled floor. Several colleagues note his path with quizzical expressions. He nods to those with whom he has at least passing familiarity. The Institute is compartmentalized, and fraternization between programs is not encouraged. A grave error, in his opinion.

He arrives at the wooden door with an opaque, frosted glass window. He taps lightly on the glass and opens the door. An attractive blonde woman regards his entry with wide blue eyes. She wears little makeup: there is a war on, after all. She rises from her desk – considerably bigger than his, he notes wryly, and adorned with several telephones – and offers her hand. He takes it. Her hand is cool, her grip firm.

"Captain Schafer. Thank you for coming so quickly. Follow me."

Without waiting for a reply, she turns and walks toward an imposing oak door at the back of the room, heels tapping sharply on the wooden floor. She raps firmly on the door. The man does not hear a response but, satisfied, she opens the door and motions for him to enter. He walks through, nodding thanks.

The director is a squat but solid man, gray tints in his hair and sagging jowls signaling the imminent approach of his fifties. He gazes contemplatively at a map of Europe and north Africa that adorns nearly an entire wall, defensive lines, vectors of attack and division insignia denoting the disposition and activity of Reich forces, their allies, and various adversaries. The man salutes.

"Director. You called for me."

"Yes, Captain. At ease." He returns the salute carelessly, his attention shifting immediately back to the map.

"Healthy advances everywhere, eh Captain? Wouldn't you say?"

"Yes, sir. Certainly. Operation Barbarossa surpassed all expectations. We are winning on all fronts."

"All fronts." The director lets the words roll around his mouth, considering them. "All fronts, indeed. And there are many fronts. Too many. Those damnable Japanese moved too quickly with the Americans. They will appear in force, sooner or later. And we are not ready."

The man remains silent. A clock ticks, loud in the sudden stillness. Even in a place relatively insulated from politics as The Institute, this is not a healthy topic of conversation.

After a pause, the Director sits behind his vast desk, spotlessly clean. He motions for the man to sit as well. He does, sitting forward and erect, eschewing the padded comfort of the chair.

"Captain, your background is in aeronautical engineering and automated calculation systems, yes?"

"Yes, sir. I'm currently working on…"

He waves his hand dismissively. "I know what you're working on. It's my job to know."

"Of course, sir."

"I am moving you to the Helios Program." He acknowledges the man's failed attempt to mask his reaction with a slight smile. "You are skeptical about this program. Publicly skeptical." He brushes away emerging protests. "Normally I do not encourage this type of dissent in the middle of the town square, as it were. However, in this case I agree with you. The Sun Gun, or whatever romantic name they have attached to it, is pure folly. It cannot work. However…"

He opens a drawer in his desk and pulls out a file, shuffling through its contents. "Something has come in. From America. New York City, of all places. They say it could solve the otherwise fatal problems of this program, problems any schoolboy could have seen months ago. I suspect they are grasping at straws, since they know they are close to cancelation. I would like someone with a fresh set of eyes - a rigorously skeptical set of eyes - to look at this material. How is your English?"

"Good, sir. I can navigate professional documents with ease."

"Mostly it's in English, some of it seems to be in Serbo-Croatian, or whatever they call it. Assuming your Serbian is non-existent…?"

The man's mouth suddenly goes dry as he considers the ramifications of these two improbable data points, and their limited possibilities for potential confluence. He wets his lips with a discreet flick of his tongue. "Yes, sir. That is correct."

"We have one fellow here from the technical university of Belgrade. A genius physicist, by all accounts. We managed to get hold of him before the Ustasi ripped his eyeballs out for soup, or whatever they had planned. A bunch of goddamn psychopaths, if you ask me. Their antics make the Gestapo blush. Anyway, he will assist you with translation if needed."

"Yes, sir. Thank you, sir."

The Director drums his fingers on the desk, leans back in his chair and sighs. "I am deeply skeptical of this, Captain… but we will need a new generation of weapons, and quickly, if we intend to confront the Americans. I fought against them in the last war. They start slowly, but once they put their mind to something, it's terrifying. We are stronger than we were a generation ago, but so are they. I do not want to leave any stone unturned. You have three months to tell me if this is workable or not. We cannot afford to spend time and effort chasing shadows and dreams."

"Yes sir. Of course."

"The material is being brought to your office now." With a resigned nod he waves the man out of his office. His assistant escorts him to the door, thrusting a sheaf of papers into his hand.

"Your new orders, Captain. Good luck."

His feet hardly seem to touch the floor as he strides hurriedly back to his office, orders gripped tightly in his hand. His pulse is elevated, and he can feel each heartbeat as a hot thud in the veins of his temples. As promised, a group of workmen are already busy unloading trolleys full of boxes. There are dozens of them. Several dozens. His pulse quickens as he examines the labels, some in English, others in a hastily jotted, angular and barbed Cyrillic font. The ember of suspicion that ignited in the Director's office blossoms into a flame; the hope that a few moments prior seemed too wild to seriously entertain is suddenly all too real and palpable. Could these boxes and papers possibly contain what he suspects? He reaches toward the uppermost box and clumsily drops it on his desk, not noticing that it knocks over the framed photograph of his pregnant wife with a clatter. With trembling fingers, he begins to tear the box open, muttering to himself: *impossible, impossible, it cannot be, it simply cannot be…*

But it can, and is.

God's country

Manchester, New Hampshire, 1990

"...and you see boy, that's why the government gone done and made the Federal Reserve a *private company*! Not a lotta people know bout that."

The thin, reedy voice of the elderly gentleman next to you penetrates your consciousness as an unexpected jolt bumps your head against the bus window. Pale blue eyes look back at you, reflected, startled, nestled under a shock of ginger hair and amidst a flock of freckles.

Your companion glances at you with watery eyes, hands folded neatly on his knee. He wears mauve-colored pants. "You been sleeping this whole time, boy? Young fella like youself shoulda have some energy bout him. Have a donut, son." He proffers you a donut, sugar coated. A fine layer of white granules decorates the brown skin of tremulous fingers, collecting in the deep crevasses emanating weblike from the joints. The brown patina of his forehead shines in the bright sunlight streaming through the window. He dabs primly at the corners of his mouth with a napkin.

"No, thanks."

"Suit yoself. Where you headin, anyhow?"

"My uncle is picking me up in Manchester. I'm supposed to stay with him for the summer. He lives out in the mountains. Granite Lake."

Your neighbor sucks his teeth appreciatively. "That's God's country up there, yes it is! You a lucky boy. An your uncle, he a lucky man. Nice young boy like you comin to visit him. Me, I got to travel to see my kin. Ungrateful sumbitches. Come on, have a donut. You deserve it."

You take the donut. Soft, still with a hint of warmth. Granules of sucrose dissolve against your tongue. Outside, rolling hills crowned with trees have started to give way to periodic houses nestled within the foliage. You see a hawk, high above, tracing lazy, wheeling circles across the sky. A sign indicates that *Manchester Park & Ride* is 3 miles away.

"Where are you going?"

"Burlington." The man shakes his wizened head sadly, and repeats the word in wonderment. *"Burlington!* Full of do-goodin white folk. I don know what my fool son think he doin up there. *Lawyerin,* he say. We gonna see, we gonna see."

The bus pulls up into the station, coming to rest with a wheezing hydraulic sigh. *Manchester,* a gravelly voice announces over the intercom. You stand up, a welcome relief for your protesting legs. Your neighbor grasps the seat in front of him with bulbous fingers and hauls himself upright with considerable effort. "Sweet holy Jesus. Gotta stretch them legs, right, boy?"

You trip along the aisle, down the stairs and take a welcome breath of fresh air after hours of recycled, climate-controlled atmosphere. It is more humid here than in Philadelphia, which surprises you. The bus driver unceremoniously tosses baggage from the hold onto the sidewalk with a series of uncompromising thumps. You extricate yours from the pile and peer around; searching for what, or whom, you are not sure.

The terminal is a far cry from the noisy chaos of the one you left, with its argumentative vendors, roving gangs of delinquents, wary but aggressive pigeons, and bearded homeless men staggering about and muttering to themselves. This is a quiet brick building surrounded by recently trimmed hedges and carefully tended flowerbeds. A parking lot with a few dozen cars and trucks occupying amply sized spaces. Lots of trucks, actually. Some have gun racks. An enormous American flag flaps fitfully in the breeze.

"Robert." A booming voice behind you makes you start. You turn and see your uncle Gunnar. A squat man, shorter than you remember, with a stout, round belly. He is nearly bald except for a few errant hairs that form a crown around the back. Powerful forearms ending in knotted hands. He takes yours in a crushing grip. Blue eyes twinkle from under a furry mass of eyebrow, nose red from years of systematic alcohol consumption. You'd forgotten his ears, protuberant, elfin, with wisps of hair extending from their summit. He looks like someone bred an elf with a gnome and, dissatisfied with the result, sent the resulting creature to live among the humans as one of them. "It's been too long."

Your neighbor is doing a bit of an arthritic jig in his purplish pants. "Gotta get the kinks outta these here legs afore we start up again." He notices your new companion. "This yo uncle, boy?"

"Yes, sir."

The old man barks with laughter. "Ha! *Sir*. That a good one. You gots a good boy here, you take care o him."

Uncle Gunnar's eyes harden with suspicion. "Let's go."

You nod at the man and wish him a good trip. He waves at you affectionately. Slinging your bag across your shoulder, you hurry after Uncle Gunnar. Though you have a good six inches on him, you struggle to catch up. Short, bandy legs carry him forward purposefully. He walks with a weird, bow-legged stride, as though with each step he is trying to clear some unseen obstacle. It looks like a lot of work, but it covers ground effectively.

"What did he want?" he grumbles.

"Nothing. He sat next to me from Philadelphia. It was a long trip. He had some theories about the Federal Reserve he wanted to talk about."

Gunnar peers up at you curiously from underneath a bush of wildly overgrown eyebrows. "The Federal Reserve? What do you know about the Federal Reserve? How old are you, anyway?"

"Nineteen."

"Hmmmph." You arrive at Gunnar's car, a newish Toyota Corolla. He pops the trunk and tosses your bag in casually with one hand, though it must weigh sixty pounds. "Did you tell him anything about me?"

"What would I tell him? I don't know anything about you."

He stares at you hard for a moment, the twinkle disappearing from his eyes. Then he claps you on the shoulder with a meaty palm, the impact nearly staggering you. "Ha! Ha, ha! Your mother told me you're a live one. Let's go."

The trip from the bus station to Granite Lake takes about forty minutes on the Monadnock Highway. You cut through the city itself, to save time, Gunnar explains. No traffic on Saturday. It's not much of a city, as the term goes. Mostly low-rise, nineteenth century brick buildings. A couple of taller structures, perhaps eight or ten stories, venture cautiously above the rest of the modest skyline. More churches than seems strictly necessary for such an unassuming town. You cross a bridge over a surprisingly wide and powerful-looking river.

"Wow. What river is that?" you ask.

"The Merrimack," he responds tersely, eyes scanning the water. "Indians used to call this place *Namaoskeag*. It meant 'the good fishing place'. Not true anymore, though."

"What happened?"

"We happened."

City gives way to suburbs which give way to rolling hills and gradually forest and increasingly mountainous terrain. Pine trees whip by. There are few cars. The sun is bright and the sky an iridescent, cloudless blue. You pull off the highway. He points out the sign, *Munsonville, see that?* Then you head up to Nelson and meander through the village. It consists of elongated one- or two-story wooden houses with trucks parked in their drives, a simple brick church with a modest white spire, and a general store succinctly labeled 'Store'. Granite Lake stretches off to the right. It's bigger than you had expected, probably a good two miles long and a mile wide. A couple of sailboats wander lazily across its surface.

You drive past the general store and the church, and make your way to Gunnar's home. This turns out to be a ramshackle affair, a sprawling structure resembling a squatting toad, painted a pale, institution green. It's a sizeable building, two stories with screened in porches on both sides. On the south side a crabgrass lawn dotted with shrubs and a few imposing granite boulders makes its way fitfully down the hill toward the lake before surrendering and giving way to tall, stately pines. A decrepit looking barn made from weatherworn, unpainted wood droops forlornly to the east of the house. The car crunches to a halt on his gravel driveway. Gunnar picks your bag from the trunk and marches toward the front door. He pushes through a rickety screen door to the porch. The main entrance to the house is more formidable, with no doorknob and a sleek looking security keypad. A red light above the door pulses menacingly. He jabs in a code. The light turns green and the door opens with a click. He glances at you.

"You'll need your own code. Think of one. Not your birthday. 6 digits."

"Why can't I use yours?"

He snorts. "No one has my code. *No one*. That'd be a fundamental breach of security." He glares at you. "Some house rules. Rule number one. We do *not* leave the house without setting the alarm. I don't care if you're just going out for milk or to pull a quick one off in the garage. If the house is empty, the alarm is on. Got it?"

"Uh, okay."

"Find a room upstairs you like. Waddaya drink? Coffee? Beer?"

"Water's fine." The house has the peculiar smell of old man, a musty mix of body odor, fitful and occasional cleaning, creaky leather couches and countless old books. You drag your suitcase upstairs. Ancient floorboards creak beneath your feet. There are three upstairs bedrooms. One of them obviously seems to be your uncle's, you glean from the clothes haphazardly strewn about and the unmade bed. The other two seem roughly equivalent, each with a double bed and a closet. You choose the one that smells less musty.

As you unpack your bags you find the closet is nearly full. *Crap*. Oddly, it is full of uniforms. They seem too long in the leg and thin in the waist for your uncle's squat form. A couple of them have what you suppose are US Navy insignia on them, others Air Force. Others are foreign, a metallic gray color with strange insignia you do not recognize. The lapels of one of the foreign uniforms bear metal pins, oak leaves surrounding a pair of crossed rockets.

You go back downstairs. Your uncle is in the kitchen, brewing a pot of coffee. He hands you a glass of water. The water is glacially cold against your teeth, with a faint taste of minerals.

"Well, make yourself at home. You haven't been here before, have you?"

"No."

"Well, walk down to the lake if you want. Or look around here. There's some interesting stuff in my study, if you want to check it out."

One of nature's great mysteries

To the right of the spacious living room lies Gunnar's study. It does not disappoint.

The dominant motif is the far wall, entirely occupied with a huge diorama of intricate earthen constructions, enclosed and seemingly filled with plexiglass. A breathtakingly complex latticework of tunnels, supports and buttresses, bisected with what appears to be a steel plate driven precisely through the middle. The remaining three walls are filled from floor to ceiling with books, mostly in English, but many in German. Others are written in some inscrutable, jagged, foreign alphabet. They seem to be primarily mathematical and physics related. Models of elegant rockets and strange, clumsy apparatus that appear to be planetary landing modules hang from the ceiling, amid occasional wispy spiderwebs fluttering noncommittally in the breeze. A whiteboard is filled with equations and diagrams entirely alien to you, last year's AP calculus notwithstanding. On a large desk are piles of charts: of the earth, the moon, and what you assume is Mars due to the prominent denotation of Olympus Mons, covered with scrawled arrows and Xs in heavy red marker.

You start as Gunnar speaks from mere inches behind you. You had not heard him approach. "I'm not mad, if that's what you're thinking." He hands you a cup of coffee.

"What is that?" You gesture at the diorama in the back.

"Ah ha! That is an interesting piece, isn't it? It's my most prized possession, boy. Do you have the slightest inkling what it might be?"

"If I did, I wouldn't have asked."

"Ha ha! You are a live one! Very good. What that is, boy, is a cross-section of a termite mound. From the outside it is merely a dumb, insensate heap of mud. But on the inside, we have an entirely different animal, oh yes we do. Ventilation shafts, breeding chambers, traverse routes for workers and warriors, fungus gardens … everything is here in all its astonishing, fractal beauty. Would you believe that mindless beasts can produce such architectural marvels? Never! But who *designs* these marvels?

Who insists that these arches and ventilation tunnels will interconnect just so, calibrated to ensure maximum airflow and a consistently stable temperature? The queen, with less processing power in her insect mind than the remote control of my TV set? From the point of view of the termite, Robert, this is the equivalent of the Blue Mosque of Istanbul, or the Cathedral of Seville, but designed by a blind, mute, desperately imbecilic architect giving orders to builders that they have no hope of comprehending! But yet... but yet... this is not just any termite mound. Oh no. Do you see that steel band which bisects those tunnels and bridges and latticed support structures?"

"Of course."

"Now, this is of great importance. This steel barrier, you see, was driven into the ground at the foundation of this termite colony, just after the new queen released her first brood into the world. This barrier *bisected the colony*, boy. From that moment on, no termite on the right side could communicate with one on the left, and vice versa. But look, look at the symmetry of it all!"

Even to your untrained eye, the most important structures are clearly built with the goal of meeting one another. Perfectly symmetric caverns are sliced in two, arches converge toward one another, bridges strive to meet, hampered only by the unforgiving steel plate driven into their midst.

"How, Robert? How? How do these moronic lumps of chiton know how to design and build such a wondrous, intricate, but above all *consistent* edifice when there is no conceivable way that they ever communicated with one another?"

"Well, I don't know. They didn't get into this in community college. How do they do it?"

Gunnar's shoulders slump. "I don't know either. No one does. It is one of nature's great mysteries."

"Why do you have it here?"

Gunnar looks at the glassy diorama wistfully. "It is ... a monument to humility. A reminder of all that we do not know. That we do not, cannot, understand."

You stand together for a few moments in silence, contemplating this intricate matrix of insectoid genius.

Gunnar looks at you slyly.

"You know what else is a mystery on this cold, lonely planet?"

"No. No, I don't."

"Fish. Fish, my boy. More elusive, and more satisfying than any woman. Do you know how to fish?"

"We don't fish in Philadelphia, man."

"Let's go then."

Aye aye, commander

The Toyota rumbles up to the general store, crunching to a halt before a bed of enormous, flowering magnolias. Gunnar hands you a ten-dollar bill.

"Go in and buy worms, boy, and a six pack of beer."

"They won't sell me beer. I'm underage. If I get arrested, I'll be in pretty serious trouble, you know."

"Tell the lady at the counter that you're my nephew. She'll sell you beer."

"Why don't you go in with me?"

Gunnar's hands clench the wheel ever so slightly. Veins of white spread across his knuckles. "Don't ask so many questions, boy. We're a navy family. You know what 'Aye aye' means?"

"No."

"It means, '*I* have heard, and *I* will obey'."

You sigh. "Aye aye, captain."

"Aye aye, *commander*," growls Gunnar.

The bell tinkles distantly as you push through the door to the store. It's not large, a few rows of dry goods, some bins of forlorn vegetables, heaps of deli meat, and a wall refrigerator full of drinks. *Fresh Hoagies!* a hopeful sign next to the register advertises. The pleasant aroma of fresh baked bread hangs in the air. You pull out a six pack of Sierra Nevada and walk to the counter.

A shrewish lady in her early sixties with close-cropped, silver hair peers at you bemusedly from above her glasses, thinning eyebrows rising in incredulous half-moons. "Seriously? Don't even show me that fake ID, boy. If you do, I'll have to call the police. Put the beer back and get out of here."

"It's not for me. It's for my uncle, Gunnar."

She emits a loud squawk, reminiscent of a stranded porpoise. "Gunny's here? Why didn't you say so!" She peers through the window behind her and waves excitedly. Even through the blinds, you can see Gunnar wince as he waves back. She looks back at you frantically, small stars of madness exploding darkly in her eyes. "Well, tell him to come in! I haven't seen him in ages."

"Well, you see, ma'am, he's promised to take me fishing. He says we have to get on the water soon and if he came in, well, you're such a fine, nice lady we'd start talking and simply never leave. So, he asked me to come in and get some worms."

She blushes a deep red. "Oh, that man. Impossible…" she continues muttering to herself as she fumbles underneath the counter. She plops a Styrofoam container in front of you. You hand her the ten.

A voice chirps behind you. "If you're that hungry, I'll buy you a sandwich. Who knows where those worms have been?"

You turn to observe this new interlocutor. A small, lithe girl of indeterminate Asian descent. The sharp triangle of her face is offset by the tousled waves of short, silken hair. She is dressed in athletic clothes, her skin iridescent with sweat, caramel-colored cheeks stained with the slightest apple red of physical effort.

"Were you here the whole time? I didn't hear the bell ring."

She shrugs, wide smile belied by black, shark-like eyes. "I don't set off the bell. I'm lighter than you are."

"Well… the worms are for fish. Not for me."

"Oh, I see. Good luck then. By the way, my name's Aurora."

"Robert."

"Nice to meet you, Robert." She tosses a bill on the counter and pushes through the door. Once outside she breaks into a swift run.

The store lady looks after her quickly diminishing form, eyes narrowing with deep distrust. "Don't know about that girl. They come here every summer. Mother's a professor at Bowdoin in Maine, you know. Lovely lady. But that girl... Whoever heard of a pretty girl like that wearing *black* nail polish? I don't know."

You take your leave of the proprietor, still glaring suspiciously through the shop window. You slide into the car beside your uncle. He puts the car into gear and you pull out of the parking lot, leaving a thick cloud of dust behind. "Looks like you made a friend," Gunnar comments with a chuckle.

"Looks like you did, too."

Your uncle snorts. "He *is* a live one. OK, another rule, boy. We don't pick up the phone, you hear? People who know, let it ring three times, hang up, then re-dial. Those you pick up. Anything else, leave it be. *Capische?*"

"*Ich verstehe.*"

A baleful glare and silence. Mercifully, a few seconds later, he pulls into a dock by the lake.

He has a small 18 foot outboard. You help him pull the tarp off and detach the mooring lines. The boat rocks precipitously under your feet as you step aboard.

"Don't get on boats much in Philly, eh? If you got to puke, do it over the side." After a couple of wheezing coughs and fitful belches of diesel smoke, the engine roars into life, and you carve a sharp crescent across the still, black surface of the lake. The sun is beginning to descend toward the horizon, taking on an orange hue as it settles toward the purpling mountains beyond the lakeshore. Gunnar slaps you on the shoulder and points at a seaplane, two docks down from his.

"Plastic surgeon!" He shouts above the insistent thrum of the engine. "Flies up from Boston every weekend in that damn thing! I think he runs it on the fat tits and asses he cuts out of adulterous housewives during the week."

You motor decisively toward a small island on the western side of the lake. He cuts the motor and you drift toward a point on the island, where a small, scrubby birch tree overhangs the water, its scabby white bark reflected in the black water below.

"Perfect," he mutters.

"What are we going for?"

"Bass, boy. They've laid their eggs, and around every nest there'll be three bass. A male and female guarding the eggs, and another male waiting to eat them if they're not careful." He snickers and gestures toward the aft of the boat. "Try that rod. It's all set up."

Gingerly you pick up the rod. You unhook the lure from one of the eyes. A red, heavy piece of plastic with three cruel, barbed hooks dangling from the tail.

"What's this supposed to be? It doesn't look like a fish."

He shrugs. "They're aggressive right now, defending their eggs. They don't even eat these days. But they'll attack, and try to murder, anything that approaches their nest. We'll get a couple of bass with these, then use the worms for trout on the other side of the lake."

You pull back the bail and flick the rod. The lure smacks violently into the water about four feet from the boat.

"Try a little further," he suggests. "Release higher. Finish the cast pointing with the rod where you want the lure to go."

You reel it in and cast again, landing a few feet in front of the shore. A fountain of white, thrashing water erupts instantly from the surface.

"Set the hook! Set the hook!" You pull back hard and feel the unmistakable, ferocious pull of a fish. You start to reel in. The line traces back and forth in lazy figure eights, the tip of the rod shaking wildly as the fish struggles to free itself. The rod bends ever more sharply as the fish approaches the boat. Gunnar cackles with glee.

"He sees the boat. Now he's pissed." He leans over the side, net in hand, watching the water intently. He takes a swig of beer, eyes never leaving the water. The rod bends even more, so sharply you think it must at any moment snap, when suddenly Gunnar lunges for the water. He lifts out the net, droplets of water sparkling in the sun, in which a good-sized, brown bass flips back and forth. He wets his hand in the water and gently pulls the fish from the net. Its eyes are a bright, fiery red, staring at you with implacable hate.

"Wet your hand before you touch them. Otherwise, they can get fungal infections and die. They have this protective coating of slime, you see..." He pulls a pair of pliers from his belt and carefully removes the hook from the fish's lip. He looks at you with sparkling, sky blue eyes. "Good work, boy. Let's say it was the first cast. That other one was just practice." He hefts the fish. "Good four pounds, I'd say."

"Uh, what do we do with it? Eat it?"

"No, I mostly let them go. This is the third or fourth time I've caught this guy. I recognize the scar. See here?" A faint scar adorns the brown flank of the fish. "Loon or something tried to eat him, I bet." He snorts and releases the fish into the water. With a flip of its tail, it disappears into the black depths below.

"What's a loon?"

"Oh, you'll hear them tonight. Neat birds. Big bastards. They make the weirdest noises. Have a beer, son." He tosses you a bottle. You twist off the top and take a sip. It's not terribly cold, but the sharp, malty taste is fine on a rocking boat as the shadows of trees begin to lengthen across the lake and the chill of evening gradually descends.

You scoot around in the boat to a few more spots, landing two more bass, until finally it is nearly too dark to distinguish whether you're casting at the water or the shore. Reluctantly, you head back to the dock and the steep climb back to Gunnar's house. It is pitch black out by the time you ascend the stairway curving through the dense pines. *The worms will keep, boy. We'll get a couple of them trout tomorrow.* Gunnar walks assuredly between the trees, while you seemingly stumble on every rock, root and stick. Whip-poor-wills begin to sing their strange, alien song, and the sharp, spicy scent of fresh pine needles fills your nostrils. Fireflies blink on and off intermittently as they trace their slow, meandering patterns through the night. You exit the woods to his lawn; above you, an endless expanse of winking stars splashes across an inky night sky, unlike anything you have ever seen.

For emergencies only

The next day you start awake. The silence momentarily panics you. No engines, no car horns, no neighbors squabbling and shouting, no police and ambulance sirens wailing in the distance. *Where am I?* Memories trickle back as you stare up at the cracked ceiling.

Floorboards creak alarmingly under your feet as you stumble downstairs. Your uncle is nowhere to be found. The smell of coffee wafts from the kitchen. The light from outside is still dim, though whether from an early morning sun, or shade from the surrounding trees, is impossible to say. You shiver in the frigid air. It's late June; in Philly, without air conditioning, you would already be sweating.

You pour a cup of coffee and walk out onto the porch. Last night there hadn't been much of an opportunity to look around. The porch is full of junk; broken fishing rods, piles of books in various languages, dartboard sans darts, anonymous cardboard boxes full of papers. You look out to the yard. A doe, white spots adorning her light brown flank, stands about twenty yards from the house. She gazes at you intently, tail pointed skyward in alarm. For a moment you stare at each other, before she turns and bounds noiselessly away into the trees.

Moments later, your uncle trudges into view out of the copse of trees on the path you'd taken the previous evening. He wears a fluorescent orange swimsuit, towel slung over his shoulder. He has a gut and his skin sags, but there is power still visible in the broad shoulders and knotted calves, and the thick boxer's neck clearly trained to absorb blow after blow if needed.

He nods at you curtly as he ascends the final stair. "You're up early. Thought you kids sleep til lunchtime nowadays. Tomorrow you can come for the morning swim."

"No thanks. It's cold enough already."

He shrugs and unceremoniously seizes your coffee mug. He takes a sip. "Hmm. Black. That's how your mother drinks it."

"I should call her." *Should have called her last night*, you think. As if on cue, the phone rings. You move to answer it. Gunnar seizes your arm.

"Don't. We need to see if they know the code."

"The code?"

"Yes. The code. We only answer people who know the code. No breach of security." The phone continues ringing. "Remember? Three times, hang up, dial again. Then we answer."

"What the hell is wrong with you, man?"

The answering machine comes on. Gunnar's uncertain baritone comes on. "Hello, we are, uh, not home right now. If you'd like to leave us a, er, message, well, go for it. Like now." A shrill beep follows. After a short pause, a familiar female voice begins to shout. "Goddamn it Gunnar, pick up the phone *immediately*. If you think I'm going to follow your stupid code, well you thought wrong. Now do you have Robbie or…"

You move quickly to pick up the phone. "Hi Mom. Sorry, Uncle Gunnar was just having me help him fix his boat."

"Why didn't you call me?"

"Oh, the bus was late yesterday and by the time we got here I thought you'd be busy making dinner." Your uncle stares at you, eyes bugging out in alarm. "Gunnar actually told me to call you but I uh, wanted to go swimming. Sorry about that." His shoulders slump in relief.

You chat about the trip for a few moments. "Now, give me your uncle." You hand him the phone and go into the kitchen to find breakfast. Three unopened boxes of Cheerios lurk in the back of one of the cupboards. You consciously avoid examining the expiration dates. In the background you hear Gunnar muttering, *yes … yes … yes, Susan. Of course. Sure. Yes…*

He wanders into the kitchen, shaking his head. He nods at you, ever so slightly. "Take whatever you want. Just don't get into my booze without asking me."

"OK. You want some Cheerios?"

He grunts an affirmation. You pour him a bowl. "So, what happened down there in Philly, anyway?"

"Lost an argument."

"Huh. Some argument, sounds like."

You crunch cereal together in the sudden silence.

"Hey, so, uh, can I borrow your car? I need to buy some stuff. I have a license."

"What stuff?"

"Stuff. I don't have a swimming suit."

He looks at you carefully. "Sure. Just don't crash it. And remember…"

"Code the door. I thought of a code. It's …"

"Don't tell me," he interrupts. "It's better that way. Breach of security. I'll help you set it. But go to Keene, probably. There are some stores there. I don't buy much stuff personally. But I get fishing gear there."

Gunnar helps you set the code and you exit the house. The screen door to the front porch bangs alarmingly as it swings shut behind you. You climb into his Toyota, pushing the seat back as far as it will go. You turn the key. After a brief, uncertain cough, the engine hums into life. You pull out of the driveway, gravel and pinecones crackling beneath the wheels. You head back the way you drove in yesterday, realizing as you do so that you don't have a clue how to get to Keene. Hopefully there will be signs, you muse to yourself.

As you drive down the road, a spritely figure lopes toward you. It's the girl from yesterday, bouncing effortlessly up the incline, her gait more reminiscent of the morning's deer than a person. She wears a white tank-top and calf-length black spandex leggings. She waves you down as you approach. As you roll to a stop she leans against the car, panting. A bright smile turns brown cheeks into tight knobs overshadowing improbably deep dimples, her chin sharp as an axe.

"Where ya goin?"

"Keene. I guess. Though I don't know how to get there. I need to buy some stuff."

"Cool. I'll come with you." Without waiting for an answer, she hops around the car and slides into the passenger seat. Although it's early, it's humid and she is coated with a sheen of sweat. She emanates a sharp, but not unpleasant citrusy smell, like cinnamon on a fresh cut lime. Her black eyes, alert under short bangs, scan the road. "Just head down to the highway. I think there's a sign there. We definitely need to go east, though."

"Right. Which way's, uh, east?"

"Follow the sun, dummy."

Fortunately, at the entrance to the highway there is indeed a sign pointing toward Keene. As you turn on to the highway, Aurora opens the window and leans her head out, smiling contentedly, short black hair blowing back like a lion's mane. After a few moments she turns her attention to the radio.

"Sometimes we can get WFNX out of Boston. It's pretty good. What are you doing here, anyway?"

"Family thought it would be a nice change of scenery for me for the summer. Get some fresh air. See how my uncle is getting on. Apparently he gets weirder every year."

She shrugs. "We all do. You want weird, you should meet my folks. Isn't his name Gunnar? He's German, right?"

"Yeah. His father was either a German war hero, or war criminal. I've heard both versions. How about your folks, what do they do?"

"My mom's Chinese. She teaches … wait for it … Chinese at a college in Maine. My dad is from Texas. He's kind of, uh, self-employed. We've just been coming here for the summer break for the last few years, so my mom can do some writing. What do you do in Philly, anyway?"

"Well, community college for now, til I figure things out, I guess. You?"

Aurora peruses the trees whipping by. "Oh, well I go to the college where my mom teaches. Free tuition, you know. Hard to pass up."

"Sounds like a good deal."

Her nails rap a quick staccato pattern on the center console between the seats. "Well, I wouldn't have minded a bit of distance from the parentals. But money talks. I mean, it's a good school and it's beautiful up there. But once I graduate, I'm getting out of here. Head to the west coast and see what happens."

A few miles down the highway is a turn-off for Keene. A Dick's Sporting Goods store is right there. You pull into the parking lot. Aurora makes a beeline for the back of the store. "Come on. The good stuff's back here."

You are somewhat intimidated by the array of footwear confronting you from numerous shelves, a kaleidoscope of brands and colors and forms. You pretend to look at them discerningly, your brow furrowed in thought.

"Do you run? I mean, have you run, really?"

"Well … everyone runs a bit, right?" She cocks her head and looks at you enquiringly. "OK, not really. I'm from Philadelphia, man. We don't run there."

"Rocky ran there." She peruses the rows of footwear. "Reebok, ugh. Who wears Reebok these days? OK, try these."

"Puma?"

"It was founded by a German, Rudolf Dassler. Your uncle will approve. Anyway, they make good shoes. Stylish."

You try on a size 11. Amazingly enough, they fit perfectly. You look at the price tag. $49. You'd been hoping for something in the sub-thirty range.

"Perfect."

"Great. Do you have clothes?"

You look down at yourself. "What does it look like?"

"Running clothes, silly. This way."

Check out is a breathtaking $143. You hand the cashier your mother's credit card that she had given you for emergencies with a tight smile. Aurora finds this hilarious, grasping your arm and nearly doubling over with mirth, laughing with a soundless, open mouthed cackle.

"Oh my god. *For emergencies only?* Are you serious? Have you seen *The Sure Thing?*"

"No."

"OK, let's find a Blockbuster or something. We have to rent it. It's the best movie ever."

The sun is high in the sky when you return to the house with bags of athletic wear and VHS cassettes. You enter your code to go through the front door. Aurora frowns.

"Wow. Safety first, huh? What does he have in here, murder victims?"

"A collection of vintage Folgers coffee cans and German folk song CDs. Plastic models of spaceships. Priceless, apparently."

"OK, well, get changed and let's go."

"What, now? You just ran. And it's like, noon. Isn't it too hot?"

Aurora punches you in the arm. "I only ran two miles before I saw you. Come on, we'll go around the lake. It's four miles. It's cool there. Piece of cake."

Over the following thirty minutes or so you discover new kinds of pain you had not been aware existed. Short, stabbing pains in your quadriceps, punchy blows to your lungs when you try to speak. Aurora prattles away relentlessly the entire time, bouncing gazelle-like as you plod along the pavement, your shins howling with every impact. After an eternity, you are at the road leading to Gunnar's house. Aurora's eyes narrow.

"This is where we *turn it on!* Hills make the runner. Let's kill it."

She sprints up the hill, balls of her feet digging determinedly into the gravel. Humiliatingly, a couple of chunks fly up and strike you as she races away. After a few staggering steps and hoarse, donkey-like, wheezing attempts to draw breath, you give up and walk the rest of the way. The artificial fabric of the shirt is slick against your skin. One of your nipples oozes blood.

Aurora waits for you expectantly at Gunnar's house, a triumphant smile illuminating her face. She holds up her hand for a high five.

"Good work. I didn't think you'd make it, city boy."

"I didn't make it."

"Close enough. You'll do better tomorrow. Let's get some water." She looks toward the house and her eyes widen with shock. "Holy shit, what's that?"

Breathing nearly returning to normal, you look toward Gunnar's house. From somewhere behind it a thick pall of black, greasy smoke billows skyward. You run together toward the back of the house, pinecones cracking beneath your feet, pain momentarily forgotten.

Konnichiwa!

Gunnar stands behind his garage with some sort of device in his hands. It looks like a control unit for a radio-controlled car. A childlike, idiotic grin of joy radiates from his face.

About twenty feet to his right is an exceedingly odd-looking contraption. At first glance it appears to be a random jumble of junk.

But the junk is moving.

The pile is made of discrete units, small tractor-like devices which climb over one another in an undulating pattern that can only be termed insectoid. Small plastic mandibles latch onto those of their neighbors, assembling themselves into temporary forms one moment only to dissolve into chaos the next. Gradually some semblance of order appears. It reminds you of your friend Jeremy solving a Rubik's Cube, where continuous small, seemingly random changes gradually discern sense from hidden geometries, and order emerges from entropy. The mass gradually forms itself into a parabola, angled obliquely via some unknown trigonometric equation toward the sun. A mass of black panels locks itself into place, each connected to its neighbor. Slowly, the small devices cease to move as each finds its proper place in the system, until the entire mass becomes motionless. Gunnar, heedless of your presence, mutters to himself the entire time, one hand moving in small erratic motions like a mad, dwarfish orchestra conductor.

The smoke rises from a burnt and blackened stack of hay bales about fifty feet from this curious amalgam. As the contraption comes to rest, Gunnar lets out something between a snort and a laugh and impatiently jabs a button on his controller with a thick index finger. There is an audible *click*, and black panels flip over, revealing a mirror-like finish on the other side. They suddenly become blindingly bright. The stack of hay immediately begins to smoke and after a few seconds, bursts into flame. He punches the same button again. Another click and the panels flip over again, while flames continue to lick fitfully at the golden stack of straw. Gunnar lets out a small harrumph of triumph.

"What the hell are you doing, man?"

It is your voice, unbidden. Gunnar wheels toward you, an unearthly, manic glare in his eyes. His gaze shifts toward Aurora.

"What am I doing? What are *you* doing? Who the fuck is this? Jesus Christ on a stick! What did I tell you?"

Before you can answer he drops the remote-control unit into the grass with a clatter and marches purposefully toward Aurora, rock-like fists balled up tightly at his sides. "You goddamn little rice eater! Where did you come from? *Who are you working for?*" Veins bulge and visibly distend across a purpling forehead. Now that you want them, words fail you.

Aurora coolly stands her ground. "I'm a sleeper agent for the Imperial Japanese Army. Hawaii didn't work out for us, so we decided to try New Hampshire this time. We figured no one would suspect. *Konnichiwa.*"

Gunnar pauses mid-stride, scrutinizing her carefully. "I've sailed to Japan. You're not Japanese."

"Well, shit. You've blown my cover, then."

Gunnar glares at you balefully. "Who is this, boy? Where did you find her? And what for god's sake possessed you to bring her here?"

"Uhhhhh…"

Aurora interrupts forcefully. "We went running. Then we saw a forest fire. As concerned citizens we came to investigate the situation."

Gunnar thankfully turns his basilisk stare on your companion. "You're that Chinese lady's daughter, aren't you? Are you really a girl, by the way? You've got the figure of a 12-year-old boy." He looks up at the sky, shaking his hands imploringly. "Oh god, why the Chinese, why now?" He kicks fitfully at the grass. "We're doomed," he announces, to no one in particular.

You look at Aurora. "Are we doomed?"

Her eyes are hard as flint. "Do you know *why* we are here, Mr. Schafer? Do you know why my mother teaches here, at one of the most prestigious colleges in the nation?"

Gunnar looks at her with the distaste one reserves for the desiccated corpse of a rodent left by one's cat. Undeterred, Aurora continues.

"My mother is considered an enemy of the state. She fled China during the Cultural Revolution and married my father, who is *also* considered an imperialist insurgent. She came here twenty-five years ago and has only tried to foster understanding between two great nations, one of which has a price on her head. That is why this rice-eating girl is standing here on your smoking and, I might add, generally unkempt lawn. I was born here. Were you? The word around town is that you're a dedicated Nazi, you know. I have nothing to be ashamed of. Do you?"

During Aurora's soliloquy Gunnar's head progresses from red to various shades of purple, veins beating visibly like drums, eyes bugging out with rage as though they would explode from his skull at any moment. Suddenly, unexpectedly, he bursts into laughter, clapping hands on his knees with a resounding slap.

"Girl, everyone in this town thinks I'm a Nazi, but you're the only one who's ever had the stones to say it to my face." He wipes tears of laughter from his eyes. "Oh, if only they knew. But it feels good to finally hear it straight up. Even if it's from you."

A note of protest dies in your throat. Gunnar continues. "Well, children, I expect you're curious what I'm up to here. I should introduce you to my robots. They are clever, but not too clever." He glances at you sharply, eyes narrowing. "And most importantly, they do as they're told."

"Now, I guess you're smart enough to observe that they have dual panels, one dark and one light. Do you have any idea what the two modes are?"

"Well, the light one seems like a mirror. Or magnifying glass. It lit the hay on fire." Your voice, asserting itself without volition.

"Yes, boy. Correct. The dark mode is a solar collection panel, the light mode a reflector. So, they have two sides which shift mechanically on command. Collect, reflect. Collect, reflect. A simple flip of a switch changes them from a battery, to a mirror, and back again."

"Why the solar cells?" asks Aurora, with a puzzled frown.

"The little robots need energy to perform their tasks, kitten. For most of their lives they are in collection mode, gathering energy from the sun so that they may move about, or do other little jobs as needed. But once in a great while, the colossal energy of our great star, our magnificent fusion generator, can be directed elsewhere. That is when my little friends become mirrors. And in the correct constellation, you see, this energy can be concentrated on a finite point."

"Like the hay bale there."

"Yes, like the hay bale. Or, more usefully, another solar power array equipped to deal with this concentrated energy. A space station, for instance. Or a base on the moon. Or Mars, for that matter."

This piques your interest. "OK, but you could never get enough of them to Mars. You'd use more energy to get there than they could ever produce. And you couldn't control them."

Gunnar's eyes light up with something akin to joy. "Ah, boy, you have hit on the crux of the problem. Well, two out of three at any rate. Which, for an urban scoundrel, is not bad. Perhaps there's hope for the country after all." Aurora looks at you enquiringly. You avoid her curious gaze.

"Now, imagine I would want to replicate what you see here…" he gestures at the small robots, which have disengaged and begun to dissipate into an unorganized mass. He picks one up. It is barely as large as his horned, callused palm.

"You see, boy, each of these has a simple function. This one's function is simply to be, to connect with its brethren, to collect and reflect." He pushes the button and the robot ceases to move, the black panels it lugs on its back suddenly flipping around with a soft flutter to display a chromium sheen. "Do you remember what I told you about the termites, yesterday?"

"Sure."

"Well, there are different types of termites. There are the queens, of course, as well as her consorts; the warriors, the builders, the farmers, the nurses… the average termite mound has eight distinct morphotypes in its population, each suited to a specific goal. Some colonies have as many as fourteen. Come, let's go inside."

In his study, Gunnar takes a key from his pocket and opens a drawer. Nestled inside are more of the small robots, each slightly differently shaped. He carefully pulls one out.

"This is a miner, for instance. It collects energy like the rest, but for a specific purpose. It wanders about and scrapes the ground when it senses silicon, and using its solar powered laser, creates a ceramic substrate which is, for all practical purposes, plastic. He has a brother which looks for minerals and, via a similar process, creates nodules of an iron-nickel-cobalt alloy. Another which melts sand to produce simple squares of glass. All of these things, children, can be found in *both* the lunar and Martian regolith. A handful of dust, and a bit of energy is all that is needed to create wonders! They deliver them to this…" He pulls another, slightly larger, spidery contraption. "This, children, is a printer. But it does not print silly words on paper. It prints things."

Aurora's eyes narrow. "How?"

"Well, it has a simple memory core with instructions how to print certain items. Now, imagine a printer, printing on paper. But it prints with materials other than ink. Silicon plastic. Fernico, our iron alloy. And it prints layer upon layer upon layer, 100 nanometers at a time. The shell and treads of plastic. Circuits and rotors of iron alloy. Solar panels – or mirrors, if we flip the switch – of glass. And so on."

Aurora mutters, as if to herself. "A self-replicating machine."

Gunnar beams. "Yes, kitten. A self-replicating machine. With 12 of these robots, each with a different function from mining, to printing, to fuel cell electrolysis, we can create a self-replicating ecosystem that can, from any surrounding environment with sufficient sun, sand and minerals, form its own community to do our bidding. The hundreds of robots you saw outside, were created from the twelve in this desk."

You struggle to get your ahead around what you are seeing, and its significance. "But… they organize themselves. How did you do that?"

Gunnar regards you cautiously. "That, boy, is a tale for another day. Do you remember the termite mound?"

"Sure."

"Enormous complexity can arise from the simplest of beginnings, given proper motivation."

The magnitude of your impending good fortune

Aurora invites you to her house for dinner. You suspect Gunnar will not have much of a plan, and in any event, you've rented a couple of videos which need to be returned in forty-eight hours.

Her mother greets you, a stocky, dwarfish Chinese lady named Chenguang. She has a broad, beaming smile and somewhat limited English. After a few pleasantries, she and Aurora begin speaking in rapid-fire Chinese. Mandarin, you later discover. Aurora beams at you after a few moments of incomprehensible discussion.

"We're going to get take-out from the Chinese place in Munsonville. Real Chinese people. They have the most *amazing* hot and sour soup." The mother jabbers a bit more. Aurora's face falls.

"Come on. We have to get money from Hal."

"Who's Hal?"

"My father."

Hal turns out to be an enormous man in a brick-colored jumpsuit with a thick Texas accent and rimless glasses. You are not small, but Hal towers over you. He peers down at you, eyes twinkling with a lively curiosity.

"Well, what have we got here?"

"It's a neighbor, Hal. Try to be normal. We need some money for take-out."

"Ah, normal. Of course. Normal, normal, normal. But who decides what's normal and what's weird, hmm?" Hal pulls out a thick roll of money from his pocket. You try not to act surprised. The only rolls you ever saw like that in Philly were carried by dealers. He peels off a couple of twenties and hands them to her.

"Thanks, Hal."

"You hain't gonna ask me what I want?"

Aurora is already walking away. "No," she shoots over her shoulder. You offer a wan smile at her father. "It's a pleasure to meet you, sir."

"No sirs round here, young feller. We live in a *democratic republic*. You know what that means?"

"I've heard the term."

"Good. Now run along, and keep my daughter out of trouble."

Aurora throws on a well-worn leather biker jacket and stomps out of the house. A decrepit and fitfully dented white Chevy Sprint is parked in front. Aurora marches toward it fiercely.

"Hey, uh, why don't we take my uncle's Toyota…"

Glittering black eyes obliterate any intention you had of completing the sentence. She throws her head back and laughs, partially offsetting her threatening countenance. "What, you don't like my baby?"

"It's beautiful. A tribute to modern American engineering."

Aurora slides in. You get in the passenger side, the black synthetic seats hot even through your clothes. The engine sputters fitfully into life and lurches down to the road. She pats the steering wheel affectionately. "She's not much, but she's mine."

Munsonville is a few miles away from the lake. A sign on the way into town announces that the population of 2,247 people greets you with open arms. The Chevy trundles carefully into a sort of central square around a small park. A couple of old ladies squint at you suspiciously from a bench where they have been chatting. The Chinese restaurant neighbors a Hallmark store to the left and a hardware store to the right. Gold dragons festoon an incorrigibly kitsch façade. *Kowloon* is spelled out in some sort of garish faux Asian script.

"The thriving metropolis of Munsonville," Aurora mutters. "Let's go down to Boston and check out Chinatown sometime this summer. We'll get real dim sum. This is bullshit."

The squat, roundish lady behind the counter begins to jabber excitedly in Mandarin, presumably, at Aurora as soon as she enters. Aurora's smile lights up the room. She answers fluently. After a few exchanges in this completely foreign tongue, she motions for you to sit with her on a padded bench across from the counter.

"We're just getting take-out," she announces. "It'll take a few minutes. I never really order from the menu, you know."

"Uh, ok. So, that was, um, kind of impressive. I mean, I've taken Spanish for years, and I can hardly order a quesadilla at Taco Bell."

"Well, when you grow up with it, it's just kinda there. I hardly even know what I'm saying half the time. But they seem to get it." She rummages through her purse, eventually pulling out a vial of black nail polish. She shoves the purse into your lap. "Hold this for a second. I need to fix my nails." She carefully begins dabbing a few spots of black on the chipped polish at the ends.

"Why the black nails? Kind of goth, isn't it?"

She shrugs, and glances at you impassively. "I like it. Goes with my eyes, they say. And I get less hassle from the townies."

There is a giant aquarium across from you filled with garishly colored tropical fish. You watch them swim listlessly among plastic plants. After a few moments, the Chinese lady at the counter squawks something and proffers bags of food at you. It seems like far too much. Aurora launches into an animated statement, leading to much mutual hilarity. She leaves forty dollars on the counter. The roundish lady clucks reprovingly and pushes twenty back at her, which she accepts after a half-hearted protest, folding it discreetly into her pocket.

In the car the warmth of cardboard boxes full of noodles and soups infuses your lap, while the distinctive aroma wafts through your nostrils. Passing cars briefly illuminate Aurora's angular features.

"Why are you up here, anyway?"

"Uh, I got in a bit of trouble down in Philly. My mother thought it would be better if I moved up here for a while."

"What's your father say?"

"Not much."

She glances at you, eyes shaded in the failing light. "What kind of trouble? Tell me if I'm prying."

You squirm a bit in the seat. "Ah, got in an argument with some people. Stupid stuff."

Aurora bursts out laughing, pounding with one hand on the steering wheel. She emits a small shriek. "Oh my god. You've got to be kidding. That's the start of the *Fresh Prince of Bel-Air!*" Another hurricane of laughter leaves her gasping for breath. "Robbie, the Fresh Prince of Munsonville!" Followed by busting into a rhyme. She does a little hip-hop dance move with her free hand.

Chilling out, maxing, relaxing all cool

And all shooting some b-ball outside of the school
When a couple of guys who were up to no good
Started making trouble in my neighborhood
I got in one little fight and my mom got scared

And said, "You're moving with your aunt and uncle in Bel-Air"

Thankfully your burning ears, surely fire-engine red, are invisible in the darkness. "Yeah, thanks," you grumble. "Real original."

Aurora dabs at her eyes. "I'm sorry. I'm sure it was all very serious." After a moment of poorly stifled mirth, she erupts in another howl of laughter, evidently infectious. You begin to laugh as well.

"It definitely wasn't over my basketball skills."

You walk into the house. A small kitchen table is set for three. Aurora's mother bustles around, setting out plates and bowls and silverware, burbling away in Mandarin the whole time. An energetic discussion begins, with ever increasing gesticulation and rising voices. It ends with a glowering Aurora carrying a carton of noodles and bowl of soup somewhere into the back of the house. The mother grins at you wordlessly and gestures for you to sit.

Moments later, Aurora stalks back into the kitchen, face like a thundercloud. "Had to bring some food out to Hal's workshop," she growls. "He's busy designing one of his board games that's gonna make us very rich someday. Let's eat."

Dinner is rather more exotic than you're used to. It is far from the garden variety Chinese take-out of fried rice and pink spare ribs. The hot and sour soup could strip paint off a car, and the noodle dishes are populated with asymmetric, crunchy, unfamiliar vegetables that smell vaguely of anise. Aurora's mother makes a few fitful efforts at conversation, usually trailing off into Mandarin. You wonder how she manages a teaching role at an elite teaching institution.

After dinner you retreat to the den, lying down on a rough shag carpet. Aurora jams *The Sure Thing* into the VCR and lies down expectantly on a blanket in front of the television. John Cusack flails his way across the nation in an insouciant attempt to mate. Aurora cackles continuously throughout, contemporaneously narrating the film, rolling on the floor when the literature teacher advises intercourse in a hammock. Apparently, she has seen the film before. Midway through the movie, Cusack's erstwhile travel companion utters the fateful line that she can't use her credit card except in cases of emergency; Aurora peers at you expectantly. "Ha! Look, that was you, man!" When Cusack finally mumbles the lines to the truck driver transporting him to California, she sings with him: "no questions asked, no strings attached, no guilt involved … *a sure thing*!"

She doesn't repeat the truck driver's muttered response. *I hope you appreciate the magnitude of your impending good fortune.*

It's nearly eleven when the movie ends. You stumble out of the front door, and turn to look at Aurora, framed in a halo of fluorescent interior light. She balls up a petite, caramel colored fist and socks you in the shoulder, hard enough that a small nova of pain explodes under the impact and radiates through the nerves of your arm. "See you tomorrow, dummy." You emit a sort of animalistic grunt of acknowledgment, and shuffle back towards Gunnar's house. The moon has risen in the north and the trees cast stark, gaunt shadows. Gravel scattered on the pavement crunches beneath your feet. A rising wind sends grayly luminescent clouds scudding past the stars, carrying with it the metallic taste of an approaching storm. A loon's haunting, quavering wail ripples upward from the lake's still, black waters. You would have surely thought it were a wolf's howl, if Gunnar had not explained the difference to you. Nevertheless, you quicken your pace.

Freedom for the pike means death for the minnows

You awake to the clatter of rain on the roof and the straining of timbers in the wind. A gray, dull light seeps in through the windows. Rain pounds against the panes in thick, dirty lashes, the glass rattling in the frames. You look at the clock. 6:30. You can smell coffee brewing downstairs. After a few moments of restless tossing in bed, you get up. The morning air is frigid; you put on jeans and a sweatshirt, and a pair of thick socks.

Gunnar is sitting on the couch, reading the paper with a steaming cup of coffee in his hands. He wears a thick sweater and a pair of waterproof pants. Gnomish eyes peer over the paper at you curiously.

"Ha!" he barks. "It's not even eleven yet! What are you doing up?"

"Getting old, Gunnar. Getting old." You pour yourself a cup of coffee. "What are you up to?"

He nods in the direction of the wall. "What do you see there, boy?"

"A bunch of old junk? Like everywhere in this dump?"

Gunnar shakes his grizzled head sadly. "Look at the barometer. You know what a barometer is?"

"Uh, yeah, I think. It measures air pressure, right?"

"Exactly. Pressure has dropped an inch since yesterday. An inch! You know what that means?"

You look casually out at the storm violently lashing the window panes. "We're in for some rain?"

"Smart ass," he grumbles. "Bait fish get active when pressure decreases. No one knows why. May have something to do with their swim bladders. Doesn't matter. Point is, active bait brings out the big boys. Pike, and muskie. But here we have pike."

"Ah. Of course."

"Anyway, this is perfect pike weather. I've got another pair of all-weathers you can borrow. Let's go."

The bright orange rubber pants have about ten inches of give around the waist and only descend halfway down your shins, but it's better than nothing. You stomp down to the lake, rain collecting in fat droplets on the brim of your hat. The wind pierces easily through your windbreaker and sweatshirt. You hop onto the boat, slightly more gracefully than the first time. Gunnar unties it and pushes off. After a few moments of fiddling with the engine and cursing under his breath in some unidentifiable foreign tongue, it roars into life.

You expect to speed directly out into the lake, but Gunnar cuts the motor almost to idle and you putter slowly along the shore. He gesticulates.

"Grab that buoy off the starboard bow!"

"Grab the what off the what?"

He smacks his forehead theatrically. "Starboard. The right-hand side as you face the front of the boat. Get the white buoy, the thing floating in the water." Indeed, a small white ball of Styrofoam bobs expectantly in the slate gray waves. You grab it and start to pull, the freezing water a shock against your skin. The line is attached to something unexpectedly heavy. A cage emerges into view from the greenish depths.

"Bait trap!" shouts Gunnar. "Show me what's in it!"

You pull the trap, a wire cage about 2 feet to a side, with a brick at the bottom. You pull it out of the water and into the boat, detaching the buoy. A dozen small fish flop desperately inside, blueish in hue, except for a splash of orange at the throat, with faint vertical black stripes on their flanks.

"Bluegills. Good." The engine roars into life and you speed off toward the east side of the lake. About 50 yards off shore, he cuts the motor. "Take out two of them bluegill and then tie the trap to the side of the boat. He takes a small fine-meshed net from his pocket and carefully ties it to one of the cleats. "Frozen chum," he calls out. "More bluegill. Ground up some of these guys' cousins last week." You inexpertly try and grab the wriggling fish; instantly, a couple of sharp dorsal spines surgically pierce the flesh of your palm. You muffle a whoop of pain and scoop two onto the deck, then tie off the trap to another cleat. Gunnar inserts a hook into the middle of the back of one as it shudders in panic and casts it out casually away from the boat. The desperately wriggling fish sails through the air and disappears with a small splash into the water. He hands you the rod.

"Look, there's hardly any drag on this now. You'll feel the little guy tugging and pulling a bit of line. Let him do it. If a pike hits, you'll know it. *WHAM!*" He whacks the side of the boat for emphasis. "Let him run for two or three seconds, tighten the drag, and set the hook as hard as you can. Got it?" You return a shivering nod and grasp the rod in rapidly numbing fingers. Gunnar casually hooks the second fish and casts it unceremoniously off the other side of the boat. He glances up at the sky.

"This should die down in an hour or so."

You sit in silence, the boat rocking in the waves, rain pelting your hats and coats in a continuous, soft pattering drumbeat. Millions of small circles expand in the water and just as quickly disappear as the clouds unleash their ceaseless bombardment. You need something to get your mind off of the cold.

"So, like, what's your deal, man?"

Gunnar looks at you sharply. A bead of water hangs off his nose. He wipes it away impatiently. "My deal?"

"Yeah, your deal. I don't know. Robots and door-locking codes and termite mounds. Foreign military uniforms in my closet. All this Nazi talk. It's super weird. What's going on with you?"

A bastardized cross of a chuckle and a snort emerges from Gunnar's chest. "Rest of the family doesn't talk about this, huh?"

"Nope."

"Well, all right, we have time, I guess. They don't necessarily know all of it themselves." Blue eyes, now calm and contemplative, peruse the shoreline. The bluegill tugs gently, but insistently, on your line.

"This all starts about fifty years ago with a man named Nikola Tesla. Do you know who he was?"

"Uh, a scientist, right? Didn't he invent the radio, or something?"

Something like respect dawns in Gunnar's eyes as he peers at you curiously. "*Yes*! Yes, he did, boy, and many other things. Well, it's more complicated than that. Tesla invented the induction coil, which you need to make a radio work. Unfortunately, he had a competitor, a goddamned greaseball Italian named Marconi. Marconi bribed the US Patent Office to give him the patent instead. He had a couple of big investors whose names you might recognize, like Andrew Carnegie and Thomas Edison. Poor Tesla was screwed. He sued and sued and lost lawsuit after lawsuit. He had about as much of a chance as our poor little bluegills out there. That's the thing about free enterprise, boy. Freedom for the pike means death for the minnows."

"Now, Tesla was one of the greatest scientists of the modern age. One of the most fundamental discoveries of the century, up there with the bomb and miracle of flight, must be credited to him. I'm talking about the *wireless transmission of electrical power and data*. Something that could have, and maybe someday will, revolutionize our existence on this silly, sad ball of dirt. But good science doesn't mean commercial success. By the time the war rolled around, I mean the big one, the big show, he was living on handouts in New York City. For the last ten years of his life, he lived in room 3327 of the New Yorker Hotel, in Manhattan. The king of Yugoslavia visited him there once." He gazes at you contemplatively for a moment, something inscrutable lurking in his pale, watery blue eyes. "Remember that number for me, OK?"

"What, 3327? Why?"

"Yes, that's the one. Just remember it. If you never forget one number as long as you live, make sure it's that one. Anyway, one day these folks came to him and said, well Mr. Tesla, it's nice that you're a famous scientist and all, but we kind of need you to pay your bill. Tesla tells them, I understand guys, but I'm a bit short of cash right now. What I can do is give you a prototype of my latest invention. It's right here. If anything happens to me, you can sell this to the government for a lot of money. It's incredibly dangerous. And he gives them this big crate, and attaches a handwritten note to it: 'Prototype death ray. Could lead to mankind's doom: do not open!' Suitably impressed, they put it in storage in the basement with a bunch of his other crap, and the poor bastard croaked two years later."

The rain indeed has begun to die down, with only a light staccato tap of drops on the fiberglass shell of the boat. The wind has slackened to an occasional, diminished gust. Gunnar removes his hat and mops his face with it.

"Well, as I said, Tesla was the greatest mind of his time, and the country was in the middle of a war. This was early 1943, or thereabouts. The Germans were doing well, and the Allies were still in serious shit. The FBI had a special team dedicated to watching Tesla, and when they got wind he'd died, they swooped in and grabbed all of his papers, inventions and prototypes. Including the box in the New Yorker. Which turned out to be full of random junk."

You snigger. "So that's where they got the idea for *Back to the Future*!"

"What?"

"Oh, it's a movie. A scientist sells some terrorists a fake nuclear bomb made out of parts from an old pinball machine."

Gunnar sighs theatrically. "Jesus. Films. But wait. The thing is, the FBI wasn't the only one watching Tesla. There was another group, a cell of German agents the Nazis had in Manhattan from 1938, with *exactly the same mission*. And they were not as polite as the Americans were. They stole a bunch of his prototypes from the New Yorker, including our 'death ray', about six months before he died, and transported it back to Europe by submarine. Leaving a bunch of boxes full of garbage in their place. Tesla himself most likely never knew anything about it."

"What, so there is an actual death ray?"

"Calm down, Darth Vader. Power can be put to any use. You can use microwaves to send data, send energy, cook a hot dog, or cook a person. So, they brought back all of this stuff to Germany for use in the *Wunderwaffe* program, the advanced weapons development division. These were the guys who made the V1 and V2 rockets, and the first jet powered fighter plane. Electrically-powered submarines that didn't need air to operate. The first acoustic homing torpedo. Neat stuff."

"Now, there have been rumors floating around for fifty years that Tesla invented some kind of death ray. The thing is, there was a kind of energy ray in that box, but not really what you, or anyone else, mean by the term. I mean, put yourself in Tesla's shoes in the 1940s. No battery technology to speak of. What are you gonna do, hook it up to a coal plant in Kentucky? Besides, he wasn't really interested in weapons. He was interested in wireless energy transmission."

You nod, sagely. "Of course." Your bluegill wanders aimlessly in circles. The rain has nearly stopped, with only the occasional circle expanding from an impacting raindrop on the surface of the lake.

"Of course, *nothing*! What he invented was an early version of these little robots you saw the other day. The things themselves are deceptively simple. Tesla demonstrated a remotely controlled boat in a New York water fountain before the turn of the century, for Christ's sake. Fuel cell technology had already existed for fifty years at that point. The thing was, he needed a more powerful fuel source. An unlimited fuel source."

You remember the diagrams of Mars and the Moon in his study. "Space."

Gunnar pauses, looks at you appraisingly, seemingly focused on a spot about a foot behind your cranium. "Yes, space. The sun is an incredible energy source, but most of this energy never reaches us. Because of the atmosphere, only a quarter of the sun's energy even reaches earth, and half of the earth is dark at any moment. So, at most you enjoy maybe 10 percent of gross solar output. And the sun shines most where people aren't, and it's too inefficient to transport it from the Sahara to London. But in space, boy, there is no atmosphere, nothing to block the endless energy of the sun. Tesla's great genius was to come up with a way to harness that massive potential, and direct it where and when it's needed."

"Building reflectors in space."

"Yes!" shouts Gunnar, pounding on the gunwale. "But not in space. On the moon. You see, boy, he had the vision, the foresight, the *inspiration*, to imagine sending a platoon of those small machines to the very moon itself, which would then replicate one another and organize themselves into a series of power stations, beaming constant streams of energy to giant collectors in orbit below."

"On the ground? But wouldn't you still lose the energy in the clouds or whatever?"

Gunnar's eyes light up. "You've hit one of the major problems, boy. Light cannot penetrate clouds well, but microwaves *can*. Tesla's idea was to tether a geosynchronous station to the moon with a huge solar collector, which would then convert the energy to microwaves and transmit down to earth. A limitless source of energy, generated by a few colonies of self-replicating robots launched toward that great orb in the sky." He chuckles.

"So? Why didn't he do it?"

"Well, Tesla was missing a few key pieces of technology. The robots themselves were simple to design. Assembling themselves into large macro-structures was more difficult, but in the end, he only needed to work out the mathematics of it – a finite problem, which could be programmed even into the primitive circuit boards available then. This took him years, but he managed. It's far easier now. Solar power cells had been developed during the war, so that was fine. He was missing two critical pieces of technology, however. Supraorbital flight, and autonomous local production."

"OK, but space flight didn't happen for ten or fifteen years after he died. Why was he even thinking about it?"

Gunnar's eyes flash with anger under the brim of his canvas fishing hat. "Don't you see, *this was his genius*. He could see that these technologies were close, even incipient in some cases. He didn't let himself be limited by the here and now. Orbital and supraorbital flight, superconductivity, remote production … these were obviously solvable problems, from his point of view. So, he designed a set of workable drones that could do the job he envisioned. He plotted the coordinates on the moon for a series of generators that would continuously target various points on the globe. The moon is tidally locked, you know. Every place on Earth always faces the same point on the moon."

You did not know that. "What does this have to do with the Nazis? And you?"

"Ah, yes." Gunnar rubs his chin thoughtfully. "All of this was delivered to an underground bunker on the shore of the North Sea, where the best and brightest minds of the German Reich were working on the *Wunderwaffe*. Tesla's papers, designs, and prototypes were delivered to a young physicist named Gerhard Schafer sometime in 1942 or 1943. Now, young Gerhard had always admired Tesla. Imagine his shock, and awe, to have the great man's unfinished work literally dumped on his desk while RAF bombers thundered overhead. And remember, he was working shoulder to shoulder with some of the scientific titans of his generation, people like Werner van Braun, who were at the same moment very close to developing space flight in the V2 program."

The clouds gradually are beginning to break, and the lake is now calm. Gunnar pulls a sandwich bag from his pocket and takes out a piece of jerky. He pops it into his mouth and chews reflectively. He offers you a piece. You accept it, placing it into your mouth. At first hard as plastic, it gradually softens into a malleable, chewable mass. The taste of chili and teriyaki plays havoc with your palate.

"It's from an elk I shot out in Idaho last year. This is the last of her," he remarks. You chew reflectively together in silence for a few moments. After a pause, Gunnar continues his story.

"Gerhard immediately saw the potential to weaponize this idea. If you ignored Tesla's desire to create a usable energy source, these stations ringing the moon could be programmed to focus the sun's unflinching rays anywhere on the planet. New York, Moscow, Paris, London, Peking. It wouldn't be as dramatic as in the movies, but he calculated that within a few months, the scale installations Tesla had planned - about a million square meters of panels - could raise the surface temperature of a ten square kilometer area by at least ten degrees Celsius. Which would render many cities in the world uninhabitable. Most cities operate on the very edge of sustainability anyway, and need to cool down at night. Adding a bit of energy to the system and preventing cooldown will quickly destroy an already fragile equilibrium. Imagine a couple dozen of these little colonies planting themselves on the moon, building a series of reflector plants which could hold any city on the planet hostage at the flick of a switch, with no conceivable defense or counter."

"So what happened?"

"Well..." You feel a violent jerk on your rod, and it bends precipitously toward the water.

"Holy shit!" you yell.

"Don't jerk yet, let him take it ... let him take it... now! Strike now!"

You fumble with the drag dial and jerk desperately on the pole. It now bends at an even more alarming angle, the tip shuddering with force. Line continues to spool out with a high-pitched whine.

"That's fine, he's on. We've got to tire him out. Keep the rod tip up, keep pressure on. If there's any slack he can spit out the hook and disappear." Keeping the rod tip up seems like a far-fetched task as the eye skips nervously on the surface of the water. Suddenly it bounces up, the line slack.

"Reel! Reel! He's swimming toward us!" You furiously turn the wheel, and again that dreadful weight appears as the fish changes direction, line spooling out wildly again and moving in a wide circle around the boat. Gunnar reels in his bait fish, leaving it flopping feebly on the deck.

"Don't want the lines to get tangled," he murmurs. "Come on, boy. Keep the pressure on." Your arms already ache with the unexpected effort. It seems for every foot of line you reel in, the fish surges away and takes two, but nevertheless the weaving line on the surface gradually approaches the boat. Gunnar climbs past you into the bow, net in hand. The boat rocks wildly. You see a flash of greenish white darting left, then disappearing down into the depths. It takes all your strength to hold the rod. Your arms throb with pain as you struggle to keep the fish from pulling the rod from your hands into the water.

"Pull, pull, pull ... pull left ... ga-ha!" Gunnar thrusts his net into the water like a gladiator dispatching an opponent with his sword, triumphantly raising your prize. A green, torpedo-shaped fish thrashes wildly in the net. Dark, tigerish stripes adorn its flanks. An oddly duck-billed mouth, bristling with needle-like teeth, yaws threateningly at you, savage, golden, feline eyes glaring wildly.

"Ho ho ho! Good work, boy! He's six pounds if he's an ounce." Gunnar pulls a heavy pair of pliers from his pocket and casually smashes the fish on the top of its head with a wet *thwack*. It immediately freezes into a stunned, quivering stillness, mouth gaping open in a howl of silent fury. He reaches into the fish's mouth with the pliers and unceremoniously rips the hook out, bringing what seems to be a considerable array of its innards along with it.

You are still panting from the effort. "Guess we're not throwing him back, huh?"

"No, he's dinner. Pike's tasty." He tosses his bait fish over the side and reaches into the trap for two new fresh ones, expertly hooking them again through the back. "Let's try a bit longer. I'd like to get one too. But you did good, kid. Nice fish." He offers you his hand. You take the hard, knotty palm in yours. It promptly crushes yours in a vice-like grip, looking you intently in the eye. He barks with laughter and hurls his fish far from the boat. He regales you with tales of fishing trips he used to take in Alaska. Steelhead trout with their strange, curved, bird-like lower jaws, and king salmon as long as a man is tall, roasted on an open fire at night on the banks of the river. Fishing next to bears so obese from the summer feast they could hardly walk, let alone pose any danger to man. Bald eagles wheeling in the sky and suddenly dive-bombing into the water, as wolves howled desolately in the distance. Moose and elk roaring at night during the autumn rut, their challenges to one another echoing among the moonlit hills. Setting out to sea for halibut early in the morning, no sound except for clanging bells of harbor buoys, the rattle of your engine and the stark cries of lonesome gulls, with the whole ocean stretching out in front of you like an endless black mirror. The unbearable joy of being alone on the water with a thermos of fresh coffee as dawn's first fingers tear the horizon asunder; anchoring up in the dark, silent sea and waiting for the first tug of a fish on the line. After an hour, he sighs and pulls in his bait fish.

"You had the golden rod today, kid. Let's go."

A Handful of Dust

At the cabin Gunnar punches in his code and you walk in. You remove your sodden clothing, draping it on the porch railing. Gunnar proceeds to the kitchen, tosses the pike into the sink and begins sharpening a knife, the mesmerizing ring of steel on stone startlingly loud in the confined space. He glances at you.

"Know how to fillet a fish, kid?"

"What do you think?"

Harumph. "City boys. Well, watch, you might need to know someday. Pike's one of the tougher fish to fillet. Up in Alaska, I used to guarantee no bones! No bones, or your money back! Ha!" He shows you how to slice the top off of the fish, above the dorsal bones, take off side fillets while avoiding the odd X shape of the primary and secondary ribs, and then the tail. He nonchalantly peels the guts from the skeleton and drops them in the trash. "We'll fry the fillets, make soup from the head and bones. It was a good fish. Be a crime to let anything go to waste. Now we need to bread the fillets."

"Finish your story," you blurt out as he begins massaging flower, salt, and pepper into the fillets. He looks at you curiously. "What story?"

"Come on man, Tesla and the Nazis. Who is this Gerhard guy?"

"Oh, that." He thoughtfully cracks open two eggs and mixes them slowly. "Well, he was my father. Your great uncle, as it were. You never met him, I suppose. He died a long time ago." He drops the fillets into the egg batter and sloshes them about absent-mindedly.

"Gerhard worked on perfecting Tesla's invention until the end of the war. He knew they didn't have the necessary rocket technology, but it was an interesting challenge. Anyway, when the war ended, the Americans swooped in and moved everyone from the *Wunderwaffe* installations to a secret site in New Mexico. They called it Project Paperclip, for some reason. Moved fifteen hundred Nazi scientists out into the desert, along with their families. One of those people was a young lady named Helga, and with her, came her newborn son: me. Hand me that jar of bread crumbs. The Japanese panko ones on the right. Then there's some Hungarian smoked paprika in the cupboard. Grab that, too."

You hand him a heavy jar of crumbs and, after some searching, a thick-glassed bottle of red paprika. He dumps out a considerable pile of bread crumbs onto the third plate, mixes in some of the pungent paprika flakes, then rolls the fillets into them until each is coated with a thick red and gold crust. "Now, Gerhard - my father - knew the Germans were never going to solve this in time. He was more interested in the mathematics of putting the arrays together, how to program this logic into simple logical gates that could be produced easily, the conductivity issues of solar collectors, and so on. Get me a pan, the thick one." He pours thick gobs of oil into the pan, far more than seems healthy, and punches the starter on the stove until it bursts into a hissing purple flame.

"Always cook on gas, son. Your mother cooks on gas. She's a good cook. Nobody ever cooked a good meal on an electric stove."

"Sure we need that much, uh, oil?"

Gunnar barks with laughter. "Go look in the kitchen of a McDonald's sometime. Hoo boy." He shakes his head, dropping a crumb of breading into the oil, watching intently as it begins to hiss and smoke. "We need to wait til it's hot."

"Where was I… ah, yes. So, he realized the potential of this idea. He knew something about the other programs – the Manhattan Project, the rocketry program – and he could see it was simply a matter of time until the technology matured. But when The Bomb was dropped on Hiroshima and fried a hundred thousand goddamn Japs in two seconds, he decided no one could be trusted with this. So, he hid it."

"Hid it? How?"

Gunnar shrugs, dropping the fillets into the now sizzling pan. A sharp hissing sound erupts from the bubbling oil. "It was a hectic time. There was a war to win. No one understood this stuff except for him. When he said it wasn't workable, nobody fussed about it anymore. Anyway, there wasn't that much to look at, actually. Some diagrams. A couple of primitive prototypes. Mostly the mathematics around constructing the arrays, the logic needed to send commands which would inform that construction around a particular target in space."

"Or on earth."

"Indeed. Or on earth." He turns over the fillets, now golden and crispy on the bottom. "Once Project Paperclip ended in 1953 - after the discovery of the hydrogen bomb - the scientists were released to find their own fortunes. My father, one of the few people who knew anything about computing at the time, joined a company known then, as now, as IBM. They moved him to New York. He managed to die of a heart attack at the ripe age of fifty-nine. My mother… joined him soon after. OK, this is probably good." He removes the golden-brown fillets with tongs from the oil and places them on paper towels. "Soak up that oil you're so worried about. Grab a couple beers and let's go out to the porch."

He brings the plate of fillets outside. The sky has cleared considerably, flashes of occasional blue fitfully appearing amidst the clouds. The sun struggles mightily to break through the overcast. You bite into a piece of fish, so hot it burns your mouth, but the fresh, firm flesh, redolent of this ancient mountain lake, is a taste like none other you have experienced.

"Good, huh? Nothing like fresh fish you caught yourself." Gunnar munches contentedly, staring out into the trees, steam rising from his mouth as the heat from the fish reacts violently with the chilly air.

"So, what happened to his stuff?"

"Well, I never got along too well with the old man. People at school found out where we were from. I got tired of being called a Nazi. Went to school in California, got master's degrees in mathematics and mechanical engineering. Old man paid for everything. So, to piss him off, I moved to Alaska, worked as a fishing guide for a couple of summers, and joined the Coast Guard." He glances at you. "That's why you call me Commander. Ran my own harbor tug, and then patrol boat, for a while." He chuckles and takes a pull of beer. You follow his lead, though it can't be past ten in the morning.

"Anyway, the Coast Guard realized I was better at math than driving boats, and moved me to their research and development center in Connecticut. I worked on mathematical models of hurricane movement together with the National Weather Service. That was right at the time the old man died, eleven, twelve years ago, must've been ...1979, I guess? My mother called me and said he had all this weird stuff in his workroom in the basement and had no idea what it was, asked me to come down and look through it to see if anything was worth saving. And there I am all of a sudden, thirty-six years old and sitting in a cellar with a bottle of peach schnapps and the lost papers of *Nikola fucking Tesla!*" He slaps his knees with glee.

"What did you do? I guess you didn't call the government."

"No, no, no. I figured it must be a gold mine. At first, I wanted to sell it all, but then I started looking at my father's later work. He made several important breakthroughs. He'd had access to some pretty advanced stuff in IBM. They more or less left him alone to fuck around with whatever he wanted. That was the deal the government made with them after the war – keep these guys happy and out of the way, and make sure the Russians don't get their hands on them. Anyway, the rocketry problem had been solved by the 1950s. Getting a payload to the moon was no longer difficult. But what to do when you're there?" Gunnar lets out an enormous belch for emphasis, wiping bits of fish carefully away from the corners of his mouth, tongue darting out, methodically probing for any undiscovered crumbs.

"The first issue was power. Without an expanding power source, you're screwed. This obviously had to be the sun. There's no oil on the moon. The photovoltaic effect had been known for over a century, but it wasn't until during the war the first functional solar panels were produced. They gradually became more efficient, and the first lunar soil samples from Apollo 15 confirmed what my father had hoped: the regolith contains *everything* you need to make a solar cell. Silicon, iron, titanium oxide, calcium and aluminum. Also, it turns out that the most difficult part of producing a solar panel on Earth – you need a near perfect vacuum – is already sorted on the moon."

You finish the last of your fish. "OK, but you still have to build this stuff up there. I guess you can't put a factory on a rocket."

Gunnar guffaws and slaps his knees again. "Ah, but now we can, boy! Don't you see? IBM had a partnership with a company called 3D Imaging which was a generation ahead of its time in stereolithography and laser sintering. Do you know what that is?"

"No clue."

"It allows you to print a solid object, layer upon layer, nanometer by nanometer, by beaming lasers at powders or liquids. My father had one of the first ones in his lab. Probably cost a million dollars at the time. After he died, I used to make fishing lures with it. They're going to be everywhere in a few years. Need a new kidney? Print one. Need a new part for your car? Print it. The tricky part though, if you wanted to reach scale, was how to *print another printer*. I need millions of these little robots for my idea to work. They take about fourteen hours to print, so one printer could make about seven hundred per year. It would take centuries, millennia even, to produce a usable installation. We need *geometric* growth, not arithmetic growth. That was the final piece of the puzzle he was missing to achieve his dream. To achieve Tesla's dream, in fact."

"So, do you have it? Do you have the last piece of the puzzle?"

"I do. Come look."

Gunnar waddles down the stairs from the back porch, stocky frame swaying with every step. You walk around to the decrepit garage, with peeling green siding. A large paper wasp nest hangs over a side doorway. Gunnar walks up to it unconcernedly and starts jiggling it.

You back away. "What are you doing, man?"

Gunnar glances at you bemusedly and tugs the nest off of the wall, tossing it unceremoniously to the ground with a plastic *clunk*. Another of his keypads is hidden behind the false nest. Thick fingers jab at it multiple times. With a click and a hum, the rickety, white wooden door swings outward. As you enter, you notice that behind half an inch of plywood is another half inch of seemingly solid steel.

Lights flicker on and you see the 'garage' is not nearly what it appears to be from outside. Desk after desk piled with electronic equipment, drones in various states of disassembly. A stack of insistently blinking servers nearly fills the back wall. The soft hum of air conditioning suffuses the room. The atmosphere feels cool and dry; somehow, you sense that it is antiseptically clean. In the middle of the room, like some sort of demented centerpiece, is a tall cube of what appears to be plexiglass, nearly as tall as you are. Various tubes and wires protrude from random edifices. Inside the chamber lurks a large, menacing object, plastic mandibles relentlessly humming back and forth, trailing sticky filaments in their wake. It looks like some sort of giant arachnid wrapping a meal in silk for later.

"What the hell is that thing? Why do you keep it in a baby bubble?"

"That, you unappreciative little shit, is the future of mankind you're looking at. It's a mobile production robot, capable of printing a functioning copy of another printer. Or of itself. One of those other ones you saw can print drone robots, but it can't print a printer. Come closer and look. Don't be afraid, she doesn't bite. But put these on." With a grunt, he pulls two cloaks of hooks on the wall. He hands you one. It is so unexpectedly heavy that you nearly drop it.

"Lead-lined cloak," grunts Gunnar. "Covers your vitals and genitals. That's a pretty radioactive environment in there. It's shielded, but better safe than sorry." His hand flashes out and taps your testicles. You emit a sharp *whoosh* and double over in surprise. "Can't just reprint those bad boys, you know." A manic smile fills his gnomish face. "Not yet, anyway."

"Why is it radioactive?"

"It's as near as I can replicate the conditions on the surface of the moon, which are, shall we say, extreme. Temperatures range from nearly 300 degrees below zero to above boiling. It's got no atmosphere to speak of, so it's a near perfect vacuum, not to mention that there's no magnetosphere shielding it from the solar wind. I'm trying to see how many production cycles it can get through without degrading. So far, I'm on seven. Which is enough. As long as each one can produce five before it croaks, it's enough to assure a geometric productivity function."

You stand next to each other, watching the plastic jaws move remorselessly to and fro.

"So what was the big idea here you were missing?"

"Ah. I'm part of various 3D printing Usenet groups. There are various communities around the planet connected on this network of academic and government facilities. I retired from the Coast Guard three years ago, but I can still use their computer facilities. So, about two years ago, this Russian kid, Evegny Dmitrov, posts a design for a self-replicating printer using *vacuum tubes* instead of transistors and a *Fresnel lens* for focusing sunlight instead of a laser! You know, like in those old television sets. Can you believe it? And a fucking *Fresnel lens*!" Gunnar roars with laughter.

"Hilarious," you comment drily.

Gunnar wipes his eyes. "Well, it was a weird idea, using this crazy old technology for something in the vanguard of modern innovation. Everyone laughed at him. Except me. Vacuum tubes are ideal for my purposes, you see. I can't imagine how I would reliably print a transistor or a laser, but a tube and a lens is simple. It's just silicon. Even if I could print a transistor, it wouldn't survive long in all the radiation up there. And, of course, we don't need to go through the complication of maintaining a vacuum in Earth's atmosphere – it's already there. It was genius. Sometimes you have to go down to go up, you know. Kid should get a medal. Except he apparently died of alcohol poisoning shortly afterwards. Pity. I'll have a statue of him put up in Sevastopol someday, though."

You look around at the thick ropes of cables, snaking past piles of haphazardly stacked electronics. Security cameras wink periodically at you from the corners of the room. "How do you pay for all of this, anyway?"

Gunnar shrugs. "I inherited some money from my parents. Retired with my 20 from the Coast Guard. Never wasted my money on women, or brats like you."

"Thanks."

"Well, I've seen worse than you, kid, that's for sure. Your father might have even been proud."

"You sure know how to charm a guy. So what's your plan, here, anyway? Just come in here every night and jerk off to your own genius, or what?"

Gunnar stares at you incredulously for a moment, then bursts out laughing. "You are your father's son, that's for damn sure. The man did not suffer fools lightly. I can vouch for that. The plan, boy, is we are going to pack up this whole circus, drive it out to Nebraska, and sell it to the man they call The Cornfield Oracle."

"Who?"

"He's the smartest, richest man in the world. He'll get this in a nanosecond."

"I mean, have you patented this? Wouldn't it be better to patent it and then try and sell the patent? I mean, don't know. Just seems simpler to me."

Gunnar looks at you askance, as though you'd invited him to sample a bowl of fried termites. "Patent? Like, as in the US Patent Office? Are you insane? That's exactly what Tesla tried to do. Look what happened to him. What do you think they'll do to me if I try and patent this thing? They'll squash me like a grape."

"Who's 'they'?"

"They? Them? *Everyone*! Have you heard a thing I've told you? Don't you see how disruptive this is? Energy production and distribution is a five *trillion*-dollar industry. If I can get a hundred *million* dollars' worth of rocket launches to put seed colonies on the moon, in a generation this technology could substitute 50% of global energy use. And can you imagine the military applications of this? You could fry any city off the face of the earth! Have you heard of the CIA?"

"Sure."

"Clowns! Clowns in sunglasses playing spy games with each other! Now, have you heard of the NSA?"

"Who?"

"Exactly. That, my young friend, is the National Security Agency. At once everywhere, and nowhere. They have ten times the CIA's budget. 'No Such Agency', we used to call them, in the service. Those guys know their shit. Hell, they know *your* shit. They know you're going to shit before you even do. Trust me, if I file a patent I'll have a cardiac event down at the lake before you can say 'Zapruder film', and a caravan of black vans will have all of this junk out of here before the sun is down. And you'd best pray they assume you don't know anything about it. No, no, we need world-class backup on this one."

"We?"

Gunnar pokes at the floor with his shoe. The tufts of hair lining his ears shine wanly in the electric light. "Well, I can't leave you here alone by yourself. Your mother would kill me. And it's always better to have someone with you in these discussions. Sometimes what gets said and what gets heard doesn't always match up, you know."

You fall into silence, watching the vaguely insectoid drone in the vacuum chamber continue to dutifully execute its instructions, moving in precise, mesmerizing, geometric patterns, plastic jaws mindlessly creating layer after painstaking layer of its own progeny; an exercise in simple brute force, but magnified by human ingenuity. The cacophonous, random symphony of DNA and natural selection, superseded by the cold, merciless order of algorithmic plastic extrusion molding and stereolithography, achieving in a few hours what evolution never could, even given countless eons.

Gunnar murmurs quietly beside you. "What are these roots that clutch, what branches grow out of this stony rubbish? I will show you fear in a handful of dust."

"What?"

"Nothing. Never mind."

Watch where you put your hands

The phone rings about 10 AM. Sunlight streams through the windows; fluffy cumulus clouds hang motionless in the summer sky. You pick up the phone, ignoring Gunnar's wail from his study. "*The code!* Wait for the *code*, you little creep!"

"Chateau Gunnar," you say.

A surprised pause on the other end. A female voice. "Oh, ah. Oh dear. I don't think anyone's ever picked up the phone before. I've only left messages," she titters. "This is Missy Eldridge. From the store, you know. Is your uncle there?"

Gunnar charges out of his study, clad only in his underwear and a tank top, institution green, festooned with numerous small holes through which wisps of white body hair protrude. Eyes bulging furiously, he waves frantically and makes cut-throat motions.

"No, ma'am. He's at the proctologist for a checkup, I'm afraid. Can I take a message?"

"Oh dear. Well, better safe than sorry at our age, I suppose. Yes, please tell Gunny that we're still counting on him to call out Bingo at the Knights of Columbus fundraiser tonight, OK?"

"Certainly. He's really looking forward to it. I hope you'll have a seat reserved for him right next to you. He's been talking about it all week."

An excited squeal erupts from the line. "Oh, of course! Tell him I'll bring a pillow for him to sit on in case his tush hurts him."

"I'll pass the message, ma'am. Thank you." You hang up.

Gunnar glares at you. "Proctologist appointment, eh? Very funny."

"Maybe you should go. Sometimes it seems like you've got something stuck up there pretty good."

Gunnar stomps wordlessly back into his study. You call after him. "I got you a date for Bingo tonight! Thank me later." The door slams behind him.

You pour yourself a glass of water. Even after a few weeks, the cold, mineral taste still astonishes you. How can simple old water be so different, you think. A light tap on the window makes you jerk your head up. A grotesque, deformed face gapes back at you from the window, eyes seemingly melting like wax, black nostrils smeared wide on the glass, tongue protruding from the mouth at an impossible angle. You eke out a small whimper of terror, and lurch away.

The face peels itself away from the window pane and rearranges itself into Aurora's angular features. She points at the door. You walk to the door and open it. She sports a lupine, mocking grin.

"Got you pretty good there, huh?"

"That was not what I needed this early in the morning."

"Oh, stop sulking. It's not a good look on anybody. C'mon, let's go swimming. It's a nice day."

"Yeah, all right. Let me get my bathing suit."

"I'll change down here."

You go upstairs and change into your bathing suit. Aurora is waiting, white one-piece suit in sharp relief against her toffee-colored skin. She holds a pair of swimming goggles and a towel. "Let's go."

Gunnar barges out again, still wearing his eclectic ensemble of underwear. His nose shines a deep maroon in the sunlight flooding through the windows. "What the…" he stops, in mid-shout, gazing nonplussed at your visitor.

"Good morning, Mr. Schafer. Would you like to join us for a swim?"

He continues to regard her appraisingly. "No. I already went." He pauses. "OK, I take it back, kitten. You don't look like a twelve-year-old boy."

She smiles sweetly. "Neither do you, sir."

He grimaces and lets out a small snort. "Fair enough. You kids have fun."

You walk down the hill to the lake. There is a small grassy landing with a short dock extending out into the lake where the boat is tied up. Aurora tosses her towel onto the grass and carefully fastens her goggles around her head. They are tinted black. She bounds down the deck and dives gracefully into the water, barely making a splash. After a few moments, her head emerges from the water and she begins to swim. She is an excellent swimmer, and fast, arms cutting through the air and into the water with machine-like precision, head turning every four strokes. In an alarmingly short period of time she is fifty or sixty yards from the dock. She pauses and turns around to look at you and waves. "Come on in!"

You jump gracelessly into the water. Although the sun is high in the sky, and it's very hot out, the water is shudderingly cold. Spring-fed, Gunnar had explained, water rising up from hidden wells nestled deep within the earth's stony roots. You struggle out to where Aurora bobs in wait for you, attempting some approximation of the breast stroke you've seen on television.

"Well," you gasp, spitting out a mouthful of icy water. "Guess we've found another sport you can teach me. You swim like a fish."

Aurora gives a noncommittal shrug, a simple achievement you cannot imagine accomplishing in such deep water. "I get to use the pool at Bowdoin. I train with their swim team sometimes, actually. I swim across the lake here a couple times a week. It's a good workout, half mile each way, I guess. Not today though."

"No, not today." A few yards away there is a small floating platform. You swim over to it. A small school of perch lurk in the shadows underneath it, flitting away in alarm as you approach. You pull yourself onto it and sit, enjoying the warmth of the sun as it drives away the chill of the lake. Aurora strikes out determinedly toward the middle of the lake. After a couple of hundred yards she turns around, and returns, switching from the crawl to breast stroke, submerging with every stroke. As she approaches the raft, she goes deeper, her shimmering form arcing dolphin-like through the water. She surfaces and pulls herself onto the raft. You note Gunnar has come to the dock at some point. His car is parked on the road and he sits in a deck chair, reading a newspaper.

You cavort on the raft for a bit, jumping into the water. Aurora tries, and fails, to teach you how to dive, the unsecured platform yawing wildly beneath you with every jump. She notices the deep, ragged scar on your right shoulder. "Wow. Guess that explains why you suck at basketball."

"It's more because I have the vertical of a snapping turtle."

After a bit, you return to the dock. Gunnar peers over the newspaper. "You're a heck of a swimmer, kitten. Why don't you try and teach this bumbling pile of freckles and limbs here a thing or two? He's about as coordinated as the fawns drunk on fermented crabapples I get staggering around my lawn every summer." His shirt is off. You notice for the first time that he has two swallows tattooed on his upper pectorals and, oddly, crosses on the soles of his feet.

"We need to get him goggles. Hard to do much without goggles."

You change the subject from your abject ineptitude at all thing athletic. "What's new in the world?"

"War's a-coming. Iraq's fixin to invade Kuwait, maybe Saudi. Hope you're ready to get called up, boy. But we're a Navy family. You'll be fine. Just lob a few missiles from a cruiser at those worthless towelheads, and they'll run back to Baghdad like the bitches they are!" He emits a contemptuous bark. "Those camelfuckers don't have a clue what they're up against."

"You know, could you like, have a bit of compassion for your fellow man once in a while?"

Gunnar peers at you curiously. "What? We didn't start this. But you can be goddamn sure we'll finish it. Anyway, who's hungry? I brought the grill down. Got some chicken marinating, and I bought some corn."

Aurora pipes up. "That sounds fantastic, Mr. Schafer."

"You can call me Gunnar, kitten. And I've got plenty, bring your parents down if you like."

"Well, that's very kind of you. You can call me Aurora. Call me 'kitten' again and you might get scratched. Even kittens have claws, you know. I'll go tell them." She strides across the thin strip of grass and onto the road, flip flops producing an equine *clop* with every decisive step.

Gunnar looks at you meaningfully once she is out of hearing, gnomish eyes suddenly possessed of laser-like focus. "Boy, she's a little firecracker, ain't she? You're doing all right there, kid. Did you get it wet in that yet, or what?"

"Jesus Christ, man. Can you be even a little bit normal for a change? Do I sit here and ask you what you do after Bingo?"

"All right, all right. A gentleman never tells. I gotcha. Susan's raising you right, boy. Don't listen to Uncle Gunnar. It'll only get you in trouble." He trundles over to his car and begins to haul out pieces of his grill and a sack of charcoal. Kneeling down, he energetically begins to reassemble it. He glances at you. "Go up to the house, bring down the chicken and the corn from the refrigerator. And a cooler of beer."

By the time you return, Aurora and her parents are already there. Aurora wears a long, light blue summer dress. Her mother is non-descript in khaki shorts and white shirt. Her father looms over everyone in blue jeans and a short button-down shirt, crew cut white hair shining in the sunlight. He wears wrap-around aviator sunglasses. Gunnar has the grill blazing and looks perfectly content, poking at the coals with a metal spatula, the serene smile of a mentally challenged child plastered across his face. Aurora's parents bob and nod at you uncomfortably.

You open a beer for Gunnar and Hal. Miraculously, you'd also found a bottle of white wine in the back of Gunnar's refrigerator. Chenguang accepts a glass gratefully.

Hal peers down at you intensely, looking like some gigantic bug with the mirrored aviator sunglasses. "I see your uncle's a sailor, Robert. Why didn't you say so? I've spent some time in the ocean's bosom myself, indeed I has."

"Yes, Coast Guard, I believe…"

Hal chortles. "Oh no no no. Did you see those tattoos? He's got two sparrows. If mine eyes be not mistaken, he done no less than ten thousand of ye ol nautical miles. Or be I mistaken, Captain?"

"*Commander,*" Gunnar mumbles, nearly inaudibly, under his breath.

"....and ye old *Commander* here has *crosses* on his soles, yes he do indeed."

"What does that mean?" Aurora pipes up, clearly interested.

"So the sharks don't eat you if you fall into the Big Blue," grumbles Gunnar. "Old wives' tale. Or sailors' tale. You know your tattoos, Hal. Do you have one yourself?"

Hal smiles broadly. "Aye, *commander*. I have one. But nowhere the likes of thee. I was Merchant Marine for a spell, meself."

You decide to interrupt. "Well, coals look about ready." You begin to unpack the chicken. Gunnar stops you.

"First the corn." He gently removes a half dozen foil-wrapped ears of corn and places them reverently on the coals. A dull hiss emanates from within the foil. Gunnar drops more coal on top, then places the grill. He fans the grill with his newspaper until the upper coals catch, and a steady orange flame begins to brightly burn. "OK, now the chicken." Gunnar's face lights up with the typical, imbecilic grin that animates his face whenever he is dealing with fish, food, or fire. "We have two kinds of chicken, folks. Habanero Double Flush, or Macadamia Nut Burp. Double Flush on the left, Nut Burp on the right. Pick your poison. *Chickenat emptor.*" He joyfully pulls out dripping bits of chicken from the two containers, some an alarming neon orange, others a more soothing espresso brown, placing them on the grill with a satisfying hiss. Even from several feet away, a bilious cloud of seared capsaicin makes your eyes water.

While the chicken and corn is cooking, Hal regales you with tales of his time in India. Aurora looks ready to regurgitate food she hasn't yet eaten, nursing a Snapple with a venomous glint in her eyes.

"So, I'm on this bus in New Delhi, back before it became what it is today, you see? And this feller next to me gets talking and wondering how come it is I *speakee* such good *Hindi*..." Aurora coughs in contempt. Chenguang beams and nods obliviously. Hal plows onward. "And this feller, he's got his arm outta window, you see. And we're talking and talking… now the roads haint too wide in New Delhi, right? An this minibus come roaring along the other side and come a mite too close to us, and what happens? Take the feller's arm clean off! Clean as a whistle! Pow!" He claps his ham-like hands together, the crackle of sound booming across the water.

Aurora gazes searchingly into the lake, waves gently lapping the shore as reeds sway in the breeze, as if wondering in which particular part to throw up.

"Thing is, it gone done and happen so fast, feller didn't even notice! He kept talking to me about differences in Urdu as opposed to Hindi, meanwhile he's got blood spurting out his elbow stump like nothing doin! I figured only polite thing to do was tell him, hey pardner, you gonna die in about two minutes here if we don't do nothin. Well! He take a look at his arm, start screaming, and well afore we could stop the bus and get a doctor, poor fella was done and done for, god rest his poor soul." Hal crosses himself reverently at this moment.

Gunnar regards Hal with peculiar interest as he relates this story, mouth gaping half open, spatula dangling loosely from his hand. Aurora interrupts, witheringly.

"Now, *Hal*, is there by any chance some kind of *lesson* you think people should draw from this *extremely* entertaining story of yours?"

"Well, *daughter*, now that you mention it, there is." He draws from his beer and gazes at you, eyes invisible behind mirrored shades.

"A man always got to be careful where he put his hands. An that God's truth."

"Hoo-wee!" screams Gunnar at that moment into the uncomfortable silence that abruptly descends after this last comment. "Who's ready for chicken and corn? And I'm warning you kind folks, when I say double flush, I'm not joking around!"

The food turns out to be extraordinarily good. The corn is otherworldly, fresh sweet corn grilled on open coals in foil, slightly burnt and infused with butter and salt and coriander. The habanero chicken is, as advertised, really very hot. You have tasted nothing remotely similar in your life. Even Hal, evidently raised in El Paso, and who makes much of having spent many years in Thailand, Korea, Hong Kong and assorted other

Asian locales, is forced to admit that it 'packs a wallop,' dabbing his eyes with a napkin as he does so, while beads of sweat form on his reddening brow. Macadamia Nut Burp is similarly foreign to your experience. After one bite of the slightly sweet, nutty crust enveloping a juicy chunk of chicken thigh, Aurora flatly declares, "Forget about your stupid robots. Open a restaurant. Tomorrow."

"*Kitten*," Gunnar growls menacingly.

Hal's eyes light up. "We've heard you are summat of an inventor, yes, a veritable *engineer*, even." Chenguang bobs her head encouragingly. "I have taken the liberty, sir, of bringing my own invention to this impromptu, ah, *meeting of the minds*." Hal pulls an anonymous white box from his pack, the size and shape of a typical board game. "I was hoping such esteemed gentlemens such as yourselves would lower hisselves to look at my, ah, impoverished efforts to *amuse* my betters. After we done *et*, of course." Aurora looks frantically at the ground nearby as though she might will into existence through pure force of concentration some crevasse willing to swallow her whole, immediately and forever. You discreetly squeeze her elbow, and grin encouragingly. She looks up at you, startled, and offers a wan smile in return.

After you finish the food, Hal corrals everyone onto a blanket to test out his board game. He calls it Sequentia. It is very mathematical and involves a set of dozens of plastic markers and a pack of cards, sort of a multidimensional *Connect 4* but using the cards to determine the vectors of influence of the markers and their effects. Once everyone gets the hang of it, it's actually quite entertaining, but fiendishly complex.

Gunnar gazes at the tableaux contemplatively. "I see what you're trying to do. Mathematically, I mean. It's a neat idea. But you overestimate people's intelligence. I mean, you're dropping Fibonnacci sequences into the mechanics of a board game, for god's sake, man."

Hal's enormous form hunches over the board, thick fingers toying with multicolored markers. "Yes! But people rise to the level of expectation! Design for troglodytes and resign yourself to humanity behaving like troglodytes! That's the whole point, my stumpy friend. We must make them think, and consider, and think again!"

"If you think you'll change people's *mentus operandi* with a board game,

Mr. Robinson, you are badly mistaken. I mean, not to be immodest, but ask my nephew here how smart I am."

Hal and Gunnar both look at you enquiringly.

"He is, indeed, smarter than the average bear."

"And what do I do to amuse myself, boy?"

"As far as I can tell he likes to fish, insult people, and masturbate to earmarked copies of 1987 *Playboy* magazines."

After a moment of frozen silence, Hal erupts into an extraordinary torrent of laughter. Even Chenguang and Aurora lose their composure and begin to giggle. Gunnar looks at you with a stony visage for a few moments, but eventually a smile cracks through. He begins to chuckle, and wipes his eyes.

"OK, OK, you got me there, boy. Anyway, my point is even a Newtonian-level genius such as myself, without a care in the world, with no hormonal brats to watch over, is not gonna spend his time parsing your overly clever board game dynamics. We seek simpler pleasures. Listen to Thoreau, Mr. Robinson. Simplify, simplify."

The sun has begun to descend on the lake and Aurora's parents begin to make the inevitable excuses as to why they must leave. You insert that your uncle has certain unavoidable obligations at the Knights of Columbus in any event involving a shopkeeper and a pillow. The Robinson clan takes their leave and marches down the road. Aurora turns and looks back at you, dress twirling artistically as she does so, and mouths 'thank you'. She shrugs, and turns, and walks on. The sun is low on the horizon, the sky a mellow medley of orange and purple hues.

You turn to Gunnar, who still gazes contemplatively at the trio walking away.

"You better get ready for your big night, man."

Gunnar ignores you, intently watching the three figures as they fade, and finally disappear, into the encroaching shadows. He glances at you. "Did you see his tattoo?"

"No. What was it?"

"He's got a dragon on his left forearm."

"So what?"

"Well, if he's a sailor like he says, it means he served in China."

"…and?"

"He's my age. No one served in China since 1949 when those Commie dipshits took over. Either he got that tattoo when he was six or…"

"Or what?"

"Or nothing. Let's go up to the house. I have to get dressed."

Tanto nomini nullum par elogium

You wake to a splitting headache. After Gunnar had left for his Bingo date, you'd drunk the rest of the beer from his cooler. You can't remember how many there had been, but given the throbbing in your head, there must have been several. Light shines through the blinds. You have no idea what time it might be. You creak down the stairs. Gunnar sits in his chair, coffee mug beside him, head bent forward in sleep.

"Wake up, old man," you shout, without response. You head into the kitchen and pour yourself a residual cup of coffee from the pot. You return to the living room. Gunnar remains motionless.

"Gunnar. Uncle Gunnar. Wake up."

No response. You gingerly touch his coffee cup. It is barely warm; it must have been there for some time. A creeping sensation of dread begins to steal upward along the length of your spine.

"Gunnar!" you shout at his still form. Again, no response. You shake his shoulder. Nothing. You place your fingers on his neck, seeking a pulse. Suddenly his eyes flash open and steely fingers lash out to your throat, choking off your air supply faster than you would have dreamed possible. Before you know what has happened, you are prone on the ground, his fingers still digging into your throat, a heavy knee driving mercilessly into your shoulder. You see a massive, knotted fist hovering above you, preparing to strike; maniacal, ice blue eyes, pupils deadly pinpricks of darkness, animated solely by a murderous rage, staring into yours.

Somehow you manage to force air you didn't realize you still had past your vocal cords. "Stop it ... you ... fucking... psychopath..."

Recognition gradually dawns in Gunnar's eyes. He stands, releasing you from the hold. He stretches and settles back into his chair.

"Don't surprise me like that, kid." He takes a sip of coffee, and grimaces. "Damn, this is cold. Musta fallen asleep."

You massage your throat, which still feels as though an anaconda is having its way with it. You want to shout, but can only manage a faint, hoarse wheeze.

"Dammit, I've had enough of your crap! What the fuck is wrong with you? You just tried to kill me. Your nephew, remember?"

Gunnar hoists himself from the chair and saunters calmly into the kitchen. He places his coffee mug in the microwave and turns it on. A stately hum emanates from the small box. He stretches his back for a second time, looks at you blankly, and shrugs.

"Military training, kid. Nothing personal. Just don't sneak up on me like that. Wouldn't hurt you to learn this stuff, you know. Might come in handy sometime."

"What, so I can accidentally murder the occasional relative? Sounds great."

Gunnar shrugs. "Ehhh. Anyway, start thinking about what you want to pack. I want to head out tomorrow."

"Head out?" You can still manage nothing above a light rasp.

"I told you. Nebraska. We're gonna pack up the lab and bring it to the richest man in the world." He peers at you and grins slyly. "Don't worry, we'll only be gone a week. It's a two-day drive. You'll still have plenty of time with your little friend there."

You continue massaging your throat. Looking through the window you note that there is indeed a sizeable orange and gray U-Haul van lurking in the driveway. "I thought you were joking. How about *your* little friend? Did you get to ah, *call Bingo*, shall we say?"

Gunnar furrows his brow at you irately. "No, but she brought me a pillow to sit on and asked some intimate questions about the health of my ass. Thanks for that."

The phone rings. You go to pick it up. Gunnar throws his hands in the air theatrically and mouths *the code*.

"Hello?"

Aurora. "Was dinner so bad that you guys are moving away? I'm sorry."

"Ah, no. Just temporarily. We're gonna do a roadshow."

"When you leaving?"

"Tomorrow, early. We'll be back in a few days."

You agree a run around the lake. Gunnar looks at you appraisingly. "All right, but get back here. I need help moving this stuff into the truck."

"Sure."

You meet down at the dock. After even a few runs, you find it much easier and even manage to wheeze out part of a conversation as you go. Aurora trots unconcernedly beside you, nearly noiseless compared to the echoing slaps of your oversized soles. The sun rises rapidly in the sky, but mercifully the trees provide shade and relief. Your hangover burns away rapidly in the heat. Cheerily colored lakeside houses nestle among the greenery. The occasional couple sitting on a porch waves to you as you pad by. Unseen robins warble at one another, hidden in the branches above.

"Sorry if my parents were weird, man."

"Relax. Uncle Gunnar isn't gonna win any awards for his dinner table manners either," you croak out in response.

"Funny part is that we'll probably end up that way. Everyone looks at the older generation and says 'not me'. Then you wake up one day, and it is you."

You glance at her. Jaw clenched tightly, she powers determinedly ahead.

"Something's kinda wrong there, isn't it?"

She does not look at you. "Yeah. Yeah, there is."

"Wanna talk about it?"

She shakes her head forcefully. "Nah."

"OK."

You complete the rest of the run in silence. You slow to a halt in front of Gunnar's house, panting with exertion and dripping with sweat. You hold up your hand for her customary high five. Instead, Aurora quickly reaches toward you and gives you a fierce embrace, her lithe form pressed against you, firm as though her body were carved from wood. After a few moments, she releases you. She flashes you a bright smile, and delivers a light punch to your shoulder.

"Drive safe, dummy. Let me know when you're back."

Gunnar is already milling around his workshop. "Ah! Ha, ha! There you are. Come on, we've got a lot to do. First things, first, we need to lock up the drones and codes." A stack of sleek silver cases with flashing digital locks stands by the plexiglass tank. "Now, take two of those inside to my study. Everything we are taking with us is piled on the floor. Once you fill a case, arm the lock, like so," he carefully points to a button with a red lock on it, "and bring it out here to the van."

You bring the cases inside and pour a glass of water. There is an enormous stack of assorted junk: folders with sheaves of papers, haphazard piles of small robots glinting in the fitful sunlight that manages to pierce the canopy of trees outside. A neat stack of black rectangular boxes sits on its own. You begin with them; they just fill one case. A few of the robots suffices for the second. You lock the cases and bring them out to the truck.

Gunnar, bare chested, is straining to wheel out the large case with the production robot inside. Sunlight glints off of the surface, momentarily blinding you. He's abandoned the protective apron, you note.

"What are those little black things?" you enquire, tossing the cases into the van.

Gunnar screams in alarm, eyes bulging fantastically. "Jesus, be careful with that stuff!"

"Supposed to survive a trip to the moon, aren't they?"

"It's not the stuff in the boxes I'm worried about, it's the *boxes*. They each have a thermite charge connected to the lock. If someone puts in the wrong code three times … *boom*. All of them. At once. There won't be enough left of anyone in a thirty meter radius to interest a coyote."

"Hope you're a good driver. Guess we better not get in an accident."

Gunnar acknowledges this point with a growl. "Yep, plus we'll make a measurable radiation event with this bad boy." He pats the case where the production drone still busily spins its webs of plastic and metal alloys. "Anyway, the boxes are solid state disk drives. They hold all the codes and coordinates and instructions. Each of the robots has a little receiver and can get instructions via wireless transmission, 2.45 gigahertz. It's a freeband. Those boxes hold the instructions."

"Kind of far to the moon to make a phone call, isn't it?"

Gunnar shrugs. "It's not that hard. You just need a powerful enough transmitter on earth. We don't need to get a signal back, thankfully – that would be a heavier lift."

After about three hours you manage to pack everything up. The huge crate with the production unit is obviously far too heavy to lift even for the two of you; it must weigh several hundred pounds, you remark. Gunnar dismisses your concerns with an airy wave. Whistling to himself, he trundles out a wheeled device ensconced under his deck with two thick metal prongs and slides this under the case. He cranks a lever a few times and the case gradually rises off the ground a few inches. He wheels it over toward the van and industriously cranks for several minutes while the contraption gradually rises to where he can slide it into the van.

"Neat," you observe. "You do plan ahead, I'll say that for you."

"Seneca teaches us that luck is what happens when preparation meets opportunity, boy. I stole this from Home Depot last year sometime. Now, run down to the store and pick up a couple of hoagies and a six-pack of beer. I'm hungry, and someone appears to have emptied my refrigerator last night." He hands you a fold of bills, damp and smelling of sweat, from his pocket.

You drive down to the store in the Toyota and park. Two elderly gentlemen with black and gold 'POW – MIA: Never Forget' baseball hats struggle decrepitly up the stairs into the store. One leans heavily on a cane. You pause behind them. The man with the cane peers at you with kindly, watery eyes. He nods at you, the flesh hanging from his throat, shaking like a turkey's wattle as he speaks.

"Go ahead, young fella. We might be awhile. Had a run-in with some Chinamen in Koh-REE-uh back in the day, you see. Done gone and crimped my style a bit."

"Take your time, sir. I'm in no hurry."

They manage to make their way into the store. It smells of fresh-baked bread and brewing coffee. You drop a six-pack of Sierra Nevada on the counter. "Good afternoon, Ms. Eldridge. How are you this fine morning?"

The proprietor leans a head on one hand and looks at you with bleary eyes. "Oh, hello there, Robert. Well, I've had better days. Sometimes those Bingo nights can get a bit hectic, you know?"

"Yes ma'am. I'm sure they can. Uncle Gunnar seems awfully worn out. He sent me down here, saying the only thing that could possibly revive him would be one of those wonderful hoagies you make."

She emits a gentle titter and rubs her temple. "Oh, of course. And one for you, I hope. Growing boy and all."

You carry the bag of food back to the car and drive back to Gunnar's. He sits cross-legged on the floor of his study, brow furrowed in concentration, sorting stacks of files and papers.

"Chow's on."

He nods at you dismissively, deeply absorbed in his own mad little world of equations and diagrams. He shakes his head and mutters to himself as he casts papers and documents into various piles in front of him, fingers dancing through the air, as though conducting some kind of spectral orchestra.

"Couple of black vans parked out front," you call out.

"Uh huh," he mumbles distractedly.

"They have NSA logos on the side."

"Right." He waves you away indifferently.

You give up trying to bait him, and eat your lunch. He hobbles out a couple of hours later to join you on the porch, long-cold hoagie in one knotted hand and a beer in the other. The sky is beginning to turn a deeper shade of blue as the sun begins its descent.

"Good beer. I didn't know it. Gotta remember this one." He rips a chunk off of his sandwich with his teeth, chewing methodically, eyes fixated on the pale orb of the moon rising in the northern part of the sky. Bird flit among the pines. You hear the machine-like clatter of a woodpecker industriously seeking grubs within the pulp of a nearby tree. "Welp, enjoy the view while it lasts. We're heading out to corn country tomorrow."

"You nervous?"

Gunnar shrugs. He seems oddly melancholy. "Tomorrow we're gonna try to change the world. It's never easy. You know who Machiavelli was?"

"Uh, I've heard the name."

"Well, he said 'there is nothing so hard to take in hand, more perilous to conduct, or more uncertain in success, than to attempt to create a new order of things.'" He ferociously tears off another chunk of his sandwich. "I saw his tomb in Italy, once. You know what's written on it? *Tanto nomini nullum par elogium*. 'There can be no eulogy for so great a name'. Arrogant son of a bitch."

"Sounds like it."

Later, Gunnar retreats back to his study to continue sorting through his junk. You settle onto the couch, where you've been struggling through *Dune* for the last several days. Around nine o' clock he returns, a shotgun casually dangling from one hand, and flicks on the television.

"Planning on winning one of those arguments you're always having with the TV news anchors this time?"

He glances at you contemptuously and presses a few buttons on the remote control. A grainy view of the U-Haul in the driveway emerges from static.

"That trailer contains a few lifetimes worth of work of better men than you and me, kid. I'll be damned if some hoodlum decides he's gonna get cute and stick his snout into it. There's a motion-sensor out there that'll trigger an alarm, but I'm not gonna run out there every time a racoon wanders by. You might want to get to bed, by the way. We ride at dawn. I'll wake you up."

You retire to bed with *Dune* and read it long into the night. Frank Herbert's tales of densely complex political machinations, and ecologically improbable monsters roaming exotic desert worlds for some reason act as a calming influence on your mind; a tale only slightly stranger than your crazed uncle lurking below in his bathrobe, shotgun cradled in his lap, staring at a grainy video feed of chipmunks cavorting over and around a dented U-Haul, implacably defending the daunting legacy of Nikola Tesla from imagined enemies, at home and abroad.

Bingo!

You awaken with a start. The instant, unmistakable realization washes over you that it is far too late, and you have badly overslept. Light streams in through the window. *We both overslept*, you think. *We should have left hours ago.* You hurriedly pull clothes on and grab the suitcase you packed the day before.

Gunnar slouches in his chair, exactly as you left him many hours before, head tilted forward in repose, shotgun still in his lap. As yesterday, a cup of coffee sits still and seemingly untouched on the table beside him.

"Wake up, man. We're late!" You pass by and enter the kitchen, pouring yourself a cup of coffee. You glance into the living room – no response.

"I'm not falling for that trap again, asshole. Not while you've got a shotgun in your hands." You stick your head around the doorjamb. There really is a non-zero chance he might wake up startled and simply shoot you, you realize.

You fill a glass with water and, aiming carefully, slosh its contents toward where your uncle sits a few feet away, immediately ducking behind the door to avoid any potential incoming barrage of buckshot. After a few seconds, you cautiously peer into the room. Your toss was on target: Gunnar's robe sports a large dark stain, and water drips from his nose and ears. A large puddle has collected beneath him. Nevertheless, he remains motionless.

"Gunnar!" you shout. No response.

Gingerly, you approach. Carefully seizing the gun's stock with one hand and barrel with the other, you attempt to jerk it away suddenly. Gunnar's hands remain partially locked onto the gun, and the motion causes his body to topple gracelessly from the chair. His motionless form collapses to the wooden floor with a dull thud; his mouth lolls open and saliva begins to drip out, forming a small, glistening pool underneath.

You toss the shotgun onto the couch and kneel beside your uncle, shaking Gunnar firmly. "Wake up! *Wake up!*" You feel his throat: you detect no pulse. His skin is cool to the touch. The body lolls on the ground at an exceedingly odd angle, which no one would naturally tolerate for any length of time, even in sleep.

You collapse heavily onto the couch next to the gun, staring at the crumpled, stilted form of your uncle lying on the floor for what seems like an aeon. He remains motionless, in spite of your best efforts to will him into animation. You hear a faint *beep … beep … beep …* from his study.

Your thoughts gradually begin to organize themselves. Obviously, you should call 911. If he's had a heart attack and is in a coma or something similar, every second is precious. Somehow, you cannot bring yourself to move. You examine the still form again, its bizarre tangle of limbs. *That's no coma*, you think. There is a small mirror on the wall: you rip it off, screws and all, and hold it close to Gunnar's mouth for a few seconds. You check: not even a tiny bit of condensation that the shallowest of breaths would surely leave.

The insistent, metronomic beep from the study continues. You check the doors and windows: all shut, all locked. The U-Haul remains in the driveway exactly where it was the night before. You enter the study, strangely uncluttered, save for a few piles of papers and models Gunnar had evidently decided to leave behind. His computer, a sleek black Compaq model, rests imposingly on his desk. It seems to be the source of the beeping. Driven by an inexplicable urge, you turn on the monitor.

Enter your security code, a window demands. For lack of better options, you enter the security code that you set several weeks ago to lock and unlock the front door. To your surprise, it seems to accept this, and the computer hums into life. Unbidden, a video opens: Gunnar. The video is not extremely recent – he sports a slightly more civilized haircut than he does now – but he is approximately the same age. It cannot be more than a year or two old. He speaks. You turn up the volume.

"…is lucky enough to be listening to this message, it means two of two things. First, the biometric sensor in my watch has registered that my heart is beating at fewer than ten beats a minute and my body temperature is ninety-four degrees or less, which means I'm either dead, or so close to it there's no point arguing otherwise. Second, you've gotten an automated call, and you've got a code to get into my house. Which means you're in my circle of trust. I don't know who this is – Keith, if this is you, you sorry,

STD-riddled bastard, I have *not* forgotten how you fucked me over in Budapest that time, and I do *not* forgive you. This is your chance to make things right, however. Sergejs, if this is you..." at this point he breaks into a foreign language you do not recognize, punctuating the discourse with a hearty laugh. He lifts a glass, more than half-full with amber liquid, and toasts the camera. *Nazdrovye*! Not German; Russian, you suppose.

"Now, to whomever this is addressed. You have to work fast; whoever did this to me didn't do it for kicks. They know about my work, and they want it. It is vitally important not to call the police, or the emergency services. They will be waiting for someone to find the body, and clear it out. They'll have made it look like a heart attack, so there won't be any forensic investigation, not at my age and condition. Over the next couple of days they'll extract my work, clean as a whistle. *This must not be allowed to happen under any circumstances.*"

"Follow my instructions as best you can in the time you have. Go to my workshop in the garage. There is a keypad under a fake wasp nest by the door; the code – write this down" – he pauses for a few seconds – "is 198653. There is a pile of suitcases on the west wall. Load my drones, disk drives and papers into these and lock them. They're armed with thermite detonators, which will go off if people try to open them three times without the right code, or break into them by force. They're all connected by a wireless near field communication network, so if one goes off or they are separated by more than ten meters from one another, they *all* go off. So, uh, be careful with them. Anyway, if you have a code to my house, you should know the PIN code as well. Otherwise, I've balled this up pretty good." He pauses, looks off to his right, then back at the camera. "In the end, it's better that all our work be destroyed than for it to fall into the wrong hands," he concludes, in seeming seriousness.

"Now, the drones are pre-programmed to set up binary colonies on the side of the moon facing Earth's eastern hemisphere. They need to be dropped approximately at the following lunar coordinates..." He rattles off a series of numbers and grimaces. "If worst comes to worst, no one is gonna fry New York off the map with my little babies. Once they've landed, if all goes well, they should be able to create a million-square meter array within five months: this is enough to generate 10 terawatts of electricity if harvested properly. They need to be sent a signal on the two-forty-five giga freeband channel; there is a simple control application on one of the drives that requires coordinate codes. Our house code plus three zeroes - in any order, the code is position neutral - will direct them to form an array which aims at a geosynchronous orbital position between the equator and the moon. Whoever is able to get up enough satellites there with sufficient solar arrays and microwave transport capacity will be a very rich man. When it's ready, send the command reflect – again alphanumerically, with your code – to switch the panels. If wholesale energy prices stick at $100 per megawatt hour, just this one dual array will generate electricity worth three *billion* dollars per year. And this can be replicated ad infinitum, more or less. If you need to turn them off, use 'collect' instead of 'reflect'."

He holds up a phone number to the screen. There is a name scrawled under it, Jack Larkinsdale. "Call this guy. I've been in touch with him. He works for the people out in Nebraska. We agreed to do a demonstration of the technology in Omaha once I've got it set up. But if someone is watching this damn video then … well, all bets are off. You've *got* to convince him to send in a team – *today, by helicopter* – to pick up my work and get it somewhere secure."

Gunnar takes another swig from his glass and smacks his lips. A wistful melancholy invades his eyes. "There should be a good payday here. We don't have anything on paper, but they're honorable men. Just… make sure they take care of my people."

"Just in case, I've set up, shall we say, an *insurance policy*. There are a number of pre-programmed subroutines in the drones. The largest cities in the eastern hemisphere can also be targeted with these little toys in case this has really gone pear-shaped and my worst fears have been realized." Gunnar smirks maliciously. "Same deal, your house code and an alphanumeric translation of the city's airport IATA code. So Tokyo is NRT, or 14-18-20. Beijing is PEK, 16-05-11. Riyadh, RUH, 18-21-08. And so on. Hopefully that won't become necessary, but we live in dangerous times. Three false codes and the drones will lock in place, where they are at that moment, and will not accept any further instructions."

"You've got the tools to do what you need to do. You can play this video one more time, if you need to write anything down, then it will self-erase. Good luck… whoever you are." He raises his glass again in a mock toast, and the screen goes black. After a moment a polite query appears: *play again?*

You lean back in the chair, mind racing. On the one hand, it all strikes you as Gunnar's typical paranoid madness. On the other, it's a hell of a coincidence to have a sudden heart attack the very day you're starting out to disrupt the global energy industry. You need a second opinion.

Trying not to look at Gunnar's sprawled form on the floor, you steal out through the kitchen. Automatically, without thinking, you arm the lock on the door. You jog across the short distance to Aurora's house and ring the bell. After a few moments, Aurora opens the door, dressed in a long T shirt and sweatpants, disheveled hair protruding at odd angles. She rubs her eyes and looks at you curiously, blinking in the sunlight.

"Sorry, you woke me up. Whatcha still doin here, dummy? Aren't you supposed to be on the road to riches? Got a flat tire or something?"

"Come with me."

Aurora cocks her head. "What's wrong? You look like someone just boiled your bunny."

"I'm serious. Now."

She blinks again. "Uh, OK. Let me put some clothes on."

"Hurry."

You race back to the house together. With trembling fingers you punch in the access code and shove the door open. Aurora crumples backwards and emits a shrill scream as she sees Gunnar's still form crumpled on the floor. Then she rushes to him, shaking his unresisting body. She looks up at you, tearful, distraught.

"Is he dead?"

"I think so. I mean, yes. I guess. I don't know."

"Oh my god, no." She rises and strides toward the phone. "Let's call 911. Maybe it's not too late, maybe they can do something…"

You grab the phone from her hand and replace it. "No. Wait. I have to show you something."

Aurora looks at you, eyebrows arching into incredulous crescents. "*Wait?* Wait for what? He might be dying, right now! What's wrong with you?"

"Come with me." You take her by the hand and lead her into the study, where you play the video for her. She calms quickly and watches it closely, black eyes darting back and forth, chewing absent-mindedly on a lock of hair. This time you have the wherewithal to take a pen and jot down notes. At the end of the video, a short routine displays itself on the monitor, brusquely noting that it is irrevocably erasing the video. The screen subsequently winks back into darkness.

Aurora sits back in the chair. "Wow. Holy shit. So you think someone killed him?"

You pace around the oddly uncluttered study, poking at sheaves of paper with your toe. "I don't know. Seems crazy, but… it's a hell of a coincidence, otherwise. We were going to leave this morning for Omaha, to sell this to the Corn Oracle, he said."

"Who?"

"Apparently he's the smartest man in the world. At least that's what Uncle Gunnar thinks. Thought. I guess that's his company he talks about in the video, or whatever he said."

"But who would want to kill him? Who would want this?"

"Well, everyone, I suppose. This can make you insanely rich, or a uniquely successful genocidal maniac…"

"Or both," muses Aurora.

"Or both, yes. What's not to like? Everyone wants this, I guess. I mean, who wouldn't?"

"I wouldn't." She drums her fingers on the desk. "Well. Let's just do it."

"Do what?"

"Drive it to Omaha. You've got everything packed up, right? If we drive in shifts, we can be there in 24 hours, I guess. I drove to Chicago once by myself in one go. It was like sixteen hours, maybe. Omaha can't be that much further."

That had not occurred to you. "What, just drive into Omaha and ask around until we find the richest man in the world?"

"Why not?"

"We're not gonna outrun the CIA in a U-Haul. Even if we do, some might say we fled the scene of a possible murder."

Jet black eyes dart back and forth, taking in the strange artifacts adorning the walls. Her jaw clenches in thought. "That's true. Depends who it is, I guess. If it's anyone. Maybe he really did have a heart attack."

"Maybe. Like I said, that'd be a hell of a coincidence."

Aurora shrugs. "Well, all right, let's just call this guy like he says in the video. Call 911, get the police here, say we suspect foul play, and why. Get them to cordon the place off til the cavalry arrives."

"If it arrives."

"Got a better idea, dummy?"

"Not really."

"Well, let's go then."

You walk out of the study and into the living room. You are startled by an enormous form in a red jumpsuit standing by a window, arms crossed and legs akimbo, regarding you amiably through rimless glasses. You stare at each other for a long moment. Aurora makes an audible gasp of surprise.

"Left the door open, son. Breach of security, don't ya think?"

You manage to force a word out. "You…"

Hal nods companionably. "Bingo." He reaches into his pocket and pulls out an impossibly long, black handgun. *How did that thing even fit in his pocket*, you think to yourself as you lunge hopelessly for the shotgun, still resting on the couch. Instead of the expected sharp *crack* of a nine-millimeter round smashing through the sound barrier and the concussive shock of a bullet ripping flesh and splintering bone, all you hear is a soft *ffffi* and a sharp sting on your shoulder. Looking down, you see a red tufted dart protruding from your shirt sleeve. As you watch, dumbfounded, another magically sprouts from your chest. You continue to scrabble for the gun. Suddenly thick, clumsy fingers that seem to belong to someone else try, and fail, to grasp at the weapon in front of you. Your mouth forms a voiceless O of surprise, your legs begin to fail, and you wobble, finally falling to the floor next to Gunnar's stiffening corpse. The world around you begins to spin, slowly at first, then faster, and faster, and finally, to shrink. As though from a great distance, you hear Aurora howl: *"Hal! Noooooo…"*

Darkness and silence, at once somehow very real and tangible entities, rush toward you, washing over you like the sea, pulling you down into an endless black pool of oblivion, and rest. You close your eyes, too tired even to scream.

A gift from a grateful nation

You awaken to the sound of a loud, deep, methodic thrum. Your mind and body feel entangled by cobwebs. A steel bulkhead stretches over you, neat rows of rivets forming stately rectangular patterns. You are lying in some kind of cot or bed that vibrates uncomfortably beneath you. Cheap, thin sheets and a gray wool blanket. A lumpy pillow inadequately supports your head.

Where am I? What happened?

Memories gradually come back. *Hal. Some kind of dart gun.* Reflexively you touch your shoulder and chest. Some soreness, a couple of tender lumps, but you are otherwise undamaged. You sit up abruptly in the bed. Your field of vision immediately begins to yaw wildly. You close your eyes for a few seconds until things settle, then open them again.

You are in an enclosed metal cylinder. No windows, just your cot and a pile of boxes. Gunnar's toys, you realize, somehow unloaded from the U-Haul and packed into wooden crates. An Asian man, dressed in a drab olive-green military uniform, sits in a folding chair among the boxes. He watches you carefully. He is armed with an ugly, but probably efficiently functional, snub-nosed pistol. A police baton rests on one of the crates. You start to get out of the cot.

He hisses at you. "*Ssst. Ssst.*" And shakes his head. He points at the cot, indicating you should stay.

The entire cylinder is shaking, you realize. The droning noise is really very loud; the shuddering vibrations penetrate deep down into your skeleton. It dawns on you that you are probably in an airplane. "Where are we? Where are we going?" Your voice is rough and hoarse.

He points at his ears, then his mouth, shakes his head, and shrugs. He points at the table next to you. There is a bottle of water. He pantomimes for you to drink. You are extremely thirsty, you realize. You sip it gingerly, wondering if it contains some new drug. But it is cool and good, and your parched throat sings in praise. You down most of it in a few long gulps.

"We're gonna have a long flight if you can't talk, man."

You examine your escort. He can't be more than 5'6". You are not restrained in any way. Even in your weakened state you figure it would be at least a fair fight, notwithstanding the police baton. The pistol is another matter. But even if you overpowered him, then what? For all you know, you're 30,000 feet over the ocean.

The soldier notices your calculations and smiles, not unkindly, the skin crinkling at the corners of his eyes. He shakes his head again. He holds up four fingers. *Four more hours? He has four colleagues somewhere else on the plane waiting to pummel you?* He folds his hands and places them by his cheek and closes his eyes for a moment, then points at you.

Not a bad idea, all things considered. You drain the rest of the water and lie back down. Sleep overtakes you immediately, mercifully.

You are jolted awake by your head banging against the steel bulkhead. The high-pitched whine of the engine is unbearably loud.

You sit up. "Dammit!" You can feel the increasing G-force as the plane apparently skids to an ignominious halt. Even without seeing outside, you can feel the body of the plane swaying left and right as it fishtails down a landing strip. You notice your erstwhile escort picking himself up off the floor. Even with deeply tanned Asian skin, he looks ashen.

"Nice fucking landing. Where did this asshole learn to fly?"

The soldier smiles briefly and shakes his head, setting up his seat again with tremulous hands.

Finally, the plane seems to come to a halt and the noise of the engine gradually subsides. After a few minutes you hear a grate at the door on the front head of the bulkhead. Hal's massive form awkwardly squeezes itself through the small opening. Incongruously, he now wears a beige linen suit and open-necked, black shirt. He shakes his head and smiles at you, blue eyes twinkling with merriment.

"They didn't build this thing with me in mind, that's fo sure. You have a good sleep, young feller? Now, don't look at ol Hal like that. This is jes business, nothing personal."

His genial eyes gaze unperturbed into your silent, death wish stare for a few moments. He shrugs and says something to the soldier - in Chinese, you presume, pantomiming the panic everyone had been in at the front of the plane. The soldier laughs and gestures how he had been knocked around like a squash ball here in the back. Hal examines the crates, securely fastened to the bulkhead with thick canvas straps. Satisfied, he pats them and pushes a red button on the wall. A hydraulic whine fills the confined space as a hatch opens in the back of the compartment. Light streams in from outside. A metallic grating sound indicates the hatch striking pavement. Hal walks down the ramp, stretching his arms out.

"Lordy! *China*! Praise be! It's been too long." He turns around, arms still outstretched. "Come on down and drink it in, son! No place on earth smells like China, for better or for worse. Smells like hope an fear an raw sewage, all mixed up and left out in the sunshine fer a millenium, or three."

Unsteadily, you walk down the ramp. A wave of hot, humid air blasts you as you approach the exit. Palm trees sway in a slight breeze. The sky is blue, but a far cry from the crisp turquoise of New Hampshire; it's a dirty, tarnished, washed out blue, fading into a brownish miasma as it apprehensively touches the horizon. There is a distinctive tang to the air. Not exactly bad, but alien and not entirely pleasant, either. A couple of other aircraft are parked haphazardly around the airfield.

A group of soldiers with unmarked cloth hats stand idly around the plane. Some have rifles slung over their shoulders. A few of them smoke. They stare at you and Hal curiously. You have several inches on most of them, while Hal towers nearly a foot over the tallest. A black sedan with tinted windows, followed by a large green van, speeds along the tarmac. The two vehicles skid to a halt by your plane. A troop of soldiers decamps from the van and races to the plane. Much shouting and gesturing is followed by them industriously lugging the crates out of the plane and into the van. A soldier opens the back door of the sedan and motions for you and Hal to get in. Hal crams himself through the door. After a moment's hesitation, you follow. As soon as the door closes, the car races away.

A tinted window separates you from the front seat. Hal raps on the glass and shouts something in Chinese. The glass lowers and a hand slips an apple through. Hal crunches into it with relish.

"You know, the food in America don't taste like nothin these days, not a damn thing. Everything genetically modified, codified, *oddified* if you done ask me. But this… this here is a real apple. Tastes though it come from the very bosom of Eden isself. You hungry, son? Wasn't a damn thing to eat that whole flight."

You are starving. "Go fuck yourself."

"Suit yourself." Hal shrugs and munches contentedly on his apple. "Now, we're going to meet…"

"I said, go fuck yourself."

"Have it your way. Ye gonna find out soon enough."

The sedan does not leave the airfield, but pulls up at a long, low brick building a few hundred yards away. It is characterized by the same sort of institutional monotony one finds the world over. A khaki-clad soldier opens the door for you. You exit the car and walk up the steps into the building. Two soldiers stand guard at the door. Inside, it is pleasantly cool, though you detect no air-conditioning. Drab brown tile hallways flanked by yellow walls stretch off to either side. You ascend one more flight of stairs and enter a large office. A Caucasian man with close-cropped gray hair in a United States military uniform sits behind the desk, busily writing. He looks up and smiles as you enter. Maps adorn the walls; a photograph of President Bush directs a rictus grin at you from the opposite wall.

"Robert! Welcome to China. I'm Colonel S… well, just call me Colonel, if you don't mind. Have a seat." You do not particularly want to sit, but fatigue overwhelms pride. You lower yourself into the chair. Hal settles into the one next to you. It emits an alarming creak of protest in response.

"But, ah, I would also like to express my deepest condolences for your recent loss. Both personally, and on behalf of the United States government. Your uncle served his adopted nation faithfully, and honorably."

You look at Hal enquiringly. "You know, Hal, I'd just about decided you're the biggest dickhead I ever saw in my life, and here you go finding an even bigger one as soon as I step off the plane. What's next? Afternoon tea with Pol Pot?"

Hal smiles faintly and adjusts the sleeves of his coat. "Boy's upset, Colonel. Understandably. Also, he haint et aught in bout sixteen hours, as I reckon. Enough to make the most peaceable feller a mite ornery. Caint abide strangers on an empty stomach, meself."

"Good lord, let's get on top of that. I didn't realize." He claps his hands and shouts something in Chinese. A few moments later, a Chinese orderly rushes in with a can of Coke and some kind of energy bar. The colonel notes your expression and smiles faintly. "First things first. Get some calories in you, son. You look like you're about to fall over on us here any moment. You can find something else to throw at me later, if you like."

You open the coke and drink, the explosion of sugar in your gut reminding you how ravenous you actually are. Tearing the energy bar open, you bite into it. It is soft and malleable in your hands, with an anonymous hint of peanut and cacao.

The Colonel drums his fingers on his uncluttered desk. Sunlight glints from the insignia on his shoulders. "Now, to business! I know what you're thinking. We didn't kill your uncle. As far as we can ascertain, he died of natural causes." You stare at him, chewing your energy bar. "Oh, I'll admit, we've had our eye on him for quite a while. You see, I work for DARPA, the Defense Department Advanced Research Projects Agency. We keep track of ah, interesting initiatives such as your uncle's, when we come across them. Most of them are cranks. But not your uncle. He was the real deal. A very impressive man. *Most* impressive."

"You think I'm an idiot," you remark, as flatly as you can manage in the circumstances, but unable to completely disguise the tremor in your voice.

"On the contrary, son. On the contrary. You're obviously a bright young man. Think about it – why would we go to the trouble of murdering him? We wanted to buy the system, not steal it. I have signing authority up to ten million dollars. It was worth far more to us with him in the package than without him."

"So why kidnap me?"

His eyes widen in surprise. "*Kidnap*? What gave you that impression? You are our guest."

"I dunno, maybe being drugged and thrown onto a cargo plane to China, or wherever the fuck we are? Let me call the embassy if I'm a 'guest' so I can catch the next plane home."

Hal pipes up. "Say, Colonel, howsabout you rustle up some more o them energy bars so as we has summat to et durin this here indubitably interesting yet *lengthy* soliloquy o yours. I gots a *hunger* on me today, I does indeed."

The Colonel sighs and presses a buzzer. He is younger than the hair suggests, you note. He can't be 40. An orderly comes in, going around the desk and pressing a piece of paper into the officer's hand and whispering into his ear. He nods with satisfaction. They exchange more words in their foreign tongue, and the orderly speeds out.

The Colonel holds the piece of paper casually up in front of his eyes and peers at Hal over it. "We found your daughter, Mr. Robinson. She's en route as we speak."

"Ah, excellent. Was meaning to ask you, son, if you knew where she got herself to. Skipped out with yo uncle's car, she done, an his credit cards, whilst I was a-taking care o you, lickety split."

"She won't say where she was heading. Seems like Chicago, maybe. They got her in upstate New York, heading west. So that direction anyway."

"Hmmm." Hal reclines back in his chair. The orderly returns with a stack of energy bars and places them on the desk. Hal takes one, peels it open like an orange, and thoughtfully peruses the ceiling. "Chicago, Chicago… could be Motorola, I suppose. They're active in satcomms. They out that way."

"Motorola's on our side. We'd know if they were in touch with Mr. Schafer."

"She call anyone?"

The Colonel examines the paper again. "Not that we know of. But she must have driven by dozens of pay phones. And we don't know her exact route. Impossible to say."

Hal claps you on the shoulder with a huge hand. "Just have to ask our young friend here, won't we? Lotta companies out Chicago way. Could be anyone."

"Do I need to repeat myself?" you ask.

The Colonel ignores you. "We have the notes she took during Gunnar's video that was subsequently erased. She tried to destroy them when we caught up with her, but we have them. Maybe they'll contain some clues. Right now we have another task for young Robert. Have another energy bar. You'll need your wits about you." He rises from his desk and ushers you out of his office and down the stairs, where the car that brought you still waits, engine thrumming expectantly.

The sedan speeds you and the Colonel through the base. Hal follows in another car. You stare out the window as your companion drones on. "Now you see, this is of the utmost strategic importance to the country! It's the *perfect weapon*. Not a US soldier within a thousand miles of a battlefield, nobody gets killed, you can flick it on and off like a light switch, in a matter of months you can bring any country on earth to its knees without a single casualty!"

"Sounds fantastic."

"But it is, Robert! Don't you see? We're preparing to send hundreds of thousands of troops to the Middle East as we speak, ready to do battle and spill lord knows how much blood into the thankless sands of Iraq, as Churchill so presciently called them. Think of the cost – economic, human, moral – which we could avoid if we had your uncle's tool at our disposal?"

"That wasn't his plan. That wasn't Tesla's plan."

"Well, plans change. Progress marches inexorably onward, and forward! As shall we!" The car careens to a halt in front of a low concrete building, more a bunker than anything. Alarming looking Chinese characters in blazing red and yellow adorn a sign above a thick steel door. The driver dismounts from the car and jogs over to the door, turning a foot-wide wheel which somehow results in the door swinging ominously open, exposing darkness within.

"Now, Robert, we would really appreciate your help." As you walk into the hallway, fluorescent lights automatically turn on. Your companion walks swiftly down the hallway, dress shoes clacking on the tiled floor. "We can make wonderful, magical things happen for our friends, you know. Suddenly, a developer decides he absolutely *must* buy that hideous row house of your mother's for an exorbitant price. Princeton develops a keen interest in your abilities, and must transfer you from that third-rate community college you attend…" At the end of the hallway is a door, opening into a large room. The contents of the crates from the plane have been carefully unloaded. Several people of indeterminate sex bustle around in what look like hospital uniforms and masks. Some take notes, others photographs. One carefully focuses on the production robot - still unconcernedly spinning its plastic webs - with a handheld video camera.

"It's a good thing we found Aurora's notes when we did," he comments drily. "We didn't know about the thermite charges and the ten-meter rule. That could have ended our project very quickly… but where was I? Yes, we take care of our friends. Our opponents… have problems. Substantial problems. That misdemeanor possession charge that got dropped last year? Suddenly an ambitious prosecutor decides to revive it as felony intent to distribute a controlled substance. Do you follow me?"

"What have you told my mother?"

"The Coast Guard needed your uncle back for a special scientific project abroad and brought you with him to assist. She's very proud, I can assure you. Now, to the matter at hand…"

"Maybe first you'd like to explain to me what a guy claiming to be a US Army Colonel is doing on some low-rent air base in China, ordering the murder of retirees, kidnapping college students, you know, shit like that. How do I know 'we' aren't a gang of pedophiles who like complicated play dress-up fantasies?"

The Colonel's faint, supercilious smile emerges again from the corner of his mouth. "Very amusing. You'll have to take my word for it, for now. You see, Robert, we are at a pivotal moment in history. The Soviet Empire lies in ruins. Japan and Europe have neutered themselves into insignificance. But *China*! China is on the cusp of an unstoppable rise. Well over a billion people, my young friend, all marching single-mindedly toward a common goal. Now that Deng Xiaphong has liberalized the market, nothing can stop this country. They are a people of supreme dedication and concentration, in ways in which we in the West do not properly even understand the meaning of the words. One way or another, the next century will be a *Chinese* century. Some of us believe that we should fight this; others, that we can manage it, or even turn it toward our advantage. For their part, this approaching conflict in the Gulf has made them realize how fragile their economy is, and how perilous is their path to prosperity…"

"Would you quit with the speeches and tell me what the fuck you are doing here exactly?" You are alone, you realize. Idly you consider your chances of overpowering him. Given the last experience with an overweight, retired and somewhat pickled Gunnar, you might need to upgrade your hand-to-hand fighting skills before engaging in combat with a trained soldier, you admit ruefully to yourself.

"DARPA – my agency, the advanced weapons agency – has an arrangement with the PLA which allows us to use this base…"

"PLA?"

"People's Liberation Army. The Chinese armed forces. At any rate, we have certain common interests in the area of non-lethal weaponry. Americans are getting squeamish about casualties, even on the other side; the Chinese have had endlessly terrible PR from their little mishap in Tiananmen Square. I'm here as part of a trust-building mission to jointly develop a new generation of more humane weapons. The Chinese have proven immensely technically adept in this area. Beamed weapons, using everything from ultrasound to microwave, which incapacitate, but do not kill. Sonic blasts for crowd control. Of course, this all pales into insignificance compared to what your uncle developed." He pauses, looks at his watch, and shouts at the people milling around the boxes and crates. They look up in surprise, gather their things and scurry away.

He picks up a pair of earphones from a nearby desk and hands you one. "There's going to be a test in about 90 seconds. Better put these on. We're probably fine in here, but this is experimental stuff. Better safe than sorry."

You put the headphones on and are engulfed by sudden silence. For the first time in your life, you experience the complete, total absence of sound. You shout as loud as you can as a test: you feel the air rush out your throat and mouth, you even sense the vibration of your vocal cords, but you hear absolutely nothing. Suddenly the silence is broken by a soft, keening wail, as though from very far away. Though you are protected by the thick walls of the bunker and these astonishing, incomparable headphones, the vibration nevertheless stirs a visceral reaction deep inside your gut. You feel suddenly ill, as though you would like to crawl into bed and curl up into a ball of fetal misery. Mercifully, it ends after a few moments. You remove your headphones.

The Colonel grins broadly as he removes his. "Feel that? Neat, huh? Now imagine you're some Greek anarchist manning a barricade in Athens and that hits you full blast."

"So the future isn't killing people, it's just making them feel like they want to die."

"Well, not in so many words, but essentially, yes. The return on investment on good old-fashioned land wars isn't what it used to be."

"You still haven't explained why we are here."

"Ah. That." The Colonel nods. "Well, Robert, we need your help here. We know these boxes are rigged with thermite charges, and that if one goes off, they all go off. I would like to kindly ask you to unlock them."

"What makes you think I know the code?"

"Aurora wrote in her notes that you have the code."

"I don't."

"Don't you?"

You look into each other's eyes. Finally, the Colonel slams his palms on the desk. "I do not have time for games. I am going to leave you in here. When you decide you're ready, open the cases. We will be watching via video."

"What if I get it wrong and they blow up?"

A thin smile. "That's why we're doing it in this bunker. I don't know how strong those charges are, but I *do* know that in that big box there seems to be a substantial chunk of Cesium-137. This is a fallout shelter. If anything goes wrong, we'll be able to seal it off and contain the radiation in here."

"Leaving me in here?"

"Well, we won't be able to open the door for a while. Cesium-137 has a 31-year half-life."

"Great. I should be almost ready for retirement at that point."

The Colonel unholsters his sidearm and chambers a round, then pops out the magazine and slips it into his pocket. He slides the pistol along the desk toward you. "Anyway, if you do set it off, you might want to use this. Radiation poisoning is a hell of a way to go. No fun at all." With that, he turns on his heel and walks rapidly down the hall, heels of his dress shoes clicking determinedly on the tiled floor. You pick up the pistol and sight carefully between his shoulder blades, holding your breath, squeezing the trigger just as he is about to turn the corner. It does not move at all. You squeeze harder. Still nothing.

He pauses, and looks back at you, a single eyebrow lifted in amusement. "Disengage the safety next time, son. And breathe out before you take the shot, not in." He disappears around the corner. Distantly, you hear the thick steel vault door slam closed.

You toss the pistol on the desk with a metal *clang* and descend the stairs to the pile of neatly stacked steel cases, each with a winking red light next to a keypad. The printer drone spins its plastic webs inside its cocoon of leaded glass exactly as it had back in New Hampshire, unconcerned by the change of venue.

"You just don't quit, do you?" you mutter. Unperturbed, its mandibles continue to churn out strings of plastic glue, imperceptibly building up a small drone, layer by layer.

A voice crackles over the intercom. "Come on, Robert. Your country's counting on you. Good luck."

You extend your middle finger and gesture at the several security cameras stationed around the room, watching you implacably with their unblinking gaze. Inexplicably, this fails to cause the cases to spring open.

You sit cross-legged in front of the pile. You realize you don't even know how many numbers this PIN code is supposed to have. You begin to punch in your house code, which at least worked on the computer application back at your uncle's. After the fourth digit, a tone sounds and the light stops blinking, remaining a fiery red.

At least you know it's four digits. *What could that maniac possibly have put there?* Birth date ... Project Paperclip ... you type in 1-9-4-3. Another monotonous tone. The light stays red.

The voice again. "Stop fucking around, Robert. I don't want to have to send your remains back to your mother in a lead-lined shoebox."

You remember the time your friend Jeremy made a batch of thermite. Quite easy, he explained, it's just iron oxide and aluminum shavings. *It has a high ignition point, but a magnesium strip from chemistry class will do the trick...* You'd used a nickel-sized pile of it on the hood of an enemy's car who'd had the ill-conceived idea to assault Jeremy's sister behind the local 7-11. The results had been spectacular. It burned through the entire engine block and then another three inches of pavement underneath. Whatever Gunnar's other shortcomings, he did seem to have a grasp of technology. You wonder if he's designed these charges primarily to destroy the cargo inside the cases, or to chastise and disfigure the person attempting entry. You remember more clearly than you'd like the pool of molten steel forming under the ruined engine block. Presumably a human body would be far more fragile.

"I don't know the fucking code, you assholes!" you scream at the camera.

"Well, you've got one more try. Maybe you'll get lucky. We're rooting for you." The voice cracks out, replaced by a low-level hum from the loudspeaker.

You pull the case off the top of the pile and bring it to the other side of the room. If they do all go off simultaneously, at least there's no reason to have all twenty go off in your face at once. You sit down again in front of the case, trying to position it away from yourself so that it is slightly less likely to melt your face off. Gingerly, you type in the only numbers that occur to you:

3-3-2-7

You close your eyes tightly as you type the last number and hold your left hand across your face. Instead of the whine of a detonator priming, you hear a soft click. You open your eyes. The display shines green. You open the box; two small drones are nestled inside.

You hear the sound of slow clapping over the intercom. "Great job, Robert! We knew you could do it." You pick up one of the drones and hurl it at a security camera. It shatters against the wall upon impact in a blizzard of brittle plastic shards. Immediately, you hear the sound of the vault opening and the approaching sound of many jogging feet. A squad of armed Chinese soldiers appears in the room. A couple approach you, rifles pointed at your stomach, while the rest form a perimeter around the remaining crates. The Colonel walks into the room seconds later, retrieving his pistol from the desk where you'd left it.

"Now, now, son. Be careful with those. It's impolite to destroy a dead man's legacy." He pauses, and looks at you carefully as he holsters his weapon. "It almost looked for a second like you really didn't know it. Did I catch it right on the video? 3327? What does that come from?" He walks over to the pile of cases, and jabs in the code to one of them. It smoothly clicks open.

"Gunnar told me it was the client number he got for your mother in the shed behind that truck stop in Reno she used to work out of."

"Charming." He turns to the soldiers and barks orders at them. The two pointing rifles at your abdomen shoulder their weapons and guide you out of the room. "Get some sleep, son. Your country will need you again tomorrow."

The soldiers escort you to the same black sedan, open the door and usher you inside. Hal lounges in the back seat. "Hey hey, young feller. They told me it was gonna be put up, or blow up time. Guess you chose the first one. Glad to see you decided to join the team." He taps on the window and the car pulls into motion.

"Some choice."

"Well, choice is relative, haint it? Some say a man falling from a window to his death has as much choice an *agency* as a young, free feller with his whole life astretch out afront a him like a thundercloud, all *pregnant*, as it were, with *potential*…"

You ponder that for a moment. "That's the stupidest thing I ever heard."

Hal shrugs. "Guy whut said it, they done tried an give im a Nobel Prize for sayin it. *Caint* be that dumb. He wouldna take it, though. But what does ol Hal know. Hal's a simple man, when all said and done. Simple man, with simple appetites."

The base is larger than you thought. After several minutes, you pull up in front of a four-story building. As if reading your mind, Hal comments, "This was an old training airfield. This was one o the student dorms. They done re-done it for the Colonel's boys and y'all. Haint much, but she'll do fer now."

He leads you into the building and up two floors, where he opens an unlocked door. A surprisingly spacious chamber awaits, looking more like a hotel suite than a student dormitory. A fan spins lazily, doing very little to move the humid, cloying air. A double bed, a table with a couple of chairs, a couch, TV, even a refrigerator. A covered platter sits on the table; even without opening it, a rich umami scent issues forth invitingly. A sliding door opens onto a small balcony.

"Well, ol Hal gonna take his leave now, Make yoself at home. Go wherever you want on base, anywhere you shouldna be at gonna be locked anyhow or they be hell to pay. They done brought you some chow. Like I say, few other youngun jarheads here in the building, workin for yonder Colonel. I expect you gonna meet them, bye and bye. Now if y'all will excuse ol Hal, he need to make preparations for his daughter's *arrival*." He drums his fingers on the door jamb at this last.

Nothing immediately strikes your attention as a usable weapon. "Get out of here, Hal, while I look for something to bash your head in next time I see you."

Hal smiles. "Heh heh. Gots a spark in ye, young feller, I'll give ye that. I see why she like ye." He bobs his head under the doorway and shuffles down the stairs.

You eat the food ravenously. It's some kind of fried rice, with bits of chicken scattered throughout. A hint of chili burns the roof of your mouth. You open up the refrigerator: there are a few bottles of water, some milk, and oddly, a six-pack of Coors. You take a bottle of water back to the table and drink deeply. It is beginning to get dark; the sun falls far more quickly than you are used to. Palm trees sway in the evening breeze. You must be considerably further south than New Hampshire. Where exactly is anyone's guess. You have only the vaguest recollection of what China looks like on a map but it is certainly gigantic. Not that it matters. Without money or a way to communicate, you could be a mile offshore from Philadelphia and it wouldn't make the slightest difference.

There is a soft knock on the door. Putting down a forkful of food, you go to the door and open it. A short girl, approximately your age, heavily made up, stands in the entrance. She smiles at you hesitantly. She is Asian, but does not seem Chinese, at least to your untrained eye. Thai, perhaps. Maybe Filipino. She wears a short, tight black dress and high, green plastic heels. She smells strongly, but not unpleasantly, of some exotic perfume with overtones of vanilla and pecan. She hands you a slip of paper. You unfold it. It is a handwritten note.

Enjoy this gift from a grateful nation.

You smile and shake your head and close the door. She peers at you, worriedly, through the diminishing crack. You strip off your clothes and lie naked on the bed, watching the fan slowly spin above you, and let sleep overtake you once more.

Sometimes the quickest path is through the mud

You wake up to sunlight streaming in through the window. You have no idea what time it is. Your feet and ankles itch tremendously. Evidently many mosquitos feasted on them during the night. You shut the door to the balcony. It's far cooler than the day before – perhaps it is early morning.

You pick your clothes off the floor and sniff them. Predictably, they stink execrably. You begin to look around the apartment, which you had not examined carefully the night before. There are a couple of closets, containing a sizeable array of clothes seemingly tailored specifically for you. A bookshelf houses a collection of dog-eared books, all in English. Agatha Christie, detective novels, spy craft... the sort of anonymous collection one finds on an aunt's bookshelf, or in a bookstore at a train station.

Another door by the entrance leads to a sizeable bathroom. You gratefully urinate into a western-style toilet; some of Hal's colorful tales of Asian bathrooms over the previous weeks had been of some concern. You relieve your aching bladder. The urine has a dull, angry golden hue. *Probably need to drink a gallon of water to even start to hydrate*, you think to yourself. A toothbrush, tube of toothpaste, razor and shaving cream are placed neatly by the sink. You are still surprised to see the familiar brands like Crest and Gillette in these foreign surroundings. There is a bathtub with a shower head attached to the faucet. You step in and turn it on. After a few fitful coughs and sputters, water begins to spray out. You turn the knob on as far left as it will go, but the water remains stubbornly tepid. Nevertheless, scrubbing the last few days' grime and sweat from your skin is a relief. You dry yourself off and wander back into the apartment.

A small Chinese lady with a surgical face mask is putting a new tray of food on your table. She lets out a small hoot of surprise at seeing your pale, naked, comparatively giant body suddenly appear. She scurries out, gesticulating wildly and jabbering incomprehensibly. You put on a pair of shorts and shirt and examine the breakfast. A pot of tea, a bowl of soup, and some pale dumplings nestled in a bamboo basket. You cut one of the latter open. It is soft and fluffy, filled with some indeterminate dark substance. You place one half carefully in your mouth. The dumpling nearly melts on your tongue, while the filling is sweet and meaty. The soup is hearty, with thick noodles and a few thin strips of what appears to be beef. A small jar of thick, pungent, brownish sauce with rings of hot peppers floating inside seems to be intended as a condiment, but strikes you as a bit volatile for an early breakfast. A thick bundle of various unfamiliar but fragrant herbs also adorns the tray. You leave them untouched, unsure as to their purpose.

Afterward, on the balcony, you brush your teeth, for the first time in days you realize. You peruse the surroundings. The base seems quite large. There is a running track behind your building: definitely not a full quarter mile, but probably half that. Three figures jog fitfully around it. They seem to be Caucasian, with shorts and gray T-shirts. A dozen or so other buildings march off in neat rows to either side. At first glance it does not look any different from a normal housing estate, except for the runway beyond the buildings and the perimeter fence you catch occasional glimpses of, which seems to be a good 12 feet high and crowned with a ring of vicious-looking concertina wire. A large, blazing yellow sign in Chinese script seems to indicate it is electrified.

Lacking anything in particular to do, you put on shorts and a shirt and leave your apartment. There is no key, and the door does not seem to lock. You trot downstairs and go around to the back of the building to where the track is, and begin to stretch your legs. The three already on the track come around to where you are after a few moments. They are older than you, seemingly late twenties. Two males, pale like you, with crew-cut hair, and a short Latino girl, with her locks pulled back in a tight braid.

"Hol up, troops," says the taller one laconically. They slow to a halt. "Looks like reinforcements have arrived. What's your name, soldier?"

You eye them warily. "I'm not in the military. I'm a kidnapping victim. But I guess you know that."

The man allows himself a placid, bovine smile. He speaks with some sort of corn-fed, midwestern twang. "Well, I'll allow as the Colonel was mighty anxious to git you out here, an may have cut a few corners long the way. Colonel's always got reasons for what he do. But I hope you enjoy our hospitality. We make is as Murican as we ken round here."

The girl speaks up in rapid-fire, Caribbean influenced English. "Larry, *pendejo*, leave him alone. He's had a long trip. Just let him run."

Larry glances at her contemptuously, then back at you, and nods curtly. "Be seeing you, friend." He walks off the track. The other male, shorter and with dark hair, nods as well and walks away.

The girl glares at them and then glances back at you. "Sorry about them. I'm Martina."

"Robert."

"I know. You want to do some laps? I've got a few more. Or you wanna be by yourself?"

"Maybe I'll run by myself. I've got a few things on my mind."

"OK, man. I understand." She flashes you a bright, white smile. "I'll see you around." She trots away, braid flipping in the sunlight.

"Hey," you call out. She looks back enquiringly. "Is there … did they, uh… did this other, uh girl, arrive? Chinese girl, about your height, short hair?"

Martina looks around. You are alone, except for an evil-looking black bird with a long tail. It looks like a mockingbird, but lacks the iridescent blue coloration you are used to; its coat is a sheen of pure, glittering, jet black. "Hey, yo, word, she's here."

"Where?"

She shakes her head and shrugs sympathetically. "I'm not supposed to talk about her. But she's all right. I saw her yesterday when they brought her in. She seemed OK. Sorry, dude." She walks away quickly.

You make a few fitful laps around the track. It's boring, and the temperature rises rapidly as the sun burns away the morning haze. After ten or twelve laps you walk back to your room, where you take another cool shower, change into fresh clothes, and begin flipping through an Agatha Christie novel. After an hour or so, there is a knock on the door. You open it to find the shorter man from earlier, and Martina. They have traded in gym shorts and T-shirts for olive-green military fatigues. They have name tags stenciled on their breast, Hanley and Gomez, respectively. No further insignia, you note. They are not armed. Hanley speaks.

"Hello, sir. The Colonel was wondering if you're not too tired from your journey, if you'd care to join him in his quarters for lunch."

"Robert. Let's not be dicks about everything. I got the feeling we're gonna be stuck here together for a bit."

Hanley flashes a brief smile. "Fair enough. I'm Mike." He glances at your shorts. "If I, er, could I suggest…"

"Pants," interrupts Martina. "Put some pants on. You don't visit the Colonel looking like that. Anyways, in Asia. only kids wear shorts. Locals gonna laugh at you if they see you like that."

Mike nods firmly in agreement. "We don't take kindly to being laughed at."

"OK. Give me a minute." You find a pair of khaki pants in the closet. They are a good fit. You wonder if they measured you while you were unconscious in the plane.

They escort you to the same waiting sedan. Mike gets in the front of the car and Martina sits in back with you. She smells of cloves. The car roars into gear as soon as the doors close. You sit in silence during the short ride as trees and buildings flash by. You drive to a different building this time, a single-story, concrete stand-alone house with a modest fence around it. You exit the car and your companions escort you in.

The interior is spartan. A maid, again rather Filipino in appearance rather than Chinese, greets you with a wordless smile and gestures for you to follow her. You pass through a living room with a couple of low couches around a coffee table. French doors lead to a small terrace where the Colonel stands, back toward you, hands clasped behind his back, contemplating the garden. A couple of palm trees rise up from a grassy plot, ringed by a series of odd-looking bromeliads adorned with a startling cacophony of pink and orange flowers. Even from a distance they produce a heady aroma. He turns and greets you with a wide smile.

"Robert! Nice to see you. Did you sleep well? I hope you're not going to try and murder me again today."

"Not at lunchtime. That would be déclassé."

He laughs and motions for you to take a seat. He gives a short command in an indecipherable language to the maid, who nods and scurries away, returning moments later with a platter bearing a large decanter of what appears to be lemonade and two glasses. She pours each of you a glass and bobs away, smiling and genuflecting as she does so.

"What language is that?"

"Tagalog."

"Ah ha. I didn't think that was Chinese. Not as tonal."

The Colonel sips at his drink, eyeing you appraisingly over the rim. "You are an observant young man. No, she's Filipino. It's part of my deal with the Chinese here. I bring my own people. My last station was in Luzon. We were helping them with that stubborn Islamist insurgency down there. Thing's never gonna end, in my opinion." He nods at your drink. "Go ahead, it's safer than anything else in this damn country. The ice cubes are made from bottled water. But don't touch anything with ice in it that you don't get here in my place. You'll regret it."

You sip the lemonade. It is actually very good, a sharp citrusy taste more reminiscent of lime than lemon, and the sharp tang of fresh ginger, but with a sweet undercurrent of some exotic sugar. The Colonel smacks his lips.

"Ah. Even better with a slug of bourbon in it, but that'll have to wait til this evening, I'm afraid."

You watch a large, cumbersome bee attempt to navigate between the flowers. The Colonel sees the subject of your attention. "Not many bees here. Most of the plants here are actually pollinated by bats. Odd little critters. You see them at night if you look carefully. Not much bigger than moths."

"I guess you didn't invite me here for lemonade and a zoology lecture."

Piercing, guileless blue eyes regard you contemplatively. "No, I invited you here for lunch."

"Where's Aurora?"

"Oh, she's safe. Her father's taking good care of her."

"That's what I'm afraid of."

The Colonel clears his throat uncomfortably, and looks away. At that moment the maid returns, another companion in tow. The second one places plates and silverware carefully in front of you, while the first gently rests a large metallic platter in front of you. She removes the cover dramatically and a redolent haze of fumes and steam burst forth. There are two bowls of rice and a larger bowl with a thick, brownish curry, teeming with chili and unidentifiable spices. A couple of smaller bowls contain various unfamiliar herbs and sauces. The Colonel thanks the maids and unceremoniously dumps out a pile of rice onto his plate, ladling a few dollops of curry on top of it. He shakes out a few brown chips from one of the bowls as a garnish.

"Rendang curry," he comments. "It's an Indonesian recipe. Got fond of it when we were stuck in Timor years back. Try these fried onions on it. If you're feeling brave you could try those little chopped red chilis; if you do, well in my book, you'll never have to prove your courage any other way."

You help yourself to some of the food, sans chilis. As abductions go, the culinary level is better than you would have expected.

"Now Robert, I feel as though we may have gotten off on the wrong foot…"

"Murdering my uncle, kidnapping me and locking me into a Chinese fallout shelter with a radiological bomb may have had something to do with it."

"Ahem. As I said, we would not, and did not, murder your uncle. We had no reason on earth to do so. He will be regarded as a national treasure one day. Personally, I feel a great deal of admiration for him. With these codes, well, I'm sure you understand that in the military we are more oriented on results than we are on process! I was sure with sufficient motivation you would find the solution. Which you did, by the way. People always rise to the level of expectation; they never exceed it!" He munches contentedly on a heaping mouthful of rice and curry, contemplating the wisdom of his statement.

He continues. "Robert, I'm going to tell it to you straight. Your country has a big ask of you. One that it may never be able to acknowledge publicly. We want your help getting this system operational."

"Why? Don't you have enough weapons? The Soviet empire collapsed. Who exactly do you want to fight with this thing?"

"Well, you've hit on the essence of the problem, actually. One way or another, there's going to be a so-called 'peace dividend'." The Colonel's lip curls in contempt. "This little war of Bush's will hold things off for a couple of years, but not forever. And in fact, we think it will lead to even bigger problems in the Middle East in the long run. Once Saddam Hussein's army has been destroyed, there's nothing to stop Iran from dominating the region. They've held each other in a workable stalemate for decades, but now the damn fool is going to invade Kuwait, and we're gonna have to stomp him in response. This has not been thought through by anyone, not at all."

"So what?"

"Hussein is Sunni. Iraq is 60% Shia, just like Iran. Once we take out Iraq's army, Iran will enjoy regional hegemony by default. Iraq will become a puppet state. We estimate they are only eighteen months from having a usable nuclear weapon. They'll be in a position to liquidate Israel and export their revolution to Saudi, Qatar, the Emirates … and before you know it, gas will be $100 a gallon. We can't let that happen."

"So you're going to pre-emptively fry Tehran off the map."

The Colonel chortles with laughter. "Robert, Robert. Of course not. The most effective weapon is the one you never have to use. We have nothing against the Iranian people. Iran is a proud and ancient cradle of civilization. But here we and China have common interests. Neither of us can tolerate a hostile Islamic power controlling ninety percent of the world's oil. But Iran is a far more formidable military challenge than Iraq is. It's worse than Afghanistan. Ask the Russians how that little adventure turned out."

You chew on another mouthful of curry, watching birds flit casually around the garden. The Colonel continues. "We believe a small demonstration of force, carefully calibrated and communicated, perhaps not even noticeable to the population, could suffice to convince them of the futility of their military ambitions." He empties, and refills, his glass. "We military men are not bloodthirsty warmongers, Robert, in spite of what you see in the movies. My father was among the first American casualties in Vietnam, you know. A car bomb in Saigon, not terribly far from where we are now. I wouldn't wish that on anyone, American or Iranian. Trust me, the dream of every honorable soldier who's ever lived is to help usher in a world free of the horrors of war."

"What do you want from me?"

The Colonel smiles beatifically. "We just need your help in programming in target coordinates. The drones are already loaded onto a small rocket. It's only a three-hundred-kilogram payload, and it only has to get to the lunar surface, not make it back. Aurora was good enough to list the coordinates of major cities in her notes… If your uncle's calculations are correct, the initial payload should develop into two sufficiently large installations within five months of landing from initial seed colonies of two hundred drones. But the thing is, the instructions on construction and aggregation into a functioning parabola are hard-coded into the drones via analogue circuits. It looks like something from the 1950s. We could try and backwards engineer this, but it might take months, or even years, with no guarantee it would work."

"You don't have any guarantee this will work, either," you note, sipping your lemonade. "It's just something some lunatic made in his garage."

The Colonel shrugs. "Our work is experimental. The brass knows that. Sometimes it works out, sometimes it doesn't. If this gets out of control, we could get an EMP device up there as a fail-safe in days or weeks. We'll take it out quietly and no one will ever know the difference. Either way, you can be sure your country will show its gratitude, in a very tangible manner."

"That sounds great."

Your plates are clean. The maids return, cooing and clucking as they clear away the plates and trays, topping up your glasses with lemonade.

"Well, give it some thought. We have a good weather window to launch in three days."

"Three days!" you shout. "How are you putting a rocket together in *three days*? And what about a launch pad?"

The Colonel looks at you with the kindly gaze one reserves for a cousin with a particularly pernicious learning disability. "We have been planning this for some time, Robert. There is an old, mothballed ballistic missile silo on this base. It's sufficient for a one-off launch. The rocket itself is nothing complicated. It's only twenty meters long. Getting there is easy, it's getting back that's difficult. There's no return leg on this mission. We were landing one-way probes on the moon in the 1950s, for heaven's sake. This doesn't even have to land. It will just drop its payload. And the payload is tiny; it's about the same mass as the first Soviet lunar orbiter, actually."

The world begins to swim a bit. Words come unbidden into your mouth. "I'd like to talk to Aurora about this."

The Colonel smirks. "You can talk to your little friend as much as you'd like... *after* we get the code and see the drones have landed safely on the moon. I'm afraid the trip disagreed with her for some reason. She's recovering in the infirmary as we speak."

"If you think I'm gonna help you clowns commit genocide..."

The Colonel holds up a hand, stopping you. "Don't say anything you, or others, might come to regret, Robert." He pauses to take another sip of lemonade, then claps his hands loudly. He continues calmly. "Did you know, China is the only country in the world that doesn't have a shortage of organ donors? It's because they don't actually execute condemned prisoners, they send them to organ harvesting farms and excise their vitals gradually as the need arises, until, well, they succumb, as it were... Ah!" Your escorts appear at the entrance to the terrace. "Corporal Hanley, Private Gomez. Take young Robert back to his quarters, if you will. I'm sure he still has some rest to catch up on. Perhaps you youngsters can bring him with you for any evening entertainment you might have planned."

"Of course, sir." The two salute and politely wait for you to rise from your chair. The two dwarfish maids smile at you benignly as you leave.

Martina sits next to you in the back seat again. She wears aviator sunglasses against the now oppressive sunshine. "Good talk?"

"Oh yeah, he's a barrel of laughs. Have you heard his jokes about the organ farms?"

She pushes her sunglasses up onto her forehead and looks at you with serious, amber eyes, fluttering under heavily mascaraed lashes. "The Colonel's one of the good guys, Robert. He's a visionary. There aren't many like him out there. He does what has to be done to keep the country safe."

"His methods are...unorthodox."

She shrugs. "Sometimes the quickest path is through the mud."

They drop you off at your building. Mike rolls down the window. "So, hey, tonight is Friday. We have a little club we run here on the base on the weekends so we don't blow our brains out from boredom. Play some pool and darts. Throw back a couple of brews. We'll come pick you up around 8, ok?"

"My dance card is pretty free."

The car rolls away, leaving a small cumulus cloud of dust behind. You watch it roll away and ascend back to your room to wait for evening, and settle down on the couch with your Agatha Christie novel. Another meal of fried rice arrives at half past six. *Hopefully this isn't going to be the whole menu for the next five months,* you think.

True to their word, the same sedan rolls to a halt in front of your building precisely at 8 PM. Not knowing what to expect, you found a black polo shirt to go with the khakis. It's a Lacoste, you note. Probably cost a hundred dollars. Mike and Martina are inside, dressed in civilian clothes. They roll down the window as the car grinds to a halt, shouting at you. Both are clearly inebriated. You get in the car. After a short ride in which your cackling seatmates try to engage you in the relative merits of the Miami Dolphins as opposed to the Nebraska Cornhuskers, a topic for which you cannot summon even the most perfunctory interest, you arrive at The Club.

The Club is a ramshackle affair, more or less a series of repurposed classrooms in the basement of one of the decaying faculty buildings. A gaggle of people, nearly all Caucasian and Mexican, lounge on a makeshift terrace out front. Everyone is very fit. They smoke cigarettes and cradle brown bottles of beer in their laps. Somehow you'd expected a younger crowd. Several sport goatees. They wear jeans and T-shirts for the most part.

"When did the army start allowing beards?" you ask.

Martina grins. "We don't. Those are the NSA guys."

You watch rippling, tattooed muscle lifting beers toward chiseled, stubbly faces with close-set, incurious eyes. "I thought they were more computer nerds and stuff."

She shrugs. "There are different departments. These guys are field ops. The dorks with glasses are back in the US looking at satellite photos, and shit like that. Anyway, come meet the guys."

A sudden silence descends as you ascend the stairs, except for strains of Lynyrd Skynyrd emanating from within the club. Mike clears his throat. "Guys, let me introduce the fellow who risked his skin to save our project yesterday. This is Robert. Let's make him feel welcome."

As one, they stand and applaud. A couple of sharp whistles erupt. A large man, seemingly cast from steel, claps you with a heavy hand and presses a beer into your palm. Coors again. "Good job, man. You got a massive fucking pair on you, that's for sure. Holy shit. I wouldna gone in that room for no man. You a stone cold killa, for a young'un." He grins and holds up his beer for a toast. You tap his bottle.

"Uh, thanks. Anything for the flag, right?"

"That's god's truth, that is! We git the job done or die trying!" He lets out a whoop. A couple of the others respond with throaty "Hoo-ahh!"

Martina takes you by the arm and leads you inside. The club is small, less than a thousand square feet. A bar, obviously cobbled together from a pile of spare plywood they'd found somewhere, takes up the far side of the room. Two pairs of men and women stand at it; the man from the track earlier tends bar. A pool table, less than regulation size and clearly second or possibly third hand, occupies the center of the room. A relatively tall, lanky Asian with glasses is matched against a determined-looking, short redhead, freckled like you, hair pulled into a tight bun. A few mismatched tables and chairs are scattered haphazardly throughout. Martina leads you to the bar, introducing you to the two couples. You forget their names immediately. One of the girls, a blonde with close cropped hair and imposing biceps, looks at you intensely.

"The man of the hour! I'd offer to buy you a drink, but drinks are free here."

You gesture vaguely with your beer. "I have one, thanks."

"That's just the warm-up. Larry, get us a round of tequila shots."

Larry serves up six shots of tequila with slices of lemon and a plate of salt. "It says Jose Cuervo on the bottle, pardner, but in China you never know what you're getting. Smells right and ain't killed no one yet, anyhow."

Having a vague notion of the ritual, you dab some salt on your tongue. The others lick around the first knuckle and jam it into the salt, coming up with a sizeable crust, which they then slurp off. The blonde girl cries out "Bottoms up! To our new comrade in arms!" You toast and throw back the shot. The fiery gasoline smell burns your nostrils and traces a path of liquid fire down your gullet. You reach gratefully for a slice of lemon and suck on it greedily.

Martina guides you over to the pool table. "Come on, let's boot off these losers."

The redhead snorts. "Bring it on. We'll take you. Winner keeps the table."

The Asian man introduces himself as Fan. He speaks with an anonymous western accent, probably California. The girl is Fiona, with a ghastly Boston dialect. Fan racks the balls and politely offers you a cue stick.

You are not a bad pool player, thanks to hours spent knocking balls around the worn out felt and gimpy bumpers of the table in Jeremy's basement. Alcohol fuels your confidence. You smash the cue ball into the triangle of colored spheres. It breaks decisively, balls angling around the small table and into each other. The cue ball makes contact with a resounding crack, leaps vertically into the air at impact, landing, spinning backwards momentarily, then accelerating into the remaining balls. Two solids go down.

"Whoa." Martina's eyebrows arch in surprise. You sink two more, one simple, the other more challenging, before you run out of good shots. You leave your opponents in a difficult position. Fan manages a difficult bank shot, but leaves himself in an impossible position. Within three turns you've cleared the table, four lonely looking striped balls still scattered around the surface.

"Ah, shit," Fiona curses, disconsolately. "Got my ass kicked by a high school kid. I'm never gonna live this down."

"It's a small table. Lot of luck."

"Luck, shmuck. Anyway, drinks are on us." They bring you another round of tequila. The second one goes down much easier than the first. Someone brings you another beer. 'Walking in Memphis' begins to play on the stereo and Larry yowls along to it from behind the bar. Fiona flicks a coaster at him. "Goddamn it, Larry, shut the fuck up!" He laughs. "Make me, little girl," he calls mockingly across the bar.

She shakes her head. "Not in front of guests." She looks at you enquiringly. "Play again? I'll actually try this time."

The rapid intake of alcohol is making you dizzy. "No, I'll quit on a high note. Need some fresh air."

A small knot of people are gathered outside. They are passing a cigar-sized joint around. The blonde from earlier sucks intently at it, peers at you with bloodshot eyes and proffers it to you. "Wanna try? It's hay, but you can't beat the price. About ten bucks an ounce." The others erupt in laughter.

You take it. "This is definitely not what I expected a military mission to look like." You suck on it carefully, the end brightening into an incandescent orange. Hot fumes fill your lungs. You cough violently. It's not strong, but it does go down very, very rough.

Martina takes it from you and sucks, brow furrowed in concentration. Releasing a substantial cloud of smoke after a few seconds, she manages to croak, "Perk of being on a FUBAR mission at the end of the world. No one knows we're here, no one gives a shit."

"FUBAR?"

"Fucked Up Beyond All Recognition!" the blonde shouts. The rest bellow their assent. Another round of tequila presents itself. Your new friends roar in approval as you down it in one gulp. The joint finds its way into your hand again. You take another careful toke and pass it on, managing to avoid another spasm of coughing as you do.

Seeking respite from the onslaught of alcohol and marijuana, you excuse yourself and walk into the yard. You relieve yourself against a chicken wire fence, while laughter and loud talk continue on the porch of the club. As you turn around, a short figure is in front of you. Martina.

"You ok?" she asks. "These guys don't stop. Just say when you're done, I'll get the car to take you back."

"In a minute, probably. I'm ok, but another hour of this and I won't be."

She steps forward and unceremoniously seizes the back of your head, drawing you down for a kiss. Her tongue probes insistently into your mouth. She tastes of pot and tequila. Not an entirely unpleasant scent, nor completely unknown. You return the kiss hesitantly, lightly touching her solid hips. She releases you and looks up with a predatory grin. Black curls, released from the tight braid of earlier, cascade beyond her shoulders, a slight halo backlit from the blazing lights of the bar.

"Want some company back at your place?"

You look down at her, tight T-shirt accentuating ample breasts, short skirt revealing muscular thighs. "I have the feeling this isn't completely spontaneous."

Martina giggles. "Colonel said you weren't dumb." She comes closer to you, pressing her hard body against yours. "Yeah, OK, so I'm on a mission." She looks you up and down, appraisingly. "But I've had worse missions in my life, that's for sure. I volunteered, if it matters."

"Not tonight. I'll just puke all over you."

She laughs. "All right, cowboy. You be you." She flips her hair, now long, loose curls, turns and struts away. She pauses and looks over her shoulder. "But in case you change your mind, you should know I *always* give a mission a hundred ten percent. I'll send the car around."

True to her word, the car arrives nearly immediately. You manage to wait to vomit until after the car drops you off, miraculously directing most of it into the bushes near the entrance and nearly nothing onto your clothes. You stumble upstairs, throwing yourself into bed without even removing your pants, wishing for sleep while the room spins around you like whirling helicopter blades.

A nice day for an apocalypse

Three days later, you see the Colonel is as good as his word. He picks you up personally in the car this time. He nods in greeting as you slide into the car, freshly cut hair iridescent in the morning sun. Although it is still early, a sheen of sweat coats your back and your shirt sticks to the seat.

"Robert! Good morning!"

"Nice day for an apocalypse."

The Colonel snorts in derision as the car lurches into motion. "Kids these days. So melodramatic. Have you been enjoying our hospitality?"

"I've had worse abductions."

He glances at you slyly. "You haven't been, ah, taking full advantage of the *amenities* on offer."

You shrug. He presses on. "Do you prefer boys? No judgment here, Robert. We're in Asia, after all. Anything you can imagine can be arranged, as well as many things you can't."

"Are you a full-time Colonel and part-time pimp, or is it vice versa?"

The Colonel shakes his head mournfully. "A man tries to be nice… ah well. Now, when I was your age…" he thinks better of the comment, trailing off wistfully.

You sit out the remainder of the short trip in silence. You go to a completely different part of the base this time, passing through a gate in another chain link fence. The gate is manned by two burly, bearded soldiers, again in fatigues without insignia. They peer in the windows and offer half-salutes.

"Morning, Colonel."

"Good morning, men. Big day today! Wish us luck."

"Yes, sir. Good luck, sir."

Your car pulls up at another squat, anonymous concrete building. About a hundred yards away is a steel blister, perhaps thirty or forty feet in diameter, covered in camouflage netting. Presumably the ballistic missile silo the Colonel referred to rests in the darkness beneath.

You troop up the stairs into the building, and immediately take an elevator down an indeterminate distance. The doors open into a claustrophobically small control room, perhaps four hundred feet square, with large screens projected onto the walls. Several Asians in white coats are hunched over incongruously modern computers, while two in army fatigues listlessly stand guard. Hal slouches in a corner, doodling differential equations on a flipchart. His face lights up with pleasure as you enter. He wears the same beige linen suit, only now with a jazzy electric blue shirt as counterpoint. He even sports a matching lapel handkerchief.

"Robert me boy! How's about ye?"

"Shut it, Hal."

"Always the charmer. Always the charmer. Gots more o ye uncle in ye than ye think, I'll wager. Y'all sure Dad was *Dad* and Uncle was *Uncle*, as it were? Or weren't?"

The Colonel waves Hal into silence with obvious annoyance and marches toward the control panel, intently examining a series of screens. On one monitor you can clearly see the sleek cylinder of what must surely be the rocket. One of the technicians murmurs to the Colonel, gesturing animatedly at the blinking lights on the screen. Brow furrowed, he asks several questions in Chinese. The technician nods enthusiastically to each of them in turn. He stands up, interlocks his fingers and stretches his arms toward the ceiling.

"Well, well, well. Looks like we have no more excuses, people. We're ready to go!"

"Where'd you get a rocket? Or did you just put it together yourself?" you ask.

Hal chortles in amusement. "Do we lookee like *rocket scientists*? No, we done bought an old Proton from the Russkies. They's places in Russia where ye can trade one for a crate of vodka these days. Or, as summa us who read the *Good Book* might say, these *end days*."

"Why are the US and Chinese militaries buying Russian rockets from garage sales?"

The Colonel intervenes sharply. "Deniability, young Robert. Well, that's the official reason. The Chinese rocketry program has yet to produce anything terribly reliable, if we're being honest with each other. These Protons have made hundreds of successful flights. Never had a glitch. Not one failure. Unlike the Apollo missions, for example."

"Huh. What's this cost, anyway?"

"Less than you'd think. We've got a small payload, it's not like we're trying to get five tons of stuff up there. The rocket's only twenty meters long, remember. As Hal mentioned, there are deals to be had these days, with the proper connections. There are about a hundred thousand gallons of jet fuel in the first stage, plus some oxidant. Second stage has another fifty thousand gallons of liquid hydrogen and oxidant. Bit more to brake when it enters the lunar gravity well, but it won't be landing. There's a self-contained unit to deposit the droids on the lunar surface. Not much gravity up there to speak of so that's not a big push. Maybe eight, ten million dollars, all told."

"So what you're saying is we're about to light a match under fifty tons of high explosive loaded onto a second-hand Russian rocket you traded a crate of Levi's and cigarettes for to some drunken border guard. Shouldn't we have a drink first?"

The Colonel stares at you, pupils like pinpricks of agate, hard enough to cut glass. Hal bursts into laughter. "Ha! Ha, ha! Hoo-wee, he got you there, Colonel!" Even the implacable, white-coated Chinese allow themselves slight smirks as they diligently jab at their controls.

"Yes. Ah hem. At any rate, Robert, we all have our own little threads to weave into this wondrous historical tapestry before us. That includes you. Have a seat."

You sit in the high-backed, artificial leather chair to which he gestures in front of the consoles. It creaks under your weight. A simple beige monitor with a green screen occupies the desk. An innocuous prompt reads "HELIOS control framework, version 1.30. Enter authorization code to submit target coordinates."

"Now, we have city coordinates from Aurora's notes." He glances at Hal. "Aurora. Very amusing, by the way."

"What's funny about it?" you ask, involuntarily.

The Colonel's lip curls in a sneer. "Don't be so snippy, Robert. You're somewhat ahistorical, if you'll forgive a moment of criticism. Those who don't know the past are doomed to repeat it. The *Aurora* was the warship that fired the gun heralding the onset of the Russian Revolution in 1917. Perhaps it will serve as a fitting analogy, in the end. But, to the point. We require the access code. She doesn't seem to know it. Either that, or she's a *very* convincing liar."

"I told you, we - I'm not participating in your little game of geopolitical domination."

The Colonel shakes his head mournfully. "Robert, Robert. I've been trying to appeal to your patriotic nature."

"Go appeal to someone else's patriotic nature."

"I'm afraid that's not an option. Now, normally I'd be the last one to favor extreme options, but…" The Colonel mutters something in Chinese to one of the white-clothed staff at the computer terminal. The man nods twice and barks a short order into a microphone.

Hal turns and advances toward the bank of computers. You notice the demeanor of the guards instantly changes, from slouched nonchalance to alertness, hands creeping discreetly toward their sidearms. "*Whut?* Whut was that I just done *heared?*" His voice is disconcertingly, jarringly loud in the enclosed space.

On the monitor displaying the rocket you see a door slide open in the silo. A tiny figure, dressed in jeans and a white shirt, stumbles out the door, which immediately closes. Aurora. She wheels around and leaps toward the door, banging on the unforgiving steel with small fists. There is no audio from the feed, but she seems to be screaming.

Hal's face sets itself into an emotionless mask. He strides determinedly toward the man who spoke into the microphone. He grabs him by the back of the head and, before anyone can react, smashes his face into the console rapidly, several times. He lifts the still form up by the neck easily, with one hand. A rope of bloody gore trails from the man's destroyed face to the smashed and broken keyboard. You note a couple of keys have detached and are embedded in the man's cheek and forehead. Hal tosses him aside like a broken toy and shouts something into the microphone.

The Colonel backs away rapidly, with a practiced noiselessness, hand moving toward his pistol. White-coated technicians scramble to get out of the way of the impending conflict. One of the soldiers stationed by the door moves rapidly toward Hal. This turns out to be a not completely thought through plan, given the vast size differential; Hal's left arm lashes out with the speed of a mongoose, grabbing the soldier by his shirt and pulling him close, delivering a crushing elbow strike to the bridge of the man's nose with a dull crunch, then hurling him into the far wall. His head makes a wet, cracking *thud* upon impact with the unforgiving cinder blocks. The second soldier's narrow eyes widen in surprise. He fumbles for his sidearm and draws it, hands visibly trembling. It's not a pistol, you note, but wider and square shaped, orange colored. He fires toward Hal with a dull pop. Hal falls immediately to the ground, silently twitching, a pained rictus grimace plastered on his face. A wire extends from his torso to the weapon. Some form of taser, you realize. It produces a rapid clicking noise.

The door bursts open and three American soldiers with automatic rifles enter rapidly. They scan the room to assess the situation. One levels his gun at you. A goateed, tattooed man with sunglasses flipped around to the back of his head pauses to assess the bloody aftermath of the conflict, then looks enquiringly at the Colonel. "Holy shit. What now, boss?"

The Colonel jerks his head at Hal. "Get him out of here."

"Right." They sling their rifles over their shoulders and swiftly move to Hal's prostate form. One grabs him by the knees, the second under the armpits. Hal makes a strangled gargling noise as they lift him with labored grunts.

"Christ almighty. Heavy son of a bitch." They maneuver him out of the room with the professional, practiced movements of a crew of furniture movers.

The third keeps his eyes riveted unblinkingly on your shoulders, rifle still pointed at your gut. Shorter than the other two, probably of Mexican descent, with a clipped moustache. His short sleeves are rolled up, revealing biceps like grapefruits. A pack of Marlboros is tucked into one sleeve.

"Stand down, Juarez. The boy's no threat. He's been very cooperative."

"Yes, sir." He clicks the safety on his rifle – you hadn't realized it had been disengaged – and cradles it in his arm, barrel toward the ceiling. His gaze does not waver from your upper torso.

"Get a medic for these two …" the Colonel looks appraisingly at the remaining limp forms on the ground. A pool of blood is slowly expanding under the head of the soldier who had first approached Hal. His eyes are half-closed, and crossed at an odd angle. "Never mind. Get a couple of, er, stretchers, I suppose. And a mop."

"Sir." He jogs out of the room. The remaining Chinese soldier has begun to tremble uncontrollably, looking at the still forms on the floor. You begin to feel ill as well, a sudden rush of intense heat in your body and skull. A sudden uncontrollable need to retch wells up inside you. You double over, heaving and hacking, but nothing comes up save the bitter taste of bile.

"It's OK, son. First time for everyone in this game. It only gets worse. I was part of the team that went in after the Beirut bombing in '83. We were scraping guys up with shovels, not mops… ah!"

A small knot of Chinese in fatigues troop in and wordlessly begin disposing of the wounded, or worse, figures on the floor. One carries a bucket and mop and begins industriously cleaning up the thick, congealing puddles of claret from the tiles.

"Anyway, have a seat." You sit down and look up at the monitor on the wall. Aurora is no longer screaming, but strides around the confined space of the silo like a panther, head jerking to and fro as she scans for a way to escape. She tries to climb onto one of the fins, but, lacking purchase, slides down. The Colonel chuckles.

"Spirited girl." He claps you on the shoulder. Involuntarily, your muscles freeze like stone. "There there." He sits down on the chair next to you. You watch the monitor together in silence; the only noise is the ceaseless hum of electronics and the sloshing of the mop in the bucket behind you.

"I'm going to be straight with you, Robert. In my line of work, we complete the mission, or cut our losses and *bug out*, in today's vernacular. It's as simple as that. One way or another, I'm firing off that rocket today and we're getting out of here. I'm not about to leave this stuff here, and we'll just try and reconstruct things from your uncle's records."

"What about Aurora?"

He shrugs. "One less thing to explain." He looks pityingly at your ashen face. "I keep telling you, *listen to me*. We're on the same side here! Help us out, and we'll help you out. Nothing would make me happier than a successful mission, delivering you two home to your families, and doing what we can to help two bright, patriotic young people attain a life of wealth and achievement. Pursuant to which, I remind you, we have considerable, and unique, resources."

"Let her out of there."

"Fine. I presume you are aware we can always put her back in. Or both of you."

"How do I know you won't do that anyway? Two problems you don't need to explain instead of one, right?"

He sighs, drumming impatient fingers on the desk. "Robert, this would make things very complicated. Not impossible, but nothing on which I have the least interest in spending time and effort. But, if it makes you feel better..." He pulls out his pistol and slides back the action to chamber a round. He releases the magazine and shows it to you. A copper-colored bullet glints under fluorescent lighting. He reinserts the magazine and slides it across the desk to you.

"An insurance policy, if you will. It's loaded. Don't forget the safety this time. Let's make a deal. I let her out, you put in the code, the rocket launches us into the history books, we get on a plane out of here. No ill will befall either of you. You have my word on that. Everyone lives happily ever after. Even that jackass Hal. He has powerful friends. Well, friends is not exactly the right word, but he would be missed, more than one would expect." He peers at you, with innocuous, sky blue eyes. Seeing something, he continues. "I'm from a military family, Robert, like yourself. We don't give our word lightly."

You take the pistol, it's cool plastic grip rough in your palm. You disengage the safety, a bright orange dot of warning suddenly visible. "Let her out."

The Colonel shrugs, leans forward and says a few words into the microphone. On the monitor you see a door open. Aurora bolts through it. It slides shut immediately after.

You look at the keypad in front of you. The green cursor blinks indifferently. The Colonel grabs a pen and piece of paper from the desk. "Slowly please, and read out the numbers as you type."

Enunciating the number of your door code, you type them in and press enter. After a few moments, "CODE VALID" appears. The Colonel allows himself a small smirk of satisfaction. He rises and walks toward one of the remaining engineers. They begin to talk animatedly, consulting notes from a thick sheaf of papers. You keep the pistol trained on the Colonel. He glances at you.

"Don't do anything foolish, son. This is a splendid moment of triumph for you, your uncle, and for your nation. Don't spoil it."

After a few minutes of consultation in Mandarin, the engineer rapidly begins typing in code to his console. Some of the buttons in front of him begin to come to life, flashing orange initially and finally settling on a peaceful green. He speaks into a microphone. Hearing some satisfactory response in his headphones, he nods affirmatively at the Colonel. The Colonel claps him on the shoulder, and flips open a small plastic shield that covers a key in the command console. He looks at you and grins.

"Final fueling. This adds the oxidant to the tanks. If anything is going to go wrong, it's this. Are you feeling lucky? Want to do the honors?"

"You go ahead."

He nods and turns the key. The engineer taps in a few commands and a clock appears on the monitor. It begins to count down from forty minutes. He claps his hands. "Excellent!"

The door rattles open and three Americans appear. One of them you recognize from the other night. Hanley. They stop abruptly, noticing the gun in your hands, and begin to reach for their own sidearms, mouths metamorphosing rapidly from Os of surprise into hard set grimaces of concentration. The Colonel waves them off amiably. "It's all right, boys, stand down. Robert and I have a deal, don't we, Robert?"

"For now we do."

"We're all set to go. Execute Procedure Zarathustra."

Hanley salutes. "Yes, sir. Charges are ready to go. We'll place them as planned. Timing?"

The Colonel gestures tiredly at the number on the screen, now reading just over thirty-eight minutes. "T plus two minutes."

"Roger." Hanley's gaze strays again toward the pistol in your hand. His eyes rise up and meet yours, questioningly. After a moment, he shrugs. The three jog back out through the door past the Chinese soldier with the mop, still working on the stubborn slick of blood on the floor. The Colonel says something to him. He nods and exits the room, mop clutched like a rifle. Only the surviving engineers remain, looking intently at gauges and monitors, occasionally adjusting a knob or dial.

The Colonel looks at you enquiringly. "Well, shall we? We have a plane to catch. Nothing more for us to do here. The die is cast, as it were."

You motion to the door with your pistol. The Colonel smiles broadly and walks swiftly toward the exit, hat under his arm. You take the elevator back up to the ground floor. Hanley and his companions are waiting there, with bulging rucksacks. Red and black wires hang out of the top of Hanley's.

"Excellent, Hanley. Just place them according to the diagram, like we trained."

"Yes, sir."

You walk down the hallway and out the door, you two steps behind with the pistol trained on the small of the Colonel's back. It has begun to get heavier with time and now wavers slightly, though you carry it at hip height. A Chinese orderly stands at the car, holding the door open. He seems nonplussed by the appearance of his passenger being walked at gunpoint by a teenager.

The Colonel slides into the back seat of the car. You fumble your way in behind him, vainly attempting to keep the gun trained on him as you do. He watches your efforts with some apprehension.

"You sure you don't want to give that back to me? That's live ammunition in there, you know. You might hurt somebody."

You eventually settle into the seat, keeping the pistol balanced on your thigh. "This seems safer for now."

"It is most certainly *not* safer. The quickest way to get shot is to point a gun at someone, you know. For God's sake keep your finger off the trigger. It's very sensitive. That's a .45 ACP. At this range and inside a car it will make hamburger out of me, and leave you with significant hearing loss."

The car lurches into motion. You do keep your finger against the outer part of the trigger guard. You admittedly do not have much of an exit plan if you roll up into a nest of soldiers with a dead commanding officer in the car next to you. The Colonel sighs and looks out the window. He says something to the driver, presumably about avoiding the potholes dotting the decrepit roads.

After a short drive you arrive back at the original airfield where you landed several days prior. A propeller-driven cargo plane waits on the tarmac, painted a deep green with a garish yellow logo on the side. A group of soldiers, American and Chinese, busily load boxes and crates into the back from a parked truck. The car pulls to a halt. Martina trots to the car and opens the door for the Colonel. Pointedly ignoring your demand to wait, acknowledging you with nothing more than a contemptuous glance, he exits the car. You open your door and move quickly around the back, trying to keep the gun trained on your target. You hear a voice cry out. "Robbie!"

You scan the crowd. Aurora stands by the truck, incongruously glamorous in jeans, a loose-fitting white blouse, and unlaced Doc Martens. *Where the hell did she find Doc Martens in the middle of China*, you wonder to yourself.

A sudden shock of excruciating pain erupts in your wrist as someone begins to bend it back toward you at an impossible angle. Somehow you find yourself launched through the air in a forward somersault, landing with a mind-numbing full body crash onto the tarmac. Martina stands over you, still holding your wrist, knee jammed decisively into the back of your elbow, straining against the joint until it creaks just shy of the edge of fracture. She still wears the heavy mascara. Hazel eyes burn coldly into yours. You feel the chrome plated barrel of the pistol jammed deep into your cheek. Aurora shrieks.

"Colonel?" she enquires, eyes not leaving yours.

The Colonel strolls over and peers down at you with amusement. "You see what I meant, Robert? Guns are dangerous toys. Best left to the professionals. As a general rule of thumb, never point a gun at someone you don't mean to shoot on the spot." His eyes turn to the left, where you can hear Aurora wailing. "Would you *please* stop that infernal noise before I decide you two are more trouble than you're worth?" Her cry dies down to a small whimper.

"Let the boy up, Gomez. I'm mostly to blame for this circus. I gave him the gun in the first place."

"Very well, sir." She releases your arm and straightens up. She clears the bullet from the chamber with a practiced hand and catches it as it flies upward, then releases the magazine. She carefully replaces the bullet into the top of the magazine and hands them both to the Colonel. He reinserts the magazine and holsters it as you struggle to stand up. Your wrist howls in pain and is immobile, but most likely sprained and not broken. The rest of your body feels as though it's just been through a bad car crash.

You limp over to where Aurora is standing. Her eyes are stained with tears, but she offers a slight smile. Larry and Fiona are standing next to her, chortling with laughter.

Fiona's hair is tied in a tight red bun. "You're a fuckton better at pool than you are at hand-to-hand, buster, that's for sure. Stick to what you're good at. That's my advice."

Larry chimes in. "Ah, go easy on him. Martina's a tough little cookie. She's from the *barrio*, you know. Five older brothers. She'll kick anybody's ass."

Aurora folds her arms and looks at you searchingly. "What was your plan there, anyway? They kept trying to convince me that you're some kind of hard-core gangster, but that was pretty friggin feeble, to be honest."

You shrug. "Just wanted to make sure you were all right."

Aurora studies the soldiers milling back and forth busily. "Well, that was very chivalrous of you. Please tell me you didn't give these chuckleheads any information on my account."

"Well, I…"

Larry interrupts, forcefully, albeit with a slow smile on his wide, freckled midwestern face. "Now, children, I'd mighty appreciate it if you could keep your conversation to *pure pleasantries*, if ye don't mind, all rightee? No business, if ye don't mind. Thems is orders."

You massage your aching wrist. A bit of mobility has returned. Definitely not broken. "Right. So, anyway, how was your flight?"

Aurora stares at you witheringly in lieu of a reply. She looks down at the ground and kicks aimlessly at a small stone by her foot. Her boots are intricately decorated with abstract purple designs, you notice. It looks as though she drew them herself.

Another car rolls up and parks next to the Colonel's sedan. Hanley and his colleagues exit and stride toward the Colonel, giving him a salute, which he returns. They speak animatedly, but you cannot hear what they are saying. At the end, he shakes their hands in turn. Looking toward the plane, he makes a whirling motion with his hand. After a few moments, the plane's engines cough and sputter into life. The propellers begin to slowly turn, gradually accelerating until they blend into silver circles. Vast clouds of dust begin to billow up from the ground.

"That's it, chilluns," drawls Larry. "Time to bug out." He and Fiona guide you into the plane. Two rows of plastic bucket seats face each other in the front part of the hold; in the back, assorted crates and packages are piling up. As an afterthought, a stack of rifles lies piled haphazardly between a couple of wooden crates. They show you to the front of the hold and gesture for you to sit. Larry sits next to Aurora and Fiona takes the seat at your side. Aurora has a small backpack, you note. She begins rummaging through it and pulls out a Walkman. Instead of the classic fixed headband, each earpiece is freely connected by a wire to the tape deck. Avoiding your questioning gaze, she carefully attaches a speaker to each ear, pushes a button and closes her eyes.

Across the hold is a solitary, small window. The thick plexiglass distorts the view, but you clearly see the truck from which packages and gear were being unloaded. As you watch, the truck bursts into flame. More soldiers enter the hold and take their seats. The Colonel sits opposite you, a beatific smile on his face. You nudge Aurora and point to the flaming truck. She half-opens her eyes, registers the sight, and closes them again without reacting. A hydraulic whine signals the final closing of the cargo bay; the engine increases its tempo, and the body of the plane begins to shudder as it moves forward down the runway.

"I didn't realize the army was this much fun!" you shout above the din at the Colonel. "You guys should advertise this more!"

Aurora hears this and opens one eye, peering at you skeptically. "Seriously? Do these guys really look regulation Army to you, dude? Do you even know anyone in the Army?"

You look around at the slouching figures in the seats, jostling and ribbing one another. The average age must be late thirties, you realize, maybe more. Many have goatees; tattoos adorn much of the visible flesh below the neck. Most are thickly muscled. They bear a markedly heterogenous array of evil-looking sidearms and knives.

"They're fucking mercenaries, man." She closes her eye and slouches down further in her seat.

While the Colonel surely cannot hear amidst the roar of the engines, he has been watching Aurora's lips closely. He gives a loud laugh and claps his hands a couple of times, then points at his head.

"Mercenaries is an ugly word!" he shouts. "*Private security forces* is the modern term! But don't worry, we're all ex-service! We still fight for the same flag! We're the good guys!"

The plane angles upward as it takes off, the chassis shuddering fearfully. As you gain altitude, it tilts alarmingly as it turns sharply to the right. *Starboard*, you think to yourself. Unwanted tears sting your eyes. Fiona jabs you in the ribs with her elbow, pointing to the window. Through it, you see a trail of incandescent, fiery exhaust arcing into the sky. You tap Aurora's knee and point to the trail of smoke and fire racing toward the heavens. She opens her eyes, frowns, and closes them tightly. The assembled men and women begin to bang on the metal hull and let out loud whoops of jubilation. The Colonel does not deign to look out the window, but closes his eyes and releases a small whoosh of breath, his fists clenching at his knees in triumph. As the plane continues to wheel through its turn, you can see the airfield from where you'd taken off. A couple of small flashes are visible from some of the buildings as some kind of charges detonate. Thick clouds of smoke already billow forth from others.

You look at Fiona, who has a manic smile plastered on her freckled face. "Isn't someone gonna, like, notice all this?" you shout.

"Sure they will!" she laughs. "But it'll take em a while to figure out what happened. We'll be long gone by then! This is a China Post cargo plane. Official manifest and everything. Don't worry cowboy, no one is gonna shoot us down. Not today, anyway."

"Going where?"

"Hong Kong, baby boy, Hong Kong. Hope you brought your party pants."

The plane finds its heading and levels off, still rattling and shaking alarmingly. The soldiers settle into various states of repose. The Colonel seems to sleep. An elbow digs sharply into the right side of your ribcage. You turn your head toward Aurora. Black, stony eyes stare inscrutably into yours. She proffers one of her earpieces. You take it, and manage to hook it around your ear. With only one speaker, the music is tinny and faint, but better than nothing. You don't know the song, but it is distinctively David Bowie.

My little China girl

You shouldn't mess with me

I'll ruin everything you are

I'll give you television

I'll give you eyes of blue

I'll give you men who want to rule the world

And when I get excited

My little China girl says

Oh baby, just you shut your mouth…

You fasten your eyes at the small oval of deepening blue on the other side of the plane, and wonder what further madness awaits. Sleep seems improbable at best, with this ungodly racket and unforgiving plastic seats, but nevertheless overtakes you more quickly than you would have believed possible.

Atlas Shrugged

It is night when the plane touches down. A hectic transfer takes place in the darkness, full of muffled shouts and curses as the soldiers struggle to move mounds of crates, duffel bags and rucksacks between the cargo plane and a couple of waiting trucks. The trucks themselves are impressive, hulking contraptions with a forbidding 'Tatra' logo emblazoned on the front grill.

Hanley sees you inspecting them and bangs on the side of one with a loud, metallic clang. "*Tatras*! Nothing like em in the world. They make em out in Czechoslovenia or some shit like that. Every year they win the fuckin Dakar desert truck rally hands down. Nobody else even comes close."

Aurora sits in one of the trucks, an oasis of calm amidst the swirl of chaos. Her legs are folded primly, both hands clasping one knee. You climb into the truck and sit next to her. The interior has a peculiar musty smell, like old socks and salted fish.

"You look pretty Zen in here."

Aurora looks at you, startled, as though woken from a trance. "What? Sorry, I was writing a poem."

"What, in your head?"

"Yeah, dummy. In my head. Where else would I write it in this dump?"

You pick up a piece of metal from the floor of the truck. You realize it's a stray bullet. You toy with the cold cylinder, which casts an occasional glint of brass in the fitful light. You've only held handgun ammunition before; the long, heavy shell in your hand is a different species entirely. Probably leading to far more ruinous consequences to a target. "Any idea where we are?"

Aurora absentmindedly drums a staccato beat on the steel seats with her fingers. "I overheard some of the Chinese guys talking. They're mostly speaking Cantonese, said something about Tung-kuan. That would make sense. It's pretty close to Hong Kong. And we're definitely in the south somewhere. If we were up north, we'd know it. Gets cold as fuck up there."

"Look, Aurora, I'm really sorry I got you into…"

Larry and Martina climb into the truck. "Hello, kiddos. Not up to any hanky panky, are you?" Larry asks with a malicious smirk.

"Some people use trucks for transport, not foreplay, you know." Aurora's icy voice slices through the tropical darkness. Martina whistles. "Ooh, *pendejo*, you want a band-aid for that one? Sounds like that mighta stung a little, no?"

Larry stretches out unconcernedly on the bench opposite. "We'll see who gits the last laugh here." At that moment the truck coughs and rumbles into life, jolting forward, great belches of black smoke billowing from the tailpipe. The stench of burning diesel envelops you. You watch out the back of the truck at the plane resting on the tarmac. As you draw further away, you see flames begin to lick around the interior of the cabin, gradually welling out and beginning to consume the chassis as you turn a corner and lose sight of the aircraft.

"These guys really like to burn their boats behind them, huh?"

Aurora glances outside, but at this point there is only darkness. "Worked for Cortes, I guess. Must be a genocide thing."

After half an hour of disjointed movement along unlit back roads, the truck rolls to a halt, brakes letting out a satisfied hydraulic sigh as the massive chassis come to rest. You jump out of the back onto a bare dirt lot. The tangy smell of the sea is heavy in the air. The moon is high and bright, but partially obscured by thick clouds. There is enough light for you to make out the swaying palm trees around you. Toward the shore, you hear more commotion as cargo is moved rapidly down a creaking wooden dock toward waiting boats. A small knot of people has gathered around the back of one of the trucks, laughing and smoking.

"Let's go, let's go, people! Stop standing around with your dicks in your hands, if you don't mind. Excuse the language, ladies," you hear the Colonel cry out. A couple of feminine voices hurl back ribald responses concerning the relative size of their genitalia. Cigarettes are quickly extinguished, ground underfoot or hurled with a brief hiss into the water. Grunting figures clatter down the wooden ramp toward the dock. You hear dull metallic bangs echoing through the darkness as heavy crates are heaved unceremoniously onto steel decks.

He approaches you and grins, angular features illuminated starkly in grayscale by the moonlight. "Very exciting, isn't it? We're going to meet some very important people now, my young friends. The animating force behind this whole venture."

"Can't wait. Where's Hal, by the way?"

Aurora looks at you questioningly. It occurs to you that she is most likely not aware of the scene in the control room. The Colonel's broad grin retracts to a tight grimace, attempting to present itself as a smile.

"He's fine. He went ahead of us. The ah, sponsors of this project wanted to have the opportunity to thank him in private." He pauses. "By the way, we've got a reasonably lengthy boat ride in front of us. The craft are, shall we say, better dimensioned in the engine department than in terms of hygienic amenities. I suggest you take care of any, ah, primal needs before boarding."

Aurora bobs her head understandingly and flits away into the night. The Colonel squeezes your shoulder gently. "Hope you've got a strong stomach, son. This will be a bumpy ride. I don't think they could have tracked us here this quickly, but best not to take chances. It will be a fast trip. Very fast."

After some time, the jostling, shouting crowd begins to migrate down the gangway toward the dock. You allow yourself to be moved along with the general flow of movement. There are three boats, all of them no-nonsense creations designed for speed, not comfort. Unpainted, elongated cigar-shaped aluminum craft, each with a pair of massive outboard engines chugging placidly in the water. They look absurdly over-dimensioned, capable of rocketing the light craft into the sky, if need be. Simple benches along the side of the craft are the only seating. You notice each place has a sturdy metal handhold next to it. Apparently, the designers had planned on bumpy rides as well.

A few last bags are tossed on board and someone gives a shout to cast off.

There is no light save for the now gauzy moon and dull red navigation lights on the bow. Shadowy, barely discernible figures on the dock unwrap the docking ropes and toss them casually aboard, jumping after them as the boat drifts away from the dock. The Colonel is at the front of your boat. "All aboard!" he roars, the unexpected volume from his slight frame cutting through the increasing whine of the engines. He takes a last look around and, satisfied, makes a forward wave and sits down. The boats curve out from the dock at a modest clip. You can barely make out the grayish mass of rocks on either side denoting the borders of the harbor. Everyone gradually falls into silence as conversation becomes impossible as the engines tick over in ever increasing intensity.

Once you are clear of the jetty, extended like a stony, accusing finger toward the heart of the ocean itself, the engines roar into full throttle. The swells are thankfully not large, but as you gain velocity the giant boats begin skipping over them, a brief moment of flight interrupted by an inevitable shuddering crash into the next. The impact of each landing rattles the boat. Heavy gushes of seawater spray into the boat with every smashing wave. The banshee wail of the surging engines combined with the incessant clap of aluminum against the unforgiving carapace of the sea quickly becomes intolerable. Within moments you are soaked to the skin. You look for Aurora, She is nowhere to be seen.

Gunnar had advised you that in rough seas, the best bet is to keep one's eye trained on the horizon. The dissonance between what your eyes and your inner ear tell you is the cause of motion sickness, he'd explained. However, no horizon is visible among barely varying shades of darkness. You close your eyes, and count the violent impacts of metal on wave. *One, two, three, four...* You hear one of your neighbors suddenly begin to retch uncontrollably, and resist the urge to open your eyes. After a few more bone-shaking crashes against the waves, it feels as though some unseen demon is gripping your bowels in horny claws, tighter and tighter as each moment passes. You feel the bitter taste of stomach acid begin to gather and well in your throat. You force it back down for a moment. It rises again, stronger this time. *There is no point*, you think, opening your mouth. Your stomach gives a mighty heave, emptying its contents onto the deck in a watery spatter. Someone across from you vomits as well. The noisome stench of bile fills the air.

The trip lasts for an eternity. From the sound of things, everyone on board eventually throws up, most sooner rather than later. No one attempts to do it over the side, preferring to vomit on their shoes while hanging on to the handles by the seat instead of taking the risk of being ejected overboard. Even if anyone noticed one of their companions bouncing out of the boat in the howling darkness, it seems unlikely the boat would turn around to get them. Thankfully, the continuous deluge of salt water washes away the residue. The first three times you throw up, something solid is expelled. The next few times you feel nothing but acid and bile, burning your throat, dripping out your nose. Eventually even that source exhausts itself and you find yourself dry heaving, your body striving mightily but vainly to expel some imagined poison, chest pressing against your knees, wishing for a quick death.

Eventually, after what seems like hours, your body utterly spent, you manage to open your eyes as you suck in ragged breaths. Behind you, the sky just above the horizon has turned to a midnight blue. A slight glint of light suggests itself, casting the faintest of glimmers across the darkened sea. You can make out the forms of the other passengers across from you, heads bowed, swaying with every swell like trees in a rough wind. Looking toward the bow of the boat, you see the Colonel standing upright next to the driver, legs akimbo, talking with him animatedly and gesticulating. He seems unfazed by the violent passage that has left everyone else reduced to shivering sacks of misery. He turns around and peers back at the huddled forms behind him, shrugs, and looks back to the instruments on the control panel before him.

The sun rises rapidly in the sky, far more quickly than you are used to. Seemingly in minutes it transforms from the smallest glimmer of dawn to a bright yellow orb ascending quickly into the sky. One advantage of being by the equator, you think. Its warmth is welcome on your sea-soaked back. With a clearly defined horizon on which to focus, your innards gradually begin to settle. Perhaps only due to the fact that they are now visible, the waves seem smaller than they had before in the thundering darkness. You briefly consider attempting to stand, but your body feels as though its muscles have withered away to nothing. You close your eyes.

After a few minutes, you feel a squeeze on your knee. You open your eyes. Martina looks back at you. You had not realized she was sitting next to you. Her normally olive skin is chalky white. Wild stripes of smeared makeup slash across her cheeks. She gestures toward the front of the boat. With some effort, you lift your head and look forward. On the horizon is the unmistakable gray smudge of land. She shouts something at you, unintelligible over the roar of the engines. You nod. Looking closer, you note that you are not actually heading toward land, but several degrees to the right of it.

You struggle to your feet and make your way unsteadily to the control booth. The Colonel wears a jaunty grin.

"Robert! How are the sea legs? Enjoying our little excursion?"

The boat collides with a particularly unforgiving wave. Fortunately, you are able to grab onto a railing before your nose smashes into the dashboard. You steady yourself.

"Where the hell are we going? Land's over there." You gesture fitfully to the black smudge to the east.

"Don't worry, we'll get off this glorified torpedo soon. Fifteen minutes, give or take." He regards your ashen countenance with concern. "Stay up here. It's easier on the stomach, and the soul." He turns back to the skipper, pointing at a map marked with red crosses and shouting in Mandarin to be heard above the deafening din. You hold on to the railing, swaying with every bump and crash, trying to remember Gunnar's advice. *Take the impact with your legs. Hold your torso steady. Imagine you're holding a tray of glasses and you can't spill them.*

After a few minutes, the Colonel picks up a pair of binoculars. He rubs them carefully with a cloth from his pocket, and scans the horizon. He taps the skipper excitedly on the arm and hands him the binoculars, pointing at something and speaking excitedly. The skipper looks briefly, nods, and hands them back. He expertly lights a cigarette in spite of the rushing gusts of wind. The scent of tobacco is a pleasant change from the miasma of vomit and diesel. You sniff deeply at the cloud of smoke whipping by you. Noticing, the man offers you a cigarette from his pack. You shake your head.

The Colonel hands you the binoculars. "She's right ahead of us now!" he shouts. "Take a look!"

It is difficult to get a fix on the horizon as the boat leaps from wave to wave. Eventually you make out a shining white object, probably a mile or two away.

"I see it. What is it?"

"A yacht!" the Colonel shouts back. "That's our pick-up point."

As you roar onwards, sunlight now glinting mercilessly from the waves like a million mirrors, the white speck in the distance gradually grows in size, taking on shape and form. Huddled, salt-crusted figures on the benches extricate themselves from their hunched poses, blearily blinking their eyes at the sparkling blue ocean. Those whose sunglasses were not ripped away by the wind begin to place them carefully over their eyes. A couple crane their necks to see the rapidly approaching craft of - as soon becomes clear - gargantuan proportions.

Short minutes later, the engines on your speedboat cut back, the thunderous roar gradually descending into a threatening gurgle as you approach the enormous ship. It resembles nothing so much as a city block jutting up from the waves. As you approach, you can see minute figures, high above you, gesticulating with flags.

"Jesus Christ," you mutter, wiping away some of the thick, viscous film that has accumulated on your lips. "You could play football on that thing."

The Colonel pulls a cigar from his breast pocket and ignites it with a silver lighter. Some sort of military insignia is etched on the side. A pungent cloud of acrid smoke billows forth. "Not quite," he corrects you. "It's sixty-eight meters long." He gazes contemplatively at the stern. The name, *Atlas Shrugged*, is stenciled on the back in black letters, each as tall as a man.

"For a guy who likes to cover his tracks, you've picked a pretty high-profile getaway vehicle."

The Colonel sucks on his cigar, the ember at the tip flaring into a bright orange. "Hiding in plain sight, Robert. We'll be hiding in plain sight. No one ever expects that. Fear not."

As if on cue, a black, rectangular gash appears on the lower half of the stern, twenty feet wide and ten or more tall. A piece of stern smoothly detaches from the body of the ship and raises itself up with a hydraulic whine as your boat bobs a couple of hundred feet away. You can make out a cavernous space within, well-lit, and with several people bustling around inside. Your boat begins to trundle carefully toward the opening. The sea has calmed considerably, and the craft merely rocks gently in the waves.

As you pass through, you see there is an internal dock inside the ship. An enterprising soldier expertly ties a couple of buoys to cleats on the side of the boat and tosses them over. Others at the bow and stern toss ropes to waiting orderlies on the dock. They are all Asian, albeit seemingly rather Filipino than Chinese to your untrained eye, dressed in red jumpsuits. They catch the ropes and efficiently pull the boat close to the dock until the buoys, caught between, squeak in protest.

The Colonel strides to the gunwale of the boat and hops off, ignoring the hands outstretched to assist him. Others follow, most badly unsteady on their feet and with faces still ranging in color from ghostly pale to light green. Most accept the help; some stumble nevertheless. A few collapse completely. You jump onto the dock, grateful to have relatively stable aluminum under your feet. Small Asian men grab you by the elbow to make sure you will not fall, jabbering incomprehensibly. You shake them off. After everyone has disembarked, they industriously begin to remove the bags and crates that have slipped haphazardly around the boat.

A man in a gray uniform with a military cut, but without medals or insignia, has approached the Colonel. They salute one another and then shake hands. The man speaks rapidly; the Colonel shakes his head and gestures at the bedraggled crew of people standing listlessly on the dock, most with dribbles of vomit on their uniforms and crusts of salt beginning to form on their shirts where the salt water has begun to evaporate. He nods. The Colonel claps his hands and bellows:

"Men! Women! Others! You will be escorted to quarters. Clean up as best you can and prepare to be on deck in T plus sixty minutes!"

A few plaintive groans arise from the crew. You look around at the docking station and wonder where they plan on putting the other two boats. It's large, but not that large. Your question is answered as two thick canvas straps descend from the ceiling, straddling the bow and stern of the boat. Once in the water, they move toward one another until each is about a quarter of the way from the end of the boat. One of the men gives a sharp whistle and points his thumb up. The pregnant whine of machinery fills the air, the straps go taut, and the boat slowly begins to rise out of the water toward the ceiling. Once it is ten feet in the air, the second cigar boat makes its way into the docking station.

Martina grabs your arm. She looks less ghostly and has washed off the residue of her makeup. "Come on, let's go get cleaned up." You trail her as she walks after the knot of people from your boat. The group ascends a set of metal stairs, footsteps echoing in the cavernous space. After two flights of stairs, the crewman in the gray uniform – who, unlike the others, is clearly of Chinese origin – taps a panel with a card from his pocket. The door clicks open and he walks through, gesturing for the rest to follow.

A narrow hallway awaits with doors every six feet or so. Another orderly in a red jumpsuit awaits with a clipboard. He ushers people into the rooms individually. They seem to be rooms for the crew members; pictures adorn the walls and clothing hangs haphazardly in many of them.

"What are we doing?" you whisper to Martina, unsure why you are whispering.

"Take a shower. Brush your teeth. Change your clothes."

You look at the man in the red jumpsuit, a good eight inches shorter than you. "This should be fun."

You are ushered into a room. The man looks at you appraisingly, and jots something down on his clipboard. The crewman in gray nods at you stiffly. In reasonably good English, he says, "You stay here. Take shower, rest. We bring you clothes." You nod and enter.

The room is tiny, but there is a small curtained off corner with a hose and showerhead. You gratefully strip off your crusted and filthy clothes and wash yourself as best you can. The water is lukewarm at best but is a relief after the trying journey. Oddly, there is Head and Shoulders shampoo. You slather it around your hair and body and stand for a few moments, head against the wall, letting the water run down your neck and back.

When you pull back the curtain, you see someone has already left a pile of clothes, a towel, deodorant, a toothbrush, toothpaste and a razor. You dry yourself off and brush your teeth. The clothes, as usual, fit perfectly.

You lie down on the bed, which is simultaneously soft and lumpy, as well as being several inches too short. You peruse the photographs taped to the wall. Evidently the owner of the bed's family: a smiling woman, surrounded by a gaggle of children, a dilapidated hut in the background. A thin dog waits mournfully for attention at the edge of the picture.

You begin to drift off, but start awake to a knock on the door. Groggily you open it. The man in the gray uniform again. He offers you his hand.

"Forgive me for before. I did not know who you were. I should have introduced myself. I am second mate Vincent."

"Robert."

He makes a motion somewhere between a nod and a bow. "Of course. Please, follow me."

He walks down the hall and to the left. With his card, he opens another door. A few steps further is an elevator. Again holding the card to a small panel until he hears a satisfied beep, he punches a button. The door slides open. He motions you in and steps in afterward. Though there are only two of you, it is quite cramped. *Would be awfully hard to get around this boat without one of those cards*, you muse. There are buttons with numbers zero through ten, though you notice the four is missing for some reason. He punches ten.

After a short trip upwards, the door slides open. Sunshine floods in unexpectedly, momentarily blinding you. You hold a hand over your eyes and walk forward. You see a small group of people a short distance away; haloed by the sun, you are not sure who they are. You look at your companion. He nods and motions you forward.

Blinking, your eyes gradually become accustomed to the light. You are on some kind of sun deck, perhaps thirty feet on each side. A couple of lounge chairs with tables are positioned near the rear. A sumptuous mahogany bar lurks to the left, attended by a man in a white shirt and bow tie. The Colonel is there, smirking genially at you, in a freshly pressed uniform, looking ready to go on parade. He still holds half of the cigar in his hand. Hal's enormous form rises above the rest. He has traded in his linen suit for jeans and a blazer, with a pale orange shirt. His expression is stoic. Aurora stands off to the side in a gaudy blue and orange sundress that would look terrible on most women, but she somehow manages to make glamorous. Her eyes remain resolutely downcast until you approach. She looks up at you, startled, and raises her eyebrows, giving a half-hearted wave from her hip. Two women in tight-fitting silk sheath dresses, embroidered with complex black and silvery floral patterns, stand nearby. They smile broadly, holding trays of champagne flutes filled with pale, golden liquor, bubbles lazily making their way to the surface. Behind them, the ocean stretches out in its infinite vastness toward the horizon; the sun, now approaching its zenith, reflects whitely on the waves. A few puffy clouds meander through azure skies.

Behind them at the edge of the deck stands a man in a blue pinstriped suit. His hands are clasped behind his back as he gazes out over the water contemplatively. The sailor in the gray uniform approaches him hesitantly, and murmurs something. The man turns toward you. He is wearing sunglasses. He pushes them up to his forehead and walks toward you, grinning broadly. He is clearly of Chinese origin, taller than most, and rail thin. It is hard to guess his age; he could be anywhere from mid-forties to early fifties, you suppose. Black hair, without a hint of gray. As he reaches you, he thrusts out his hand.

"Robert. I've heard so much about you!" His English is impeccable, with a polished British accent. "Welcome onboard *Atlas Shrugged*. Allow me to introduce myself. Lee Ho Shan."

You take his hand. It is warm and dry. "Nice to meet you, Mr. Shan."

"Please, call me Lee. You've been through far too much on my account to indulge in formalities." His brown eyes twinkle.

"That's one way to put it."

He chuckles. "Well, I surely owe you and Aurora an explanation. But first, let's have a drink to celebrate your safe arrival." He motions for the girls. They shuffle forward, steps constrained by their form-fitting silver dresses. He takes two drinks and hands one to you, then brings the other to Aurora. She reaches out grudgingly and takes it, holding it nearly at arm's length, as though it were a dead rat. The girls float toward Hal and the Colonel, who each take one.

Lee raises his glass. "To a safe arrival, and a successful mission!"

Not knowing what else to do, you raise your glass and touch his. It is deceptively weighty, in contrast to its delicate proportions. You have never heard the slight, but instantly recognizable, ring of real crystal before, which reverberates longingly in the air as he touches everyone's glass in turn. He lifts the glass to his lips. Seeing you hesitate, he smiles.

"Let us relax for a moment and enjoy the view. There will be plenty of time for explanations on the way home."

"Home?"

"Yes, home."

No harm, no foul

The champagne is cold and crisp on your lips, as though a chilly but sun-soaked fall morning could somehow lay claim to a taste, and importantly, light enough that it does not further agitate your still violently upset innards. Lee smacks his lips with relish.

"Dom Perignon. From 1984, I believe. Very drinkable, at any rate."

"You're far too modest, sir," chimes in the Colonel sprightly, his hair shining in the bright sun like a halo. "It's a marvelous vintage. Simply exquisite."

Lee nods acknowledgment. Looking over your shoulder, his eyes widen in delight. He claps his hands together lightly. "Oh, look, a pod of dolphins! Wonderful!"

Grudgingly you turn. A couple of hundred yards off the port side of the yacht you do indeed see the shimmering gray bodies cavorting through the water at breakneck speed, breaking to the surface for air every several yards. There are at least thirty of them.

You note that the yacht is in motion, albeit slowly. "So, what's our heading, Captain?"

Lee's eyes twinkle. "Hong Kong. It's our home port, though the *Atlas Shrugged* is flagged in Cyprus. Tax reasons, you see."

Hal pipes up. "Haint nobody ever git rich like the good Mr. Shan here by payin his taxes, young Robert. Take a lesson here, this is what we call a *teachable moment*."

Your host's eyes narrow in annoyance. "Everything is legal and above board, Mr. Robinson. We don't write the tax code, we just follow it. Well, we write very little of it, at any rate. Only the essential parts." He turns back to you with a genial smile. "But that is neither here nor there. I would be very pleased if you all would be my honored guests for a few weeks, until this little project of ours has drawn to a close, this ... Colonel, what was that damned unpronounceable name you came up with?"

"*Zarathustra*, sir."

Lee chuckles and drains his glass. "Yes, of course. You military types are fond of your Nietzsche, aren't you? Needlessly messianic in my opinion, but there you go. They say in the Great War, no German soldier's knapsack was considered complete without a copy." He motions for the silk-clad girls to refill everyone's glasses.

"Well, Mr. Shan…"

"Lee. Please."

"Well, Lee, enjoyable as this sounds, I'm afraid I do have to get back to the US. I have some things to do. Tell my mother I'm alive, bury my uncle, start the fall semester…"

Lee takes you by the arm and leads you away from the others. "Excuse us for a moment, my friends." He brings you to the rail, overlooking the endless expanse of azure sea. "Robert, I understand this is a very difficult and stressful situation for you. You have handled it with a maturity few could muster at your age. However, there is a greater destiny at stake here than yours, or mine."

"Is there?"

"There most certainly is. Do you know what is scheduled to happen a few years from now?"

"Uh, no. No, I don't."

"Less than seven years from now, my home, Hong Kong, will be 'returned' to Communist China from the United Kingdom. *Returned!*" Lee's lips curl in disgust. He practically spits his words. "*Hong Kong!* One of the great economic and cultural engines of Asia. Seven million souls, currently basking in freedom under the protection of the world's founding democracy, are to be handed over with barely a whimper as slaves to a ruthless, totalitarian regime. Now, of course, they have given certain assurances about the independence of Hong Kong after this date. My colleagues and I do not believe a word of this. *Not one word*. Not after the massacre at Tiananmen Square. They will wade in blood if they need to when the time comes to subjugate my home. In their minds, it is merely a dress rehearsal for retaking Taiwan. So, several years ago we decided to take matters into our own hands. If Great Britain will not defend us, we will defend ourselves."

"Who is 'we', exactly?"

Lee's eyes follow a gull traversing in great circles off the stern of the boat. "I represent a small consortium of my countrymen, who both share the determination to prevent this abomination, and possess the means to do something about it. You may not be aware that eight of the thirty richest people in the world are citizens of Hong Kong…"

"I wasn't."

Lee beams with joy. "We are a peaceful people, a nation of shopkeepers and merchants, but we, what's that lovely American turn of phrase? *punch above our weight*, economically speaking."

"Well, Lee, I certainly sympathize with your position, and admire your patriotism…"

Lee nods at you, even allowing himself a slight bow. "And of course, we in Asia feel a keen debt of gratitude toward your great nation. You have sacrificed much blood, and much treasure, to fight the scourge of communism in faraway lands of which you know little."

You clear your throat. The gull high above emits a shrill screech and plunges toward the sea, disappearing into the waves with a slight splash.

"Ahem. Yes. However, I'm afraid…"

Lee reaches out and gently touches your arm. "A wise man listens to an offer before he refuses it. Let me explain what will happen over the next few weeks. You and Aurora will be my guests in Hong Kong, and spend the first semester of the school year in the American University in Hong Kong. I doubt your education will suffer in comparison to that gang- and vermin-infested warren you currently attend in Philadelphia. Just before your return, your mother will be contacted by a lawyer, who will inform her that unfortunately your Uncle Gunnar has passed away, but had an offshore equity fund worth one point seven million dollars, which he has left to the two of you in equal measure. My foundation will make an exceedingly generous donation to Bowdoin College, to fund a new tenured chair in Chinese studies. Aurora's mother will be appointed to this post. Both of you will receive scholarships to complete your studies at the universities of your choice, anywhere in the world. Finally, both of you will receive offers to join my company once you have finished your studies." Lee looks at you searchingly. "Robert, I don't know what your life plans might be, but I expect this may advance them considerably."

"And what do you want from me?"

He spreads his hands away from his body, palms down. "Absolutely nothing. Stay in Hong Kong for a few months. Enjoy yourself. Learn. Forget everything you saw before you boarded this boat. Never speak of it again."

"That sounds nice. I assume the alternative is correspondingly unpleasant."

Lee regards you with alert but calm brown eyes, half hidden under drooping eyelids. You note the occasional overly drawn-out vowel, and hint of a lisp, inserting itself into otherwise pitch-perfect Oxford English.

"You seem like a perceptive young man. I see no reason to waste time on depressing hypotheticals, which help no one achieve what they want." He pauses, adjusting the white silk kerchief in the breast pocket of his jacket. "You know, I'm actually quite glad to have met you. I really do hope you will accept the offer upon graduation. I can imagine a stellar career for you in our organization."

"What do you do, anyway? What pays for the boats full of mercenaries, and the Dom Perignon?"

Lee's eyes twinkle with merriment. "We have many interests. The family began in shipping. Iron ore, grain, pork bellies. The occasional odd bit of opium, or guns, when times demanded it. Now it's mostly petroleum and natural gas transport. But by the time you join our organization, Robert, I hope to be the biggest supplier of electricity on the planet. Thanks to you, and to your incomparable uncle." He drums his fingers on the railing of the deck. "Robert, *work with me* on this. Help me. Help me free my people from the tyranny of Communist China, and then the rest of the world from the curse of Middle Eastern oil. Help me do this, and I swear I will make you and yours wealthy beyond your wildest dreams."

You peruse the azure waves receding away toward the horizon. The faint smudge of land to the north rests mutely, offering no counsel.

"Not much of a choice, I'd say."

Lee grins broadly, displaying flawless, bleached teeth. He offers you his hand. "We are men of the sea, Robert. Our word is our bond. You have mine. Do I have yours?"

You take his hand in yours. It is warm, and soft, not unlike a woman's, but with a tensile core of masculine strength.

He sends you back to the small knot of people under the canopy, with instructions to ask Aurora to join him. You walk toward her. She listlessly holds the flute of champagne, seemingly untouched, at her side.

"You should try it. It's not bad."

"Meh. What does Right Said Fred there want?"

"A word with you. He's got an offer you can't refuse."

"You'd be surprised what I can refuse." She lightly tosses her glass over the railing toward the waves several stories below, and strides toward the man in the pinstriped suit with the genial, immaculate smile. One of the hostesses notices this, her eyes widening in panic. Presumably the glass was worth several days of her salary, the contents likely more.

The Colonel approaches you, smiling from ear to ear. "Robert, you have exceeded all expectations! Well done! Well done, my boy."

"All they want is for me not to do anything." You note that, magically, your glass has been refilled.

"Well, sometimes nothing is something. Lao Tzu teaches us that 'water is the most yielding of all things, yet over time erodes even mountains'. You have befriended the Ancient Eight, the most powerful families in east Asia. Many successful people in the West go their whole lives without even knowing they exist. Yet you, at this tender age, they invite to their very bosom. Unheard of."

Hal watches his daughter carefully as she confers with Lee by the railing. He speaks animatedly, hands slicing through the air. You call out to him.

"Didn't even thank me for saving your daughter, Hal. That's not very polite of you."

Hal's lower jaw clenches. After a moment, his scowl relaxes into a half smile. He tosses the remainder of his champagne into his mouth. "Well, little feller, now that ye mention it I am mightily obliged to ye. An Hal never forget his debts, no he *does not*, no sir." He directs this last, with considerable menace, at the Colonel.

The Colonel's eyes sparkle with derision. "Now Hal, take it easy, big man. Nothing personal. Just business, as you like to say. We did what we had to in order to complete the mission."

"Once you gits my daughter involved, it caint help but be personal, to mah mind."

The Colonel airily waves this away. "Your daughter is just now negotiating your family's ticket to a life of wealth, power and luxurious indolence. You can spend the rest of your life puttering around with your board games without a care in the world... ah, here they come now!"

Lee strides toward you, beaming contentedly. Aurora shuffles behind him, eyes downcast. "Wonderful news, folks! Everything is agreed. Aurora has decided to attend the Hong Kong Gifted Students Academy for the semester, instead of the American School, so she can work on perfecting her Cantonese. It's a live-in program, very intensive. I admire her ambition. The Academy was founded with a not inconsequential donation from my family, by the way."

You try to catch Aurora's eye. She gazes implacably at the deck, probing some seemingly fascinating splinter of teak with the toe of her sandal. Her toenails are also painted black, you note.

The Colonel smiles genially at you. "Well, I guess all we have to do is head to shore and wait for your uncle's little robots to do their magic, and start lighting up Hong Kong at night, free of charge."

Aurora starts violently. She stares incredulously at the Colonel. "What do you mean, 'light up Hong Kong'? We're *going* to Hong Kong. I thought the idea was to free Hong Kong, not burn it. With us in it, by the way."

Lee chuckles. "Well of course, my dear girl. Our objective is to free Hong Kong. But we must be subtle. If we tried to hold Beijing hostage, we would just start a war that no one wants, and no one could possibly win. But by targeting Hong Kong…"

The Colonel breaks in. "We fired that rocket from the Chinese mainland. Western intelligence forces will have observed the launch. They will conclude the Chinese are trying to force an early handover, or preparing to subjugate the island once they have it. However, it's still a UK territory, so this is no different than an attack on the UK itself…"

"NATO member, by the by," muses Hal. "Means UK might trigger Article 5 and ask for ye ol *US of A* to come runnin in to help."

"Oh, we're counting on it, Mr. Robinson. We're counting on it. The Americans are the only ones with the technical wherewithal to knock out that installation in a matter of days, before our lovely city becomes too stuffy for comfort."

Your glass has been refilled again. You sip at the cool, crisp liquid. Your head is spinning, though you're unsure if it's from the alcohol, or trying to follow the logic of this mad scheme.

Aurora chimes in. "But the Chinese know where it was launched from. They'll trace it back to you."

Lee smiles. "Well, my dear, they can try. You see, one of our subsidiaries really *does* have a contract with the PLA to develop crowd control weapons there. Western intelligence will determine that it was an active PLA facility. Which, for all practical purposes, it was. As for the company working there … well, suffice it to say we have extensive experience with managing such affairs via shell corporations. This particular investigation will lead them around the Cayman Islands, to Panama, and finally to a post office box in Cyprus, where the trail will unfortunately run cold."

"What do you actually want?" you ask. "I mean, what do you think is going to happen, really?"

"My associates have been engaged with Her Majesty's government for years, pressing for what is effectively direct annexation and incorporation into the United Kingdom. We have drawn up articles of association. Everything has been vetted by the best constitutional lawyers in London. However, there has been limited enthusiasm for this initiative in the current government, though certain members of the royal family are cautiously supportive, behind the scenes. Nevertheless, Thatcher's opposition was implacable, and the government has kept this position. But once the true nature of the criminal Chinese regime is exposed, the pressure on the British to accept this plan will be irresistible."

"What if it doesn't work? What if the cavalry doesn't ride to the rescue?"

Lee nods in your direction. "Well, we give it a week or so and then our good friend Robert stands down the system. No harm done. We're back where we started. No harm, no foul."

"Back where we started," you mumble.

"In a manner of speaking, of course. Now, let's go greet the troops, shall we?"

Toward the stern of the yacht is a staircase heading down to another deck, and then to another. This one is a sort of broad balcony underneath an awning. Below you is a large open deck where a number of figures mill about. The Colonel's ragtag band of mercenaries, you realize, in freshly laundered fatigues. They cluster in small groups, hooting and laughing, while more of the young women in silk sheath dresses glide amongst them with flutes of champagne and platters heaped with seafood canapes. On cue, *Sweet Home Alabama* begins to blare from hidden speakers. The soldiers begin to bob and hop with the music. Some of them notice the small knot of people standing above them and begin to nudge and point. After a few moments, the music dies down to a lower level.

The Colonel steps forward and bellows "*Ten-hut*, soldiers!", the penetrating volume, as always, at odds with his thin, dapper form. The crowd below instantly stands to attention.

He looks at them approvingly in silence for a few seconds, cigar chomped in the corner of his mouth. He removes it and gives a wide smile.

"Men, it gives me great pleasure to report this mission as having changed status from FUBAR to *goddamn fucking accomplished*!" War whoops rise from the assembled crowd. "Now, The Boss would like to have a word. Give him a warm welcome, please."

A deafening roar erupts from the crowd. "*Hoo-ahh!*" Followed by applause, punctuated by piercing whistles.

Lee steps forward. He nods at the Colonel. "Thank you, Colonel. Now, troops, I am not fond of long speeches. Suffice it to say that not only I, but an entire nation, are deeply in your debt. As an organization, we are settling the financial aspect as we speak. But in recognition of your extraordinary performance under challenging circumstances, here is a small personal gift from my consortium…" The silk clad ladies, who had discreetly moved to the back of the crowd, now begin moving among the soldiers, distributing golden envelopes to each of them. Even from a distance, there are audible gasps as they are torn open.

"Now, you have certainly all earned a bit of what I believe you military folks call 'R&R'. Once we dock in Hong Kong a slightly more anonymous boat will transport you to Macao, where my concern operates a number of modest entertainment facilities…" Bawdy hoots rise from the audience. "You will have three nights there as my guests. For those of you who enjoy games of skill and chance, there is something in the envelope to get you started. Four days from now, Tuesday, there will be a boat back to Hong Kong, and a charter flight to Los Angeles International Airport, arriving Wednesday morning." He pauses, eyes twinkling. "Don't miss the boat, folks, or you're on your own." A wave of laughter, punctuated by a few lewd comments, rises from the audience. Lee raises his glass. "But now, a toast, my friends! To a free Hong Kong: a bulwark of liberty, now and forever! And to her dear friends, who work diligently in the shadows to keep her that way." A cheer erupts from the crowd. The Colonel claps his hands vigorously.

You sidle over to Aurora, who is staring intently at the horizon, seemingly oblivious to the surrounding pandemonium.

"Hey," you say, unable to think of anything more intelligent.

She starts as though woken from sleep. Black eyes regard you coolly. "Oh. Hey, dummy."

"So, uh, I guess I'm not gonna be able to copy off you during tests at the International School, huh? Too bad."

Aurora plucks a canape from the tray of one of the passing waitresses. The waitress pauses, bobs her head and smiles encouragingly, offering you the tray as well. You select a giant butterflied shrimp, crusted in black pepper, coriander and garlic, nearly as big as your fist.

"Might as well make the best of a shitty situation. I'll never have another chance like this to get my Cantonese together." She pops the canape in her mouth, chewing reflectively. "Foie gras," she comments through a mouth full of food. "Amazing stuff, but it's awful how they make it. They stick pipes in the gullets of these poor geese and force-feed them til they practically burst."

You take a bite of the shrimp. The meat is firm and sweet, with a hint of garlic and chili. The consistency reminds you more of lobster than the pale, tasteless blobs of boiled flesh found in American supermarkets.

"Damn, that's good."

"Give me a bite." Without waiting for an answer, she expertly plucks the shrimp from your hand and pops the remainder in her mouth. She closes her eyes and chews rapturously. Opening them, but unable to talk, she jabs you in the ribs with her elbow and points toward the bow. Leaning over the rail, you can see that you are coming closer to land; shore is perhaps three or four miles away. You can make out the rolling hills and even discern some of the larger buildings jutting up above the skyline. More ships have come into view; some smaller yachts akin to yours, others massive cargo ships loaded with thousands of multihued containers stacked on top of each other like gigantic Lego blocks, a few fishing trawlers maneuvering awkwardly through the waves with cranes extending off each side for lowering and raising nets to capture the ocean's bounty.

"Is that Hong Kong?" you ask. Still unable to talk, Aurora nods.

"Hmm. Neat. Well, let's hang out sometime."

Aurora finally manages to force the lump of shrimp down her throat. She nods noncommittally. "Sure, we'll run into each other. It's a small town."

You stand together in silence atop the giant white monolith gliding noiselessly through the waves, the other multimillion dollar yachts heading with you toward the harbor looking like tiny toy boats in comparison. The terrain around the city is quite hilly. The hills themselves are largely unbuilt on, and are carpeted in a deep, verdant green. As you approach, you can gradually begin to make out the towering buildings in more detail, marching off in all directions. The city is not small, you note, not small at all.

Time will tell

A line of long black limousines awaits you at the dock, chauffeurs in gray uniforms casting their eyes about anxiously for luggage. A young man, perhaps a year or two older than you, greets Lee at one of the cars with a broad smile and they embrace. He is clothed in the deceptive casualness of the very rich, in Armani jeans and a black T-shirt, doubtless costing hundreds of dollars. Lee laughs boisterously, clapping him on the back. He looks at you, eyes bursting with merriment.

"Allow me to introduce my nephew, Roger. The pride and joy of our clan. I've asked him to help you acclimate." Roger extends his hand. You shake hands. "Now, unfortunately I have to attend to a few things at the office. Board meetings, and other insufferable trivialities. Roger will escort you to our modest domicile." A diminutive chauffeur holds a door open for you. You note Aurora being bundled into an identical car a few places behind yours. You slide into the car, luxurious tan calfskin seats enveloping you in a cool embrace. Roger climbs in behind, sitting across from you. He taps on the glass and the car glides into smooth, silent motion.

"Good trip?" he enquires with a laugh. His accent, unlike his uncle's, is purely west coast American. "Just kidding, man. I know you've had a shit couple of weeks. We'll make it up to you, don't worry."

You crane your head to look back at the other limousines in the caravan, some of which are already peeling off toward other destinations. "Where's Aurora going?"

"She said she wanted to go straight to the school. They have a summer program before the official school year starts." Noting your stricken expression, he claps you on the knee. "Don't worry, bud. There's plenty more where that came from. Hey, let's get a drink." Tapping an unseen button, a box rises silently from the seat next to Roger. He opens it and peruses the contents.

"Hmm, maybe a gin and tonic ... oh, it's *Tanqueray*, you have got to be kidding me, what kind of low rent bullshit is this? Oh well." He pours a hefty slug of liquor over a couple of ice cubes, and fills the rest with tonic and pops in a couple of wedges of lime. The tonic is Canada Dry, you note. He pours himself one as well, and proffers his glass. "Cheers."

The glass is pleasantly cold in your hand. You regard the bubbles fizzing up toward the surface. A segment of lime bobs uncertainly among the ice cubes. "What time is it, anyway?"

Roger makes a noncommittal circular gesture with his glass. "You know what they say, it's five o'clock somewhere. I don't know, maybe two in the afternoon."

You sip the drink. The alcohol creates a noticeable burn on your palate, but the coolness of it is refreshing. Looking out the window, you note that you have entered into the city proper. A slight grayish haze seems to permeate everything. Buses surround you, many of them double-decked, while mopeds zip improbably between, some precariously occupied by three or even four people. The windows seem designed to drown out sound, but you can detect hints of the manic honking and shouting. Huge buildings rise to either side, gray and tan monoliths with black windows marching toward the horizon. Garish signs in Chinese script adorn every conceivable surface, nearly stacked on top of one another. An astonishing number of people scurry over the sidewalks.

Roger chatters amiably. "We're gonna have a good time. Uncle Lee said to take care of you. Wait til you see some of the clubs we're gonna hit, you haven't seen anything like it… where are you from, anyway?"

"Philadelphia."

"Huh. Never been there. Spent some time on the west coast. LA, Berkeley. San Diego. You ever been out there?"

"No, we didn't travel much."

"Well, buckle up. You're gonna see some wild shit, dude."

Formidable city blocks gradually give way to smaller buildings and, as you climb toward the hills, single family homes. In an odd reverse function, as you progress the buildings at once begin again to increase in size, modest duplexes turning into stately villas settled discreetly behind ornate steel gates.

Lee's compound in the hills overlooking Hong Kong is vast, though screened by trees so its true scope is not evident to the casual passerby. A uniformed guard in a gatehouse scrutinizes the driver and passengers with care before nodding and opening the gate. A shotgun is slung over his shoulder. The gate is decoratively wrought but clearly thick and solid steel. The hinges are massive things, the size of basketballs. Anything short of a tank or APC would probably fail to breach it.

The limousine crunches up a gravel drive between immaculately trimmed hedges and imposing trees, foreign to your eye but casting welcome shade. After a hundred yards the driveway – or road, driveway is too modest a word – ends in a circular roundabout with a fountain in the center. Two bronze figures dance together, surrounded by four smaller ones emerging from the water.

Roger chuckles. "Copy of the *Joy of Life* fountain in London. Says it represents our family philosophy. He's got a copy of the Trevi in some villa he has in Tuscany that he never goes to. Totally tacky, if you ask me."

As the limousine slows to a halt, white-clad servants rush to open the door. A blast of hot air streams into the car, a stark change from the air-conditioned coolness, bordering on frigidity, of a moment before. Roger hoists himself from the cream-colored seats and stretches in the bright sunlight. You exit the car, disregarding proffered hands of assistance. Roger trots up stairs toward the main building, its white surface now blinding in the tropical sun. You realize that you desperately need sunglasses, as you follow him up the stairs.

The cadre of servants open the door and you enter a vast foyer with a double staircase leading up to the second floor. Another man in a white uniform, older than the others, waits to receive you. He bows as Roger approaches, then to you. Roger claps him on the shoulder.

"Five years I've been telling Hai not to bow to me. Pointless." The man's face relaxes into a crinkly, kindly smile. "Anyway, Hai is chief of the household, chief of staff, jack of all trades, whatever you call it. He'll arrange anything you need, solve any problem." Hai nods and softly delivers a few words in Mandarin, his hands fluttering like nervous butterflies as he does so. Roger answers, then turns to you with a bright smile. "Everything is arranged. You've got the best guest house. Let's go check it out." He strides purposefully forward to a large oak door between the staircases, reaching it and opening it before one of the servants manages to scurry in front of him.

A short hallway leads to a large living room. Several constellations of white leather couches settle next to glass coffee tables. A piano, also white, waits patiently in the far-left corner of the room. The wooden floor seems almost to glow warmly. Mahogany, you surmise. On the right-hand wall is a gigantic television, larger than anything you have seen or would have previously thought possible. In the center of the wall are French doors, which one of the servants manages to open before you reach them. Roger converses amiably as you walk. "We never use that TV. He's got a whole separate movie theater downstairs. Wait til you see that; he actually gets the studio film reels at the same time the theaters do, sometimes before…"

Through the French doors you come to a terrace, dotted with a few tables and chairs under white umbrellas. It overlooks a shimmering pool. Twenty-five yards long, you estimate. "Lee's a swimmer, you know. He was on the swim team at Stanford. You walk past a small house where another smiling man in white bobs his head and smiles. "Towels and drinks from this guy. He'll rub sunscreen on your private parts if you ask. What a job."

Halfway along the pool a path heads toward the right. "This is us…" Several bungalows nestle among the trees. Roger peruses the signs as you walk past them. "Ares, Dionysus, ah, Apollo. That's you."

"How appropriate. The sun god."

Roger laughs and claps you on the back. "Uncle Lee has an eye for detail. That's how he got where he is. Anyway, I'll be next door for a few weeks to help you get settled. Told my girlfriend she'll have to entertain herself for a while."

"I certainly don't want to impose…"

Roger grins impishly. "No bother. It's not the worst assignment I ever got from The Man. She'll keep. The unlimited credit card keeps her busy." He pushes the door open.

The bungalow is larger than it looks from the outside. A sizeable room seems designed to combine dining and relaxation, with a table for six and another of the leather couches facing another laughably over-dimensioned television. A small working desk has a sizeable monitor on it, with a computer resting on the floor. A neat stack of programs sits beside the monitor. Roger looks at it appraisingly. "Compaq. Pentium II processor. Plus I told them to get you games. Some awesome ones came out in the last couple of years. *Quake II, Age of Empires, Total Annihilation*, wait til you see that. *Civilization* if you want to go old school. Ooh, *Command and Conquer, Red Alert*! Have you played that?"

"No. We, uh, don't have a computer."

Roger looks at you with a fleeting moment of pity, which he immediately transforms into a genial smile. "Well, we'll get you caught up. Start with *Command and Conquer*. It's awesome. I don't know how many hours I wasted on that friggin game. Anyway, let's check out the bedroom."

The bedroom is small but functional, with a double bed surely too short for you but probably manageable if you sleep diagonally. Sleek pearl white closets fill an entire wall. Roger opens one. They are full of clothes. Silk shirts, dark, elegant jeans, khaki pants, sport jackets, even a suit. Even without close inspection, it is obvious that the cost of any of these items must far eclipse that of anything you have ever worn. Roger runs his fingers through and clucks disapprovingly. "Well, this will do for now. We didn't know what your style is, what kind of threads you like… Try the suit when you have a chance. It's a Brioni. Those things are awesome. It's like wearing a dream. Bitches just melt into a wet spot when they see one. Anyway, if you need it adjusted, let Hai know."

There is a phone by the bed. Roger notices your gaze. "Room service. Just tell them what you want. Otherwise, they'll just bring you something." He pauses. "You want to make a phone call, bud?"

"I'd like to call my mother. She must be worried sick."

"Well, it's 3 AM on the US east coast right now, so let's leave it a few hours." He pauses, his jovial countenance suddenly searching. "Look, let's get real. It's an outside line. Call your mother. Call whoever the fuck you want. Someone will be listening, and there'll be a time delay. If you say anything weird the line will cut. Just be cool, keep up your part of the deal, and Uncle Lee will be the best thing that ever happened to you."

"Right. Got it."

"Anyway, what do you want to do? Chill out? Go out?"

"I'll just hang out here for today. Call my mother in a few hours, if I make it that long. I'm exhausted. Long day."

Roger places a hand sympathetically on your shoulder. "I bet. OK, I'm two doors down, and if I'm out, just get me on my cell phone." He hands you a business card, jet black with silver text. Apparently he is a Vice President of something. He flashes an impossibly white smile and starts to leave. Pausing, he turns.

"Almost forgot." Reaching into the pocket of his jeans, he fumbles for something. After a few seconds, he pulls out a silver ring and hands it to you. It has the form of a stylized ship on the top, and is deceptively weighty and cool to the touch.

"Wear this when you go out. It's the family insignia. No one will fuck with you. Cops will pretend you're invisible. You can throw up on a bouncer at the hottest club in town and he'll just smile and call you a cab."

You regard the ring. "How come people don't just copy it? I mean, if it's a get out of jail free card, or whatever."

Roger smiles, the warmth belied by a hint of steel. "No one would dare. Anyway, get some rest, and we'll hang out tomorrow."

You explore the bungalow a bit further, playing with air conditioning and cycling through a seemingly infinite number of television channels. You stop for a few minutes at CNN. Apparently, during your adventures, Iraq indeed invaded Kuwait and US troops are massing in Saudi Arabia for a devastating counterattack. *Hmm, Gunnar was right*, you think ruefully. A sliding door leads to a small porch, adorned with a couple of comfortable chairs and a sizeable refrigerator stocked full of beer, soft drinks, juice and assorted snacks. Palm trees sway gently, fronds whispering in the breeze under a darkening sky. The sun has begun the abrupt descent peculiar to these equatorial latitudes. A cabinet contains a surprisingly full bar. The gin is Bombay Sapphire instead of Tanqueray. You pour yourself a Coke, go inside and turn on the computer. After a few moments you figure out how to insert a DVD. You put in *Command and Conquer*.

A black and white scene fills the screen. A laboratory, a scientist demanding calculations and coordinates. You cannot help but laugh at the ridiculous serendipity of the scene with your own recent experiences. They have developed some sort of time machine, apparently. The scientist disappears in a flash, transported back to Germany in 1924. *I wonder if it will be raining*, he mumbles as he disappears.

There is a man, his identity unmistakable from the narrow moustache and black hair sweeping across the forehead from a high widow's peak. *Herr Hitler*, the scientist asks. Taking his hand, mankind's most monstrous spawn disappears in an instant. The scientist returns to his own time. *Hitler is out of the picture*, he says to his assistant, calmly. Resignedly, perhaps.

"That's wonderful! Wonderful."

The scientist, wiser and more careful, shakes his head. "Time will tell. Time will tell."

Hours speed by. Your mother wakes in Philadelphia, but she is forgotten for now. You play long into the night: Tesla coil defense installations, ironically, saving your troops from many a dark fate at the hands of your enemies.

It really is a very good game.

Smoking up with Peter the Great

You finally manage to reach your mother after two days of recuperation from your adventures on the mainland. She is far calmer than you expected. Evidently someone has been in touch with her and managed to convince her this is a unique opportunity, and not to ask too many detailed questions. She mostly wants to know what Hong Kong is like. You inform her you haven't had much of a chance to see the sights, but you'll report back when you know more.

"How on earth did you manage to get in? You've never even had a *passport*, for God's sake!" she asks worriedly. You assure her it's the government, they are perfectly able to manage such things.

Roger drops by after your call. He wears khakis and a sky blue polo shirt, black JanSport backpack slung over one shoulder. You assume the timing is not a coincidence. He clasps your hand warmly. "Hey bud. How was breakfast? OK?"

"It was amazing," you answer, truthfully. The morning had exposed you to new horizons of culinary wonder. Strange fruits guarded by dragon-scaled leathery skin, creamy scrambled eggs, some esoteric kind of Danish cinnamon buns, soft and rich and chewy, with small crumbs of salted nuts hidden among the rivers of caramel. Fresh squeezed orange and pineapple juice bursting across your palate like a rainbow. A smokey espresso with hints of cacao and a layer of brown cream on top thick enough to rest a quarter upon without sinking.

"Cool. I mean, anything you can think of, just tell them. They'll make it for you. Good talk with your mother?"

"She's fine. Surprisingly unstressed. You guys have been managing her, I see."

Roger nods noncommittally. "We manage. It's what we do. Anyway, you've had a couple of days to relax. What do you want to do? I usually do a workout at the gym Thursday morning. Let's do that, then we can go into town."

You find some athletic shorts and top in your closet. Roger chatters on about the brand, some new wicking technology designed to help you cool faster, as he places them in his bag. You leave the bungalow into an unexpected wall of tropical heat. Sweat begins to bead on your brow. Roger strides along the path, this time taking a different route leading to a long, low, unassuming single-story building with white stucco and narrow, vertical windows. You enter the building through a black glass door. The temperature is a good twenty degrees lower than outside. You wonder how healthy moving between these extreme thermal gradients can be. A diminutive girl, dressed in an identical silk dress as the hostesses on the boat, greets you with a bow. She offers you bottles of Evian, and motions for you to follow. You pause to open it and drink. The water is ice cold, enough to make your teeth ache.

Roger's body is lithe and well-defined, and completely hairless. He appraises your shoulder carefully as you change shirts. "I heard about that shoulder. You want someone to look at it? We can get you an appointment at the best orthopedic surgeon in Asia."

"It looks worse than it is. Doesn't seem to be a problem, functionally anyway. It works as well as it ever did."

Roger nods. "Well, think about it. The offer stands. Might come back to haunt you when you're thirty."

The gym is as well-equipped as any commercial establishment. Vast glass windows in the back look out into an expanse of forested hills. The two of you are alone, except for three male attendants with towels and water who bob and smile at you encouragingly. You spend half an hour on a running machine. Roger runs at a pace twenty percent faster than yours, and keeps up a constant chatter as you wheeze and gasp. You have never spent much time lifting weights. Roger demonstrates the proper form, assisting you as you struggle to lift alarmingly wobbling bars. Bench press, curls, squats, hamstrings, Romanian dead lifts … Roger burbles on about the importance of exercising opposing sets of muscles to avoid injury. In spite of the chilly atmosphere, by the end of an hour you are drenched with sweat. Instead of changing, Roger charges directly out of the gym and sprints up a path between swaying palm trees. You trot after him, losing him after a few seconds. The pool comes into view; Roger strips to his underwear and catapults himself into the water. You struggle to pull off your sweat-soaked shirts and shorts, and slide into the pool.

The water is cool and refreshing, without a hint of chlorine. You touch a finger to your tongue; the pool is filled with salt water, you realize. You lie back and float, easily, unexpectedly buoyant. Roger has exited the pool, you note, and is engaged in animated conversation with another figure in swim trunks. Lee, you realize. You make your way to the side of the pool and hoist yourself out. An attendant hurriedly brings the two of you white terrycloth bathrobes.

Lee regards you kindly. "Robert. I hope you're settling in comfortably. Is everything up to your expectations? Is Roger taking good care of you?"

"Everything's wonderful, sir. This is an amazing place. I have no words."

"Good, good. Now, excuse me, boys. I need to get a bit of exercise whenever I can grab a moment for myself." He slips a pair of goggles over his head and slides into the pool. He submerges for a few moments and begins cutting through the water at a remarkable clip.

You settle into a lounge chair next to Roger. He waves at the staff, one of whom beelines toward you at a rate just short of a run. He mumbles a few words in Cantonese and slides on his sunglasses. The man bobs in understanding and jogs away. A few moments later he is back with a pair of copper mugs, straws and sprigs of fresh mint jutting above their surface.

You take a sip. There is an unexpectedly fierce tang of ginger and lime, sharp and brutal on your palate. The alcohol is barely discernible, however. "Wow. That's got a kick. What is it?"

Roger sips his as well. "Moscow Mule. Ginger beer, vodka, lime juice. Good summer drink."

Lee is racing back and forth in the pool at a clip that would shame Aurora. He alternates crawl and breast stroke, at the end of every lap turning underwater like a seal and rocketing back through a third of the pool length before surfacing. You realize you are watching in person, for the first time in your life, a truly elite athletic performance. The difference between these precise, piston-like strokes and an ordinary person swimming is like watching a falcon next to a chicken attempting to fly, you muse.

"Holy shit, look at him go."

"Like I said, he was a competitive swimmer in college. Stanford. Can't buy your way onto that team, I'll tell you that. I think they even went to nationals or something."

"Why the British accent if he went to school in the US?"

Roger titters slightly. "Well, he went to the British school in Hong Kong when he was younger. Developed a slight complex there studying next to all the sons of diplomats and executives and what have you. At some point he decided he was going to be more British than the British. He's been quite the anglophile ever since."

After half an hour, Lee emerges from the pool, smiling broadly as he removes his goggles. An attendant rushes to him with a towel and a glass of water. "Ah, lovely. The saltwater pool does wonders. One is so buoyant…it feels so fast." He pads at his eyes gently.

"Well, you are awfully fast, sir. Lee. That was something to watch."

He shakes his head theatrically. "Not anymore. In the distant days of my youth, perhaps. But! Every age brings its own joys, and its own rewards. Anyway, I suggest you take a shower. The salt might bother you later, otherwise." He leads you to a small cabana where there is in fact a shower head. Your clothes are stacked neatly on a bench. "Wash up, boys, and then let's head to my office. I want to show you something which you may find of interest."

You enter the shower, with its stone floor and cedarwood siding. Sunlight streams in from above. The shower head itself is a giant square, two feet to a side. It's more like standing in a warm rain than a shower. Roger and finally Lee follow, after you emerge. You briefly wonder what to do with the pile of swim trunks, exercise gear and towels scattered around, before dismissing the thought. There seems to be a small army around the estate employed to deal with such things, charged with ensuring that not a moment of the family's or guest's time is wasted on life's mundane details.

Lee strides ahead of you purposefully, clad in khaki pants and a white polo shirt. Roger gestures for you to follow. You head into the main house, multiple servants lowering their heads respectfully as you pass. He trots quickly up the marble staircase, where one of the ubiquitous servants holds a door open to a long hallway. At the end is a massive wooden door. Lee holds his watch to a sensor next to the door. There is a soft click and he pushes it open.

You enter what you presume to be Lee's personal office. The room is circular, with the far half of the room almost entirely glass, with a sweeping view of the hills outside and the white spires of the city in the distance and, beyond that, the hazy blue of the ocean merging indistinctly with the sky. The desk is spotlessly clean, occupied only by a few pictures and three massive monitors. Colorful pieces of abstract art adorn the walls. Several leather-backed chairs surround a low coffee table, which bears a carafe of water and a platter of fruit. Roger motions for you to sit, and takes a second chair.

Lee takes his seat behind the desk and begins to rattle away at a keyboard with the speed and precision of a professional stenographer. He gazes searchingly for a few seconds, then motions to you. "Come, come."

A gray expanse fills the screen. The image seems pixelated, as though zoomed in and past the highest resolution possible. A few dark spots are visible, some fading to black. Lee glances at you, eyes twinkling with amusement.

"Any idea what we are looking at?" he enquires.

"Um, a gray blob."

"Well, not exactly. This is the surface of the moon. One of the landing sites for our little project."

"Hmm. Doesn't look like much."

"Well, it's not supposed to at this point. We have an arrangement, shall we say, with the people who run one of the largest telescopes in the eastern hemisphere. Roger's brother has even entered an astrophysics program at the institution housing this telescope to give us sufficient cover for our program. *That* is dedication. Dedication that will be well rewarded, one day. At any rate, they will send us periodic views of what is happening. However, the resolution is only a few hundred square meters or so. It will be a few months before we know if anything is happening."

You struggle to remember the figures. "I don't even think the installations are supposed to be much bigger than that, are they?"

"No. We will be looking at shadows, mostly, as the sun rises over the moonscape. The slightest change by these shadows here, and here," he points at two smudges "will mean that a large enough structure for our purposes is being constructed."

"How will you know it works?"

Lee grins. "When we turn it on. Exciting, isn't it? We're not quite sure what we'll see when it starts, if anything. There are varying opinions as to whether anything will be visible at all, due to atmospheric distortion. Anyway, two packages were dropped to ensure that we have twenty-four-hour coverage of any potential target. It could begin to be visible in fourteen weeks, and operational a month later. So, there is nothing to do, but wait, watch, and see."

Roger raps on the desk with glee. "Amazing, uncle. Simply amazing. The vision to undertake this, and the ability to pull it off, the will to surmount all obstacles… I'm speechless."

Lee moves his head sideways and gives a half laugh. "Speechless? You? That would be a first. But now, boys, if you will excuse me…" his attention drifts back to the other monitors, full of rapidly changing numbers and incomprehensible characters. Roger tugs on your elbow and leads you discreetly away and through the door.

Once through, he exhales slightly. "Lee likes me, and I'm family, but I still get nervous going in there. A lot of people's lives have changed - drastically - in a couple of minutes in that room, for better or worse. Anyway, let's go to town. I've got a car waiting."

A sleek, black BMW seven series is parked at the front. As usual, a servant waits smiling, holding the door open. Gratefully, you slide into the air-conditioned comfort next to Roger. The door shuts and the car purrs into motion.

"I prefer the BMW to those damn limousines. So ostentatious. This is a better ride, and attracts less attention. Hold on, I need to make a couple of phone calls." He picks up a receiver embedded into the back of the driver's seat. Brow furrowed, he taps in a few numbers. Someone picks up on the other end, and an animated discussion in Cantonese ensues.

The car eases out of the hills and into the city proper. Roger spends the entire trip making calls, which vary in tone from laughing and banter to barking orders and the occasional screaming rebuke. A couple of them involve the other person making lengthy speeches and Roger making the odd murmur of assent. After the last call, he raps on the divider between you and the front. The divider lowers itself with a discreet hum. Roger speaks briefly, and the divider rises again.

"Sorry, we need to make a quick stop at the harbor. We have a big boat coming in. I need to countersign the manifest."

"What's your day job, anyway?"

"Oh, I work on the oil and gas part of the company. It's our main operation, you know. We move a lot of LNG from Indonesia to refineries across Asia."

"LNG?"

"Liquid natural gas. It's the future of energy production. Or was, until your uncle came along. But right now, it's starting to displace coal all over the world. Those coal miners in West Virginia are in for a big surprise in a few years. Dead men walking, unfortunately. They just don't know it yet."

It takes some time to maneuver the giant automobile through the city to the harbor. A pair of guards at an imposing looking gate check your identification, and wave you through with alarm when they realize who is in the car, bobbing and smiling apologetically. You pull to a halt by the harbormaster's office, where Roger excuses himself. The office is a far cry from the dingy, rusted facilities you've seen around Philadelphia: this is a sleek, compact building of glass and brushed steel. Beyond it, you can see what you assume is the ship in question, a massive structure, towering over the buildings by the docks, with the distinctive bulbous reservoirs of an oil ship. Probably enough latent explosive power in it to level most of the city, you muse idly.

After a few minutes, Roger slides back into the car, muttering to himself. "Everyone's always got their hand out… anyway, let's get lunch. Let's try Yan Toh Heen. It's right here by the harbor. Amazing food."

The restaurant turns out to be in the Intercontinental Hotel. White gloved, red-nosed Caucasian doormen in traditional English morning suits greet you. You cannot fathom how uncomfortable such an ensemble must be over the course of hours in this devastating, humid heat. The restaurant is on the top floor, with a sleek, modern gold and black design, with a sweeping panoramic view of the harbor and city. The floor seems to be entirely made from marble. A hostess escorts you to a round table with high-backed chairs next to the window.

There is some immediate commotion a few moments later as a stout Chinese man in a chef's uniform, replete with hat, charges out of a back room toward your table. He makes a deep bow. Roger smiles, stands, and embraces him. The man's face erupts into a crinkled smile. Roger turns to you.

"Robert, let me introduce you to the best chef in Hong Kong. He's only got one Michelin star but by God, if anyone in the world deserves all three, it's him." The chef bows to you. Not knowing what to do, you rise, awkwardly, and half return the bow. The hostesses giggle in amusement, poking each other and whispering.

A voluble, incomprehensible discussion ensues. After a few exchanges and some wild gesticulation, the chef retires, beaming, to the kitchen. The hostesses bring you water and retreat, smiling brightly. You notice waiters begin to discreetly move the surrounding tables away from you.

"Not your first time here, I guess."

"Yeah, they know me here. Anyway, let's keep it simple. We'll have some dim sum appetizers, and the Peking Duck. It's what he's famous for."

A slight Caucasian man with a thin moustache approaches the table. He holds a thick leather binder under his arm. He nods at you. "Welcome, gentlemen. I am Bernard, the chief sommelier." He speaks with a moderate French accent. "I understand you will be having the duck. May I recommend a wine to go with it, or do *les messieurs* have something in mind?"

Roger spreads his hands. "I am sure your judgment is impeccable, Bernard. Guide us. We are in your capable hands."

A slight smile. "Monsieur is kind. Well. The correct choice is surely a Chenin Blanc. We have several vintages from Loire. If I may, I suggest *le cuvee Constance*, from le Domaine Huet Vouvray. It is a vivacious, impudent little wine, which dances upon the palate and provides the perfect counterpoint to the plum sauce. At the same time, it is light and refreshing, raising the spirits and giving messieurs the, ah, fortitude to go forth and do battle with the richness of the duck."

Roger looks at you, a half smile on his lips. "Robert? How does that strike you?" The sommelier looks at you expectantly.

"Well, Bernard, I have to admit my experience with wine is limited to purple, orange and green. I trust you completely."

"Very well, messieurs. One moment." He sweeps away, striding purposefully into the next room.

Roger chortles as he leaves. "Purple, orange and green! Ha. Good one. What's that, Mad Dog?"

"Night Train."

"God, we did have that stuff a couple of times in college. Truly awful."

"Yep. Awful, but efficient."

"Well, sometimes there's something to be said for efficiency."

A gaggle of waitresses approach. One carefully sets up a table next to yours, upon which the next places several small, intricately woven baskets. They place silver trays in front of you, and on top of those narrow, white ceramic platforms. Small dishes appear around them, filled with indeterminate fluids of varying shades of rust and brown. Opening the baskets, a cascade of steam wafts forth. The waitresses delicately place some of the contents before you: fragile white globes with slivers of vegetable and crab protruding from the top, cups of dough, filled with fragrant meats, alien-looking, lime green tubes adorned with intricately laced slivers of mysterious vegetables, spring rolls, completely transparent, proudly displaying the generous hunks of lobster occupying most of the interior. You reach out and pop one of the open-topped cups into your mouth. The taste is indescribable, tangy and sweet, just the right dose of umami, fragrant herbs and a slight, lingering burn of chili.

Roger looks at you reprovingly, one eyebrow raised. He makes the slightest motion to the side, where the sommelier stands with a bottle in his hand, another white-suited attendant behind him with glasses.

You dab at the corners of your overly full mouth with a napkin. "Ah, sorry, Bernard. My bad. Barbarians at the gates, you know."

"Of course, monsieur. Not to worry." He uncorks the bottle, sniffing the cork deeply, eyes slightly rolled back nearly into his head. Finally, he lets out a small sigh of contentment and nods at his companion, who places the glasses in front of you. He dribbles a small amount into Roger's glass. Roger swishes the liquid expertly for a few seconds, the wine approaching the rim of the glass but never rising above. He drinks, swishing it in his mouth, and finally swallowing. He closes his eyes for a few moments in concentration. A fraught silence descends, where even the ticking of the wall clock is distinctly audible. Finally, he opens them and beams a wide smile at the sommelier. "Wonderful, Bernard. Perfect!"

The attendant fills your glasses and leaves the bottle in a bucket of ice next to the table. Roger raises his glass. You touch it with yours; again, the unmistakable, lingering bell-like ring of real crystal reverberates in the room. The wine is a delicate joy, even to your virgin palate, with hints of pear and jasmine, dry but with a slight undercurrent of honey.

Each dumpling is a peculiar breed of magic. Roger guides you through which sauce to pair with each. You save the spring roll for last, with its fist of lobster meat, nuts and grilled watermelon, which is in itself an impossible explosion of flavors.

Roger munches contentedly. "Whenever I'm in a place like this and I see something totally weird on the menu – I mean, lobster and grilled watermelon, what the fuck, right? – I always get it. They must have stumbled onto something extraordinary."

Dishes are whisked away and new ones magically appear. A solemn looking waiter brings a platter of sizzling, reddish brown squares and places it between you. Reverently, he puts a small bowl of creamy sauce next to your plate.

"This is the duck skin," Roger explains. He expertly grasps a square with his chopsticks. You try, and fail, to do the same.

"Look," he says. "It's easy. Hold one firmly the whole time, like this…" he places it between the base of his thumb and tip of his fourth finger. "This never moves. It's your base. The second…" he grasps with his thumb and second and third fingers. "This is the part that moves. Grab the food like so…" He picks a piece of skin from the plate, dips it in the sauce, and reaches across the table. You lean forward and suck it into your mouth. It is firm and crispy, not as oily as you expect, with a tangy, sugary taste of plum infused throughout.

Roger crunches contentedly into his own. "This is the traditional way to serve it, you know. Skin first, then meat. Most places can't be bothered and just give it to you all together."

One bottle of wine disappears as you fumble inexpertly through the skin. The main dish follows, thinly sliced meat, artful arrangements of slivered vegetables, paper thin pancakes, and a sweet, fragrant sauce. The sommelier discreetly opens another bottle and replaces the empty one. Roger shows you how to make a small roll from the various components. Thankfully, no chopsticks are involved at this stage. You bite into your inartfully constructed roll; the rich duck, faintly spicy vegetables, delicate herbs and smoky, sweet plum sauce combine together into an extraordinary cacophony of taste.

"Oh my God," you finally manage to say, after consuming the small cylinder. "That gets you one Michelin star? What do you have to do to get three? Comes with a blow job or what?"

Roger laughs. "They're conservative. Three stars go to restaurants in Paris that have been open since the French Revolution. But it will change, someday. And it will be places like this that change it, mark my words."

You exit the restaurant to much bowing, laughing and embracing. Roger does not seem to receive or pay a bill, as far as you are able to tell. As you exit the hotel, you realize darkness is descending. You slide into the waiting BMW.

"Where to?" You are somewhat drunk, you realize.

"Oh, let's wander around Temple Street for a while. A market springs up when the sun goes down. Then we'll go to Lan Kwai Fong. Totally degenerate."

The market is not far, but in the heavy Hong Kong traffic it takes half an hour to arrive. Walking would surely have been faster. The market is a garish affair, packed with people and shops selling everything imaginable, from pirated CDs to knock-off Gucci handbags to fried insects. Numerous Caucasians prowl the stands, but nevertheless your gangly height, freckled countenance and red hair draws considerable attention. A pair of diminutive girls drum up the courage to ask for a photograph together with you, amidst a torrent of hysterical laughter.

Roger guides you to the fish, poultry and meat section. "Check this out, this is wild…" The fishmonger section alone is astonishing, whole swordfish and tuna, six or seven feet long and surely weighing hundreds of pounds hang from hooks, prepared to be auctioned to buyers from the city's restaurants. Unimaginable fruits of the ocean are piled on ice in every stall: from the familiar football sized yellowfin tuna, albacore, heaps of mackerel and snappers to strange elongated eel-like forms with enormous eyes, gigantic barracuda with gaping, snaggle toothed jaws, brilliantly colored dolphinfish with their strange, bulbous skulls, huge grouper, catfish ranging from the size of a small trout to behemoths that could probably swallow a human whole, piles of shark fins, barrel after barrel of salted squid and rancid fish heads. Bins full of shellfish and crustaceans, some recognizable, others bizarrely alien.

Meat and poultry is weirder still. A disconcerting amount of the produce is still alive, from lambs and goat kids to piglets to puppies, gazing at you with doomed, hopeful eyes. Otherwise, every conceivable part of any animal is for sale, from brain to nose to tail, of everything from rodents to yaks. Cages full of birds flutter about next to the corpses of their eviscerated and plucked brethren. The sweltering miasma of blood, entrails and feces is horrendous. Swans, ducks, geese and chickens along with dozens of unfamiliar species call and cluck in alarm. After the poultry are the insects, heaps of fried and roasted locusts, crickets, mealworms, maggots and scorpions, which people busily inspect and buy by the pound. The vendors call and shout at passing customers. You feel ill. You nudge Roger.

"Let's go somewhere else. This is weirding me out."

"Yeah, I got you. This way." Roger guides you through a series of stalls, away from the stomach churning, ammonia-laden stench of defecating animals and decomposing fish. Animals gradually give way to vegetables, which in turn surrender to clothes and trinkets, yet more pirate CDs and knock-off handbags and purses. You make your way through an impossible maze of stalls, finally arriving at an anonymous doorway. Roger knocks assuredly on the door. A slot opens at eye length. After a moment, the door opens. You pass through, Roger pressing a note into the hand of the doorman. The doorman is a hulking mass of muscle, nearly as tall as you but twice as wide, dressed in a black suit, bald save for a braided tassel of hair extending from the rear of his scalp past the lapel of his jacket. He grunts at you and gestures for you to follow him.

A short hallway leads to a plain wooden door. The giant knocks lightly, leaning forward, ears cocked intently to hear a response. You hear nothing. Evidently your escort does. He opens the door and brusquely indicates you may enter. Dead, soulless eyes watch you intently as you pass.

A slight, elderly man sits behind a nondescript wooden desk. He rises, and bows. "Mr. Lee. This is an unexpected pleasure." He nods at you. "Forgive my English. I presume you do not speak our language."

"No, sir. I'm afraid not."

"Sit, gentlemen, sit." There are two leather-backed chairs. They creak gently as you settle your weight into them. "Had I known you were coming, I would have prepared…"

Roger interrupts. "Oh, don't worry. Robert is a friend of the family. I'm just showing him around town. Do you have anything interesting to look at?"

The man steeples his fingers and frowns. "Hmmm … on hand … well, there is a constant flow of items from the former Soviet Union and its unfortunate satellites. Times are difficult, controls are lax. One moment…" He rises carefully and moves toward the door. Opening it slightly, he murmurs a few words to the vast shadow beyond. He then returns to his desk, smiling benignly. After a few moments, the door clicks open and two slight men in suits enter, bearing steel briefcases. They place them reverently on the man's desk and hand him keys. He opens one, then the other, perusing their contents with furrowed brow. Satisfied, he turns them toward you.

Both are inset with black velvet, within which nest numerous treasures. The left-hand briefcase holds gems and jewelry: emeralds the size of almonds, an intricately wrought silver or platinum brooch of an angel holding diamonds in her hands, a matching set of earrings and a necklace bursting with rubies. In the second are small, delicate, but breathtaking works of art. Jewel encrusted Faberge eggs, or something similar, elephants and other more fantastic animals carved from ivory and wreathed with gold, and some kind of elongated pipe with an absurdly small receptacle, made from an odd, yellow translucent material.

"What's that?" you ask.

The man laughs gently. Roger takes it reverently, turning it over carefully in his hands. "It's an opium pipe, made of pure Baltic amber. Early eighteenth century. It was sent to us as a sample by a gentleman in Poland who claims to have found one of the great lost treasures of the war. The so-called Amber Chamber, gifted to Russia by Prussia in 1716. He sent it as a sample to substantiate his claims. The fellow says Peter the Great himself used to enjoy this pipe."

"The *Bernsteinzimmer*," Roger says quietly, lost in thought.

The man's eyes crinkle in pleasure. He slaps the table lightly, with both hands. "Mr. Lee, you never cease to amaze me. How you know such things at your young age… Yes, *der Bernsteinzimmer, auf Deutsche*. An entire room, constructed of amber by the finest Prussian and Danish craftsmen of the day, and sent to St. Petersburg as a token of eternal friendship between two great powers. I suppose I do not need to comment on the irony of it being seized back by the German war machine a couple of generations later, and subsequently lost forever. Until now, perhaps. Time will tell, of course."

"Extraordinary. How much would you like for this?"

The man manages to execute a small half-bow while still seated in his chair. "A gift, Mr. Lee." He waves away incipient protests. "It is a small thing, and I have no way of verifying its provenance. Should our colleague from Gdansk succeed in getting more of such trinkets to us, I will invite you and your uncle for a private showing in a more appropriate setting."

After much ceremony and protests, you take your leave. Settling into the BMW, Roger pulls the velvet case from his pocket, in which they gave him the piece for safekeeping, and inspects the intricately carved, slender wonder. "Breathtaking."

"He just gave it to you?" Roger shrugs. "It happens."

"Huh. This is an under-reported aspect of being rich I didn't realize. All the free shit people throw at you. Kind of ironic, almost. It's not like you need it."

"Mmm. Well, no one ever lost money by staying on our good side, let's put it that way." Roger pulls a small plastic bag from his jacket pocket. A knob of a brown, clay-like substance rests within. He grins at you impishly.

"Be a shame not to smoke up with the shade of Peter the Great, wouldn't you say?"

"What is that?"

"Hashish. Straight from Morocco. Good stuff. Not entirely, ah, overpowering, like some of the stuff nowadays. We need to keep our wits about us, after all." Roger carefully breaks off a piece of hash and crumbles it into the reservoir. He rummages through his pockets until he pulls out a gold-plated lighter. He opens it with a satisfying metallic clink and a thin staff of flame emerges. He holds it to the hash, sucking furiously. The hashish takes on a bright orange glow, infusing the length of the pipe. Roger exhales, releasing a small but pungent cloud of smoke. He hands you the pipe. The small pile still smolders, so you suck at the pipe without relighting it. The hash is clean and light. An effusive warmth settles over your body like a weighted blanket as you exhale.

"Nice. Smooth."

Roger casually knocks out the ash and residue from the pipe onto the creamy carpet at his feet, and places it back in the velvet case. The car crawls slowly through the teeming streets. Looking through the tinted windows, you see night has fallen. Garish neon lights adorn every conceivable surface. Men on motorbikes weave in and out between cars. Gaggles of well-dressed young people have begun to emerge from buildings, walking and chatting and jostling one another on the crowded sidewalk. Roger takes his phone again.

"Just a couple of phone calls, on the way to hit the bars, OK?"

"Sure." You half-close your eyes, allowing kaleidoscope of neon colors wash across your retinas, while next to you Roger delivers commands to the family empire in his peculiar tongue. *What a day*, you think. And it's hardly just begun.

It's Snowing in Cambodia!

July gradually seeps into August. The weather is less pleasant that you'd expected: the heat of Philadelphia during a particularly bad summer, but far more humid. The city is soaked with regular torrential showers and the occasional thunderstorm crashing and banging violently throughout the night, wind ripping through the trees and causing the very buildings themselves to creak and moan. A completely sunny day is rare.

No one seems to have particularly high expectations of you. Nevertheless, you settle into a routine of working out and swimming every day in the morning, as the sun fitfully attempts to burn through the gauzy humid haze, and playing video games and reading in the afternoons when the heavens open and rain gushes down for a few hours. At night it's easy to lose yourself in the infinite variety of global satellite television. In Philadelphia you didn't even have cable, just an analogue antenna fitfully picking up eight or ten channels, depending on the weather. Here you can watch semi-nude German game shows, imams ranting from Central Asian madrasas, and gloriously violent, inchoate Thai and Indian epic adventures.

Every few nights Roger manages to cajole you into a couple of drinks which not infrequently turns into an evening of carousing with his cadre of other wealthy scions and their hangers-on. Today he has dropped by with a six-pack of beer. Tall green bottles with a complex, baroque font on the labels. It's about three in the afternoon.

"Pilsner Urquell," he explains. "From Czechoslovakia. They say it's the best beer in the world. Used to be impossible to get hold of, but they've started exporting it now."

You open two and retire to the porch. Exceptionally, the sky is clear and deep blue, a stiff, steady wind blowing from offshore, carrying with it the tang of the sea.

"Tropical storm brewing," he remarks. "They might upgrade it to a typhoon. We should go out and enjoy the weather while we can. Could be a hell of a blow."

"I'm OK here. This is nice." The beer is really very good, with a full, rich, nutty flavor and a sharp, hoppy finish. Palm trees wave and rustle in the unusually consistent breeze.

"Janice and her friends will be at Dome de Cristal. We could go there and drop a couple grand. Take them to Club 97 after. See what happens."

"And watch those girls throw up after guzzling a magnum of Cristal? Oh god."

"Come on. Some of those chicks are dying with curiosity about this mysterious, scarred, blue-eyed American killer with the Special Forces or wherever their imagination is leading them."

You have a brief flashback to lying on the ground with a chrome-plated .45 jammed into your cheek as a couple dozen grizzled mercenaries hooted at you with mirth. "Well, so far my percentages in the killing department aren't that great."

"They don't know that. I think they've got a pool going about who's gonna get your pants off first."

"Hmmph."

Roger looks at you curiously. "You still hung up on that girl, bud? What was her name? Aurora?"

You shake your head. "Nah. I haven't thought about her in weeks."

"Forget about her. I mean, she's hella hot, I'll give you that. But come on. There's plenty others around."

Roger's gentle but insistent pressure finally succeeds in getting you into your Brioni suit and an iridescent blue silk shirt. He whistles to himself. "Fu-u-ck me, you really carry that with those big ass blue eyes of yours. I couldn't wear that."

"Are you kidding? *I* can't wear this. It's fucking ridiculous. I look like one of those gay escorts at the club."

"Come on, knock it off. You look great, killer. Let's go."

Roger's girlfriend, Janice – fiancée, you have learned in the meantime – is there, as advertised, with a coterie of aspiring models and heiresses. They giggle and squeal with laughter as you approach. You are not sure if these western names are actually given, or some kind of affectation, or perhaps an effort to make things easier for westerners, or some combination of the three. It feels impolite to ask, so you don't. Janice gives you a warm embrace. She releases you but keeps her hands on your elbows. Her eyes sparkle with merriment. Electronic music thumps through the establishment, the bass rattling your bones.

"So, Roger finally managed to drag you out of that golden cage of yours, I see."

"Well, I prefer the monastic existence, but his hospitality is sometimes just too generous to turn down." Janice titters with laughter. She turns to her group of friends, splayed out on leather couches in chiffon and silk dresses, champagne flutes dangling insouciantly from bejeweled fingers. An oversized bottle of Cristal rests in a cut glass bucket full of actual snow. You briefly wonder about the logistics of transporting snow to Hong Kong in August for the purposes of entertaining teenagers, but abandon this line of thinking. Devoting thought to any particular aspect of this whirlwind of absurdity cannot lead anywhere productive.

You find an unoccupied patch of couch. A waiter instantly flits to your side and pours you a glass of champagne. One of Janice's friends gazes at you with a predatory smile, and makes a small ball of snow, tossing it at you, striking your shoulder.

"Gotcha."

"Nice shot. I didn't expect it to snow in Hong Kong." You drop the small snowball into your glass and offer her a toast. Her smile widens. "I'm Melissa. Nice to meet you."

"Robert."

"I know who you are."

A small band of waiters approaches bearing silver platters of food. In a single, impeccably choreographed swoop they remove the covers and place the steaming trays gracefully on the tables between you. It's finger food:

bruschetta with tomatoes and basil, doubtless flown straight in from some Tuscan farm that morning, plump, seared scallops wrapped in Parma ham, delicate rolls of sushi, coated with a black, thick crust of toasted sesame, spring rolls fried to a delicate golden sheen, toast with thick slabs of foie gras, tuna carpaccio, and a vast plate of oysters, shrimp and impossibly long crab legs nestled in heaps of ice.

You try and minimize the velocity of the staff refilling your drink, always a difficult proposition when they are thoroughly trained to distribute alcohol as efficiently and pleasantly as possible at fifty dollars a glass. The girls are difficult to talk to, even more than usual in the thumping music, excusing themselves en masse to go to the bathroom with startling frequency and spending far more time there than would seem strictly necessary. While dark, narrow Asian eyes effectively camouflage pupil dilation, the bright red cheeks and jabberingly incoherent speech make you suspect alcohol is not the only culprit behind the gradually increasing mania. The girls are now dissatisfied with sitting and stand in little groups, swaying with the music, stomping at the floors with Louboutin heels and cackling with laughter.

At a certain point they simply dispense with caution and someone's makeup mirror is passed around the table, thick lines of white powder carefully railed out. Roger intercepts it and frowns, gazing around to see who is watching.

"This could get us in trouble."

"What is it? Coke?"

"Nah. Coke's really hard to get here. It's this artificial stuff, mephedrone, I think it's called. They synthesize it in labs in Cambodia. *Cambodian snow*, they call it. Some kind of methyl cathinone derivative."

"Well, aren't we quite the chemist."

Janice emits a small war cry and twirls around, heels clacking on the teakwood floor. "It's snowing in Cambodia, guys! Let's go *dancing*!"

Roger pulls a silvery, metallic straw from his jacket pocket. He looks at you seriously. "We gotta get rid of this before we get kicked out of here. I can't buy my way out of everything. Well, actually I can, but sometimes it's more hassle than it's worth. I'll do half, you do half, OK?"

"Uh…"

Without waiting, Roger snorts three of the six lines on the mirror in rapid, practiced succession. He shakes his head, tears forming in his eyes.

"Jeeee-sus, Fu-u-cking Christ, that hurts." He hands you the straw. "Come on, quick. Someone's coming."

Hesitantly, you bow your head toward the mirror. You sniff deeply, first one line into your left nostril, then the second into the right. It's like snorting powdered glass mixed with strychnine. A sharp pain stabs through your nostrils, as though a knitting needle pierced deep through your sinuses and into your cerebellum. You emit a gigantic, uncontrollable sneeze. The third line disappears in a sudden cloud of dust.

"Well, problem solved. Sorry man, I should've warned you. That stuff goes down rough. Works though. Here…." On the other side of the makeup mirror in place of blush or eyeshadow is a small plastic bag with white powder. Roger shakes half into your drink and the remainder into his.

"Do it like this. It's way easier. Lasts longer, too."

The powder is already exerting an effect. An irresistible wave of munificent, universal good will washes through and across your body. The music, already intense, seemingly takes on a new life of its own, battering its way through your cranium deep into your subconscious. Colors flare with new life, pulsing with a sudden inner strength previously absent. You lock eyes with Melissa. She breaks into an impossibly wide, imbecilic smile which is surely mirrored by your own. She walks toward you, teetering unsteadily atop thousand-dollar heels. Looking searchingly into your eyes, she raises maroon-painted nails to your cheek. A trail of sparks follows the slow travels of her fingertips. Unbidden, your hands snake through her hair; *so strange, you think, it looks so smooth and silky, yet is so thick and rough to the touch, like you imagine a horse's mane might be…* You kiss, decisively, both of your bodies suddenly moving of their own volition, hands moving rapidly across hitherto unexplored territory; you are empty, mindless vessels, nothing more than cytoplasmic shells barely able to contain a deep yearning toward a quick, febrile, animalistic coupling that simply must take place *here*, and *now*.

You see Roger sitting on the couch, watching you intently, Janice lying with her head in his lap. He smiles benignly, stroking one of her breasts with one hand, raising his glass in a silent toast with the other.

Melissa's nails stab into your palm. She looks up at you, eyes like inky saucers of liquid midnight. Her small bosom thrusts against your sternum. She pulls your head toward hers, hot breath like a tornado in your ear

"Let's go somewhere. Now. *Right now*."

She pulls you insistently toward the lady's room, which seems simultaneously like a fantastically brilliant idea, as well as supremely idiotic and impractical. You feel as though you are watching yourself somehow bemusedly from a third person perspective as this gangly body, purportedly yours, is hauled toward an uncertain fate. An obsidian-tiled hallway with yawing mirrors leads to the toilet; the door, coated in gold lame, waits at the end of the seemingly interminable hallway. The two of you stumble down its length like newborn deer attempting to cross a frozen pond, collapsing in laughter against the wall every few steps. Just as you reach the door, it opens, seemingly of its own volition.

Aurora stands there, regarding you and your companion with bemusement, blinking in surprise. She wears a sheer, peach colored cocktail dress that leaves her shoulders and neck bare. Her hair is longer than you remember, curling now over her ears and around the base of her slender neck.

"Well, hello, Robert. Fancy seeing you here. What a surprise."

"Uh, Aurora, hi. I didn't expect you, ah…"

Melissa looks up at Aurora appraisingly, eyes like an ebony void. "Jesus, where the hairy fuck did you come from? You're hot as shit, though, all right. You wanna join us?"

A blonde Caucasian girl in an electric blue, sequined dress emerges from the door. She is at least as tall as you are, even without the heels. High, ridged, Nordic cheekbones underpin eyes seemingly chiseled from the blue ice of an arctic glacier. She has the sculpted arms of a dedicated athlete. An intricate silver armlet encircles her upper left arm. Her gaze darts around, taking in the situation. She slips an arm around Aurora's waist.

"Everything OK, hon?"

"Yes, it's fine. Just ran into an old friend. I'll join you in a minute." She stands on her toes in an effort to plant a kiss on the blonde girl's cheek.

"OK. See you soon." She stalks away, directing a look of withering contempt at you and your companion as she does.

"Ah, Melissa, could you…"

Melissa doubles over with laughter, squeezing your arm. "Of course. You've got business here. Just come find me in one of the stalls when you're done. Bring your friend along if you want. I'm not picky." She pushes through the door, clattering across the tiles.

Aurora inspects you impassively. In heels, she is nearly as tall as you are. "Nice suit. I see you're fitting in just fine here."

"Seems like you are too."

Her lip curls in contempt. "You've gone a bit more native than I have. I know who you're here with. You're making quite a name for yourself."

"Aurora, I…"

She reaches out her hand and puts a finger against your lips, looking you intently in the eye.

"Robbie, I hope you're OK. Really, I do. But I don't want to talk to you when you're fucked up like this. What I *do* want is for you to remember who your friends are, and who your enemies are, though, all right? This fight isn't over yet. *Our* fight isn't over yet."

"What fight? What are you talking about? Is there something going on I don't know about?"

Calm brown eyes look deeply into yours. "Time will tell, I suppose. Good night, Robbie. Take care of yourself. No one else will." She tosses a light punch at your wounded shoulder as she strides away from you down the hallway.

You rub your eyes for a moment. Thankfully you haven't drunk from the spiked glass; your head is gradually beginning to clear. You retreat back down the hallway and into the club, collapsing onto the leather couch next to Roger. Janice has abandoned him and twirls, shrieking, on the dance floor. He looks at you enquiringly.

"That was quick. Did it go OK? Do we need to order her up a Plan B for tomorrow?"

"Oh yeah, all good. Not used to this stuff is all. Packs a bit of a wallop the first time you do it."

Roger laughs. "That's for sure. Wears off quickly though, at least." Except for his unusually expressive eyes he behaves nearly completely normally.

"So, what do you want to do?" you ask. "Head back to the ranch?"

Roger looks at you quizzically and laughs. "Are you kidding? We're just getting started! Bottoms up." He hands you the champagne flute from earlier. You can see the dusky residue of the powder from earlier sloshing around the bottom. "Drink up, pardner. Then we'll head out to Club 97 and get really crazy."

You watch the dancing motes of dust circling in the $50 glass of Cristal, and swill it back. The combination is supremely awful, like carbonated battery acid.

"Snowing in Cambodia," you croak. Roger touches your glass with his, and drains it as well.

"Snowing in Cambodia. Now let's go and get truly twisted."

Vacation is over

The school year officially starts in September. This provides structure and a nice change of pace. Your classmates at the International School adopt a studied position of distant friendliness combined with a complete disinterest in any invasive questioning, which suits you fine. The teachers seem prepared to pretend that your conjuration from thin air with no accompanying school records is absolutely normal; after a brief period of ascertainment where your relative strengths and many deficiencies lie, they seem to work out a quiet accommodation among themselves in terms of how to deal with you in the least problematic fashion until the moment when you inevitably disappear.

You have discovered, later than you'd like, that part of Lee's empire includes a small fleet of charter fishing vessels. Hai, the kindly maître domo of the mansion, arranges for you to be transported down to the harbor every Saturday morning where a listless crew awaits you with a mix of resignation and hostility. Apparently the business is a front for some sort of smuggling operation – drugs or people, you are not sure which – and your Saturday excursions are an unwanted spanner in the works. You are long since past caring about such things, however.

The weather has significantly improved in the fall, with less wind and clearer skies. The grossly overpowered 480 horsepower of engineering underneath the fiberglass hull allows you to rocket along the waves at sufficient speed to induce the tuna and mahi-mahi swarming in these southern seas to strike.

You roar out of the harbor at 7 AM toward Lamma Island. After half an hour of cruising toward the south end of the island, the sullen crew cuts the motor and you begin to let out lines. You have four rods in total, two with artificial surface lures and two with mid-depth dead bait.

"If we don't get anything here, let's go to Po Toi," you shout at the captain. He takes a drag on his unfiltered cigarette and looks at you with complete disgust, which pleases you. The idea of making these jerks do a 30-kilometer circle around Lamma to Po Toi and back again is absolutely delicious. The captain screams something at his crew, who begin chucking buckets of chum into the water behind the boat. Apparently the captain does not want to spend hours heading to Po Toi.

As if on cue, one of the surface floating rigs snaps down at an alarming angle, line whizzing out with an intense whine. The captain cuts the engine to a low burble to allow you to fight the fish on equal terms. You grab the rod from its holder, tighten the drag and jerk upwards with all your strength. The fish on the end of the line responds with an awesome display of power, slashing through the depths while the drag on your reel screams in helpless abandon. Each shuddering thrust from the fish pulls the tip of your rod closer to the water; you try vainly to stabilize the rod against your hip as it creaks and yaws, precipitously close to the point of snapping. The crew watches with grim amusement as you struggle to master your rod, slowly reeling in the other rigs so as not to get tangled with the fish on your line.

You feel yourself physically skidding across the deck as you vainly attempt to control the fish. "Put the fucking engine in reverse, fuckwit!" you shriek. "Can't you see what I'm dealing with?" The captain glares at you, sucks on the last of his cigarette, and throws the clutch backwards.

You release a bit of pressure on the drag. The dreadful force on the end of the line isn't the typical twenty-pound bonito tuna or dolphinfish you'd been expecting, but something vastly more substantial. Line continues to spool out at an incredible rate. All you can do is hold on and pray the fish tires before you do. The sun is rising in the sky and its reflection from the water begins to crackle across your retinas, making your eyes water.

"Get me sunglasses and a bottle of water, fuckmuffins," you croak.

A bottle of water appears. Sunglasses do not. Interminably, the proportion of line spooling out to that reeled in begins to change ever so slightly in your favor. After forty minutes, you even begin to believe the fish might be closer to the boat than at the beginning of your battle. The line makes lazy figures a few hundred yards from the boat, instead of the sullen whine of escape toward the depths. Suddenly, the line goes slack. Previously bored sailors begin to shout and gesticulate to reel; the great fish is swimming toward the boat in an effort to eject the cruel hook from its gullet. You reel ferociously for what seems like eons, until the line once again goes taught. A hundred yards from the stern of the boat the fish finally breaks water, shimmying into the sky, perhaps for the first time in its existence.

The crew breaks their silence, yelling something incomprehensible. You cannot understand their words, but their meaning is clear. You all saw the same fish; a marlin, with exquisite, purplish blue coloration, surely over two hundred pounds, perhaps close to three hundred, leaping free from the ocean in all its magnificent, tensile strength.

After a few more efforts at escape, it gradually becomes clear the contest can have only one end. The scimitar-like edge of its dorsal fin is now constantly above the water, lazily trailing back and forth. The great fish makes the occasional half-hearted flip into the air in an attempt to shake the hook loose from its bill, but to no avail. Once perhaps a quarter mile from the boat, now it is a hundred yards, now eighty, now fifty… One of the sailors prepares a gaff to strike a final, killing blow once it comes within range. Even the captain beams with joy. To bring such a fish into the harbor, hanging proudly at the stern, will be a great honor, notwithstanding the ugly white boy with the ginger hair and leopard-spotted skin who hunted it.

As the fish nears the boat, a gradual thudding impinges on your consciousness. A sleek, black helicopter, hewing close to the waves, approaches the boat.

"What the fuck…" you mutter. Your concentration lapses for a moment, jerked back to reality as the marlin makes a last, desperate effort to escape. The force of its sudden flight pulls you against the railing; the rod slams against it with a bang, catching your fingers in between. You howl with pain, but somehow manage to raise the rod tip again, grunting with the strain. The fish breaks water again, savagely shaking its head, razor sharp bill slashing through the air, crescent shaped tailfin shuddering with fury.

The helicopter is now very close to the boat. The whirling blades make an incredible racket, concentric circles of waves spreading out from the force of compressed air. Something begins to gradually descend from the machine toward the waves. You notice out of the corner of your eye the captain speaking into his radio, hand pressed against his other ear to block out the noise from the blades. He has cut the engine completely. After a few seconds he nods and drops the radio, a resigned look on his face. Walking toward you, he shrugs apologetically, pulls out his pocket knife and casually severs the line on your rod. The rod, an instant before bowed precipitously toward the water, catapults upward as hundreds of pounds of force is suddenly released. You watch in disbelief as the tip of the rod quivers in mid-air like a guitar string.

This manages to be at once shocking but not surprising. "What ... you – you – fucking..." you stammer.

With a smug smile, the captain points at you, then at the slowly approaching helicopter. At the end of the line descending from the machine is a bucket seat and harness. A crewman leans over the side and snags the edge of it with a gaff and pulls it on board. Cursing, you wedge yourself into it while the crew buckle you in. Your hand aches tremendously from where it struck the rail earlier; you suspect one of your finger bones may be fractured. The helicopter peels away and accelerates, the wind rushing past you and dousing you with a fine mist of salt spray. Someone begins winching your seat up into the body of the aircraft. Above you is an opening in the hull through which you see several faces peering down at you intently. You close your eyes, considering what could possibly be so urgent to necessitate this sudden extraction. The list of answers is short, and mostly unpleasant.

"Looks like the vacation is over," you mutter to yourself as the line completes its journey into the hull. The outer door slams shut, and multiple hands begin to detach you from the safety harness. You keep your eyes squeezed stubbornly closed.

No going back

The helicopter lands on top of a downtown skyscraper. You had intended to keep your eyes closed the entire trip out of spite, but curiosity gets the better of you. The view of Hong Kong from above is breathtaking, endless rows of pearly white spires marching off in all directions toward the azure sea on one side, verdant green mountains on the other.

A young man, presumably one of Lee's functionaries, awaits you by the landing pad. He wears a western style suit, fingers steadying his sunglasses against the buffeting waves of wind from the rotor blades as you descend. You disembark as the engine slowly whines to a halt, the thud of the blades gradually reducing in noise and velocity. The man offers his hand and shouts something unintelligible at you. You shake his hand and nod. He motions you to follow him, and jogs across the roof to a doorway leading to a stairwell.

The man shakes his head in relief as the door shuts behind you. He removes his sunglasses. "Well, that's a relief. I'm Jimmy, by the way. Not sure if you heard me back there." Another flawless west coast American accent. He begins to jog down the stairs, patent leather soles rhythmically slapping the concrete. You follow.

"What's so urgent that you had to go for a helicopter rescue at sea? I had a hell of a fish on, you know."

The man shrugs. "No idea, honestly. Mr. Shan said he wanted you here as soon as possible. This fit the description of 'as soon as possible'."

"Hard to argue with that."

After descending a couple of flights of stairs you exit into a non-descript hallway. The man stops in front of a pair of anonymous elevator doors. He presses the button and the doors open. The elevator is large, and not particularly clean, seemingly designed for freight rather than people. You step inside.

"We going to pick up some bushels of soybeans, or what?" you enquire.

The man chuckles, punching in a complicated combination of floor numbers. "The part of the building we're going to is, let's say, a bit off the books." As he completes the sequence, all of the numbers of the floors flash once, then twice, then go dark. The elevator trundles downward for a seemingly endless period. Finally, it shudders to a halt. The doors creak open and you step through.

The room beyond is a control room similar to the one the Colonel had blown up in China, though far sleeker and more sophisticated. Giant screens dominate the front of the room; two gray, undifferentiated pixelated images, which are presumably the lunar landing sites with shifting red polygons on them, plus a representation of the moon and the earth, with angles of incidence to different parts of the globe. Instead of the bank of terminals in the previous iteration, there is only one, with a high-backed leather chair. It swivels around at your entrance. Lee fixes you with a steady gaze, his customary grin notably absent. You cannot make out much of his expression in the dim light.

"Welcome, Robert. I apologize for disturbing your weekend relaxation."

"I'm sure you have your reasons, sir. Lee. How can I help? Is everything all right?"

"Aurora has disappeared." A familiar voice speaks to your left. The Colonel. He has abandoned his affected military uniforms, you note, and adopted the local custom of tailored Armani suits. "You wouldn't happen to know anything about that, would you?"

"You caught me. She's hidden in the bait box of the fishing boat your guys just pulled me off of."

Lee makes an irritated slashing motion with his hands. "Gentlemen. Time is precious. It's the one thing I cannot buy. Let us not waste it. Robert, we know you saw her a few weeks ago, briefly. Did she say anything? Any hint or suggestion of a plan?"

"No, sir. We only spoke for a few seconds in a club. It was very difficult to hear. She didn't seem particularly happy to see me, to be honest. Certainly not in any mood to share her secret escape plans."

"Hmmm." Lee forms a triangle with his fingers and places them at his lips. "This is very troubling."

"What about Hal?"

The Colonel answers. "Mr. Robinson proved particularly, ah, difficult to manage in some respects. We thought it would be easier for everyone to keep him out of Hong Kong. He's been amusing himself in one of the concern's properties in Macao these last few months. We've kept a close eye on him. He played no role in her disappearance. I'll vouch for that with my life."

Lee speaks slowly, deliberately, choosing his words with care, looking fixedly at steepled fingers. "*Everyone* who works for me vouches for the quality of their work with their lives, Colonel. I hope you realize that."

"Yes, sir. I do."

You clear your throat in the sudden, uncomfortable silence. "Well ... where did it happen?"

"School. She excused herself to go to the restroom, and seemingly disappeared into thin air..."

Lee interrupts. "We don't need to bother the boy with details, Colonel. Clearly he knows nothing. Nevertheless, Robert, I did want to tell you this personally," he says, kindly. "I know you are friends - or were - and rest assured we have deployed considerable resources to finding her and will pursue every avenue available."

"I understand. Thank you, sir."

"However." Lee drums his fingers on the side of the chair. "The fact that these considerable resources have shown *absolutely* no result concerns us deeply, and leads us to conclude that someone else was involved in this. Someone sophisticated, with substantial means at their disposal. We will need to accelerate our plans slightly. Colonel?"

The Colonel gives a discreet cough. "Yes. According to our calculations, the installations should be nearly complete and at any rate should continue to grow even after activation, albeit far more slowly, as we are taking most of the energy out of the system. So, our plan is to initiate activation tomorrow night. We will need you to be on hand."

He opens a briefcase and removes a thin folder with a sheaf of papers. "Here is a copy of the notes Aurora made." You note that odd phrase again, *Aurora's notes*, but remain silent. "Please take them home and study them carefully, and re-familiarize yourself with them. It's been a few months."

Lee adds, "From now on, you will be accompanied by a bodyguard at all times. This is for your own protection. I hope you understand."

"Yes, of course. If someone kidnapped Aurora, I'd be a logical target too."

"Thank you for your cooperation, Robert. I'll see you here tomorrow."

The Colonel guides you to the elevator and presses the button. The man from before is waiting inside. "Jimmy will escort you home. There is already someone in position there, so don't be alarmed when you see him lurking at your door. If you recall anything which might be of assistance to us, do let us know."

Jimmy attempts to make small talk with you during the trip home, which you largely ignore. You resist the urge to look through the notes you were given. A quick glance earlier showed that they were written in someone else's handwriting than yours, presumably Aurora's. This makes no sense, as you took the notes while she watched the video.

Outside your bungalow, as promised, waits a large man, who looks less like a human than some sort of golem loosely cobbled together from slabs of stone. He wears an earpiece, curled wire wending its way down into his ill-fitting suit jacket. The man nods at you solemnly as you approach.

Once inside, you sit at the kitchen table with a Sprite and spread the notes across the table. You are keenly aware that if there was not a camera hidden here before, there surely is now. The handwriting, while clearly jotted down hurriedly, is nevertheless neat, flawless and legible - not yours, in other words. From what you can remember, the gist of the notes seems faithful to the original recording. As you peruse them more carefully, however, you note several differences. Some key facts and names have been omitted, such as references to Omaha. Numerous codes are written down, far more than Gunnar had actually mentioned in his video. The IATA code key is not mentioned.

"What are you up to?" you mutter to yourself. Why - and more to the point, *how* - would she neatly transcribe your notes while inserting obviously carefully curated misinformation into them while racing across the country in a stolen automobile?

A slight rap on the door startles you from your reverie. Opening the door, you are taken aback by the thick, grim figure of the guard. You'd forgotten about him in the meantime. He shifts his bulk to the side and Roger slips in with a grin. He holds up a tall bag and pulls out a bottle of wine with an intricate gold and maroon label.

"Lee told me to bring you a study aid. I grabbed a 1982 Brunello di Montalcino from his wine cellar. From Il Poggione itself. What a year! Can't drink this in the summer, but it's a nice fall vintage."

"Ah. Thanks for thinking of me."

Roger wrestles the cork out of the bottle with a dull *pop*. He hands you the cork, slightly withered and discolored with age. It has a warm scent, redolent of coffee, blackberries and pepper.

"Wow. Nice."

"Should be, at four hundred dollars a bottle. We should really decant this for a couple of hours, but fuck it, right?" He pours a couple of splashes of wine into water glasses resting by the sink. He holds his glass up. You touch it with yours.

"The future begins tomorrow. No going back."

"No going back."

Roger sits opposite you. The wine is really extraordinary, the taste a gorgeous velvety cacophony of forest fruits and dark chocolate.

"You know, I'm looking forward to getting home, but this lifestyle has its advantages."

Roger peers at you curiously. "Well, no one is forcing you to go, Robbie. Stay here if you want. You've acclimated pretty well. Transfer to a university somewhere here, then take a job in The Firm. Marry an heiress, or a tennis star, or whatever. Buy your mother a beach cottage on Cape Cod. There are worse paths in life."

"Yeah, I know. I saw a couple of them."

You drink in silence for a few moments. Roger shifts uncomfortably in his seat. "So, ah, anything interesting in those notes?"

"Nah. I mean, it's a good refresher. It was a while ago, and I got shot by a tranquilizer dart right after I heard the tape. My memories were pretty fuzzy. This clarifies things."

"Good. Good."

After a few minutes, Roger leaves, half of the bottle still undrunk. You rifle through the notes a couple more times, searching for any further clues or hidden meanings, but nothing presents itself. Polishing off the rest of the wine, you go to bed. You lie awake for many hours, tossing and turning and staring at the ceiling, plotting out various constellations of what tomorrow might bring.

Oh captain, my captain!

A car arrives to pick you up at five in the afternoon the next day. After an hour or so of tortuous wending through the traffic of Hong Kong rush hour, you arrive at Lee's office tower. New functionaries usher you into the control room from the day before. More screens are lit now in addition to the two feeds from telescopes monitoring the lunar installations; there are a couple of other views of the moon at various magnification levels, CNN Asia occupies one monitor, while on three more screens are apparently feeds from cameras around some of the main public squares in Hong Kong. You recognize Statue Square and Exchange Square, the third you do not know. There is a buffet table set up with finger food, sushi and open-faced sandwiches, seared bits of beef and tuna, and various exotic fruits and nuts. Seemingly no one has touched any of it.

Lee and Roger are present, as well as the Colonel and a few other functionaries. A few bespectacled figures sit behind the terminals. You note Hal's looming presence in the corner. He has gained considerable weight, you note. You nod at him.

"Hal. Good to see you. Looks like crime does pay."

Hal gives you a thin smile. "Robert, me boy. It do be good to see you after many a moon. I been meaning to ask ye what you know bout the whereabouts of my daughter."

"As little as you do, hopefully."

Lee walks between you, breaking a fragile silence. "Enough, gentlemen. We are here to observe an historic moment." He has abandoned his customary tailored suit for jeans and a turtleneck sweater. He looks at you searchingly. "Robert. I assume you have reviewed Aurora's notes. Have you made any observations? Is there anything we should know before we proceed?"

"No sir. I didn't notice any discrepancies between her notes and my recollections."

"Well, there is nothing left but to cast the die. Robert, we've put you through much turmoil. Would you like the honor of initiating the sequence?"

"No, thank you. Igniting a weapon pointed at eight million people isn't anything I want on my conscience, if you don't mind me saying."

The Colonel coughs, and interjects. "I don't mean to presume, sir, but it would be a great honor for me to strike the first blow at those who would make Hong Kong a communist puppet state."

Lee nods munificently. "Go right ahead. The codes are at the terminal. We've set it up so it must be entered twice identically and simultaneously at each terminal before the transmission is sent."

The Colonel glides toward the terminal, his suit a silken rustle as he does. It is the same suit as yesterday, you note, though he wears a different shirt. He mutters a few words to the engineer at the terminal, who whispers something back. The Colonel straightens up, and sonorously pronounces in Lee's direction:

"Oh captain, my captain! Our fearful trip is done

The ship has weathered every rack, the prize we sought is won."

You notice Roger visibly rolling his eyes at this performance. Hal stifles a guffaw, ineffectively. Having concluded, the Colonel pauses a moment for some unclear reason; possibly he expects applause, or that someone is recording the moment for posterity. After a few seconds, he shrugs and rattles in a series of commands in the one terminal, faithfully repeated by his companion on the neighboring device. He strikes the concluding key decisively.

You scan the terminals. Nothing changes. You look at Roger, who is intently devoting himself to solving some sort of issue with his watch. Lee stands, legs akimbo, hands clasped behind his back, regarding the screens. You move discreetly toward him.

"What are we looking for," you ask, whispering for some reason.

"Well, Robert, we don't exactly know." He pauses, removes his glasses and rubs his eyes. "We've got one feed from the moon installations, we have CNN, some of the public security cameras around Hong Kong, audio feeds from security agencies..."

Two of the screens abruptly flare into a bright white. The technicians at the terminal start in surprise. Hal gives a low whistle of surprise. "Whal I'll be..." Lee clenches his fists in determined delight. Roger gives a whoop of joy. "You've done it! Amazing!" The Colonel gives a few claps of applause. "Wonderful!"

"Well, it's too early to say what is happening, but let's look..." The naked eye view of the moon reveals nothing, but there are shining pinpricks of light clearly visible at the higher resolutions which were not there before. Something has surely happened. Nothing is visible on the video feeds from Hong Kong, however.

"Hmmm," muses Lee. "It's odd. I would expect something to be visible on the ground. Not much maybe, but something."

Roger interrupts. "I have someone on the roof of the building with a photometer. Let me see if he's registered any change." He fiddles with the dials on his watch and speaks briefly into it. A voice crackles back. After a few more exchanges he lowers his wrist from his mouth.

"No change thus far. They will keep measuring. We knew there was a chance nothing would be visible to the naked eye. It doesn't mean the system won't have the heating effect we want. The infrared and ultraviolet spectra are more important than visible wavelengths."

"Of course, of course."

You pick a couple of pieces of tuna from the buffet table. Marinated in teriyaki and crusted with toasted sesame seeds, seared nearly black on the outside but left a dull red within, it is a simple but gorgeous dish. Roger sidles up to you and takes a spring roll.

"Good work, bud. We'll have to go celebrate."

"I don't see much to celebrate. I mean, I hope this works out as you plan, but it seems..."

The distinctive chime from CNN interrupts your discussion. "We interrupt our regularly scheduled programming for a special report."

The video cuts to a split screen, with the US anchor on the left and a nervous-looking male reporter standing in some kind of city square you do not recognize. While it is obviously night-time, a ghostly, bluish light illuminates the scene. "Live from Shanghai, China is our reporter Wen Jibao. Wen, what's going on?"

"Shanghai?" screams Lee. "Did she say *Shanghai?*"

Hal begins to guffaw with laughter. "Whoops. Looks like yer coordinates be a bit off, Colonel."

The Colonel fixes Hal, then you, with a murderous glare. "*You*...you little..."

Roger intercedes, a tight smile fixed on his face. "Now, now, I'm sure this is just a small glitch. A *fixable* glitch. Am I correct, Robert?"

You shrug. "You guys put in the codes, not me. It's not my fault you don't know how to type."

Hal continues to chuckle with mirth, and perhaps pride. "Hain't it obvious, Colonel? The boy's got nothing to do with it. Mah *daughter* gone an done a bait and switch on y'all. She done gone an burnt you purty good. At's mah girl."

The Colonel looks at Hal incredulously. "You're saying she switched all the codes? When? How? She was still driving when we caught her! There are dozens of codes here, it would have taken her hours..."

"Well, we don't know if she were driving the whole time now, do we? Or if she haint gone an met somebody."

You clear your throat. "Hey, let me see those codes. I think I remember at least a couple of them. I didn't check the other night, just assumed they were correct..." Lee gesticulates abruptly at the papers by the terminal. You sit and shuffle through them.

"Hmmm, I think I remember Riyadh for some reason ... it was 21 08 18 on the end. The other six digits are common. Here you have ... no, that's not it. Yeah, these are definitely wrong." Lee collapses into a chair, ashen faced. Roger picks up the papers and scans through them.

"Hey, Tokyo is listed as 18 08 21. She switched the coordinates from different cities. But the order is different."

Hal nods sagely. "Position neutral numerical code. Not sure why he'd do that. Mathematically, they easier to crack than fixed position. But he weren't a dumb man, no indeed. He had a reason, you can be sure o that."

"Well," you pipe up, "we can always aim it at Riyadh instead now, if you don't want a war with China."

"Fantastic idea, Robert," Roger grates, neatly bisecting a spring roll with white teeth. "Let's fry our company's largest customer off the map."

Hal furrows his brow. "Lemme look at those codes." He grabs the papers and purses his lips. He takes a pen form his pocket and begins rapidly scratching off numbers. "OK, these common ones ... eighteen, five, twenty-two, sixteen, eight, nine ... Well, they's alphanumeric, for one thing. Range is from 1 to 26 everywhere. The other three denote the city. Can't see a straight association though. R and H match up a bit to 18 and 08 with Riyadh, for instance, but assuming she's switched em up, Tokyo is the code at Riyadh, which she got at 09 14 04. Don't make no sense nohow, caint get TKY or TOK from that. I need more data points to find the key."

CNN is still broadcasting from the center of Shanghai. Crowds of people have gathered, necks craning up to look at the sky, wondering what the source of this weird, ethereal night-time light is. People do not seem to be panicking, as there is no obvious threat. They've managed to motivate an astronomy professor at some university on the west coast to get himself out of bed for commentary. *Well, obviously this is a completely new phenomenon for us which will require careful study...*

Lee is slouched in a chair, rubbing his eyes. "How long until they know the source, Colonel?"

"Well, I'm sure this has already been spotted by amateur astronomers. Presumably hundreds of them around the world have called into local authorities already that something odd is happening on the moon. People will start putting this together soon. The main question is who noticed the rocket launch and what they made of its trajectory. Anyway, I'd say we have hours, maybe days at best before the Chinese government figures out what's happened and its likely source."

As if on cue, CNN cuts to a video from somewhere of a high-resolution video of the moon. A brilliant light source can clearly be seen emanating from one pole. The astronomy professor perks up and begins nattering away, uninformedly but excitedly.

There is a soft knock on the door. An Asian woman, in a gray suit, opens the door cautiously. She addresses a few words to Lee. He rubs his eyes and sighs, pushing himself up from the chair with effort.

"The Prime Minister's chief of staff. That was faster than I expected. See what you gentlemen can do before I return. I'll hold off the wolves as best I can. I'll tell them it's the Chinese just shooting themselves in the foot as far as I know." He strides out of the door.

The Colonel prowls around the enclosed space like a trapped cougar. "Robert! Come on, son. Let's fix this. You must remember the code for Hong Kong! Think, boy."

"Actually, I think I do remember. Try these numbers." You rattle off some random figures. The technicians at the terminal dutifully punch them in. A flashing window appears. *Invalid code.*

"Oh, sorry. That seven should have been a nine."

The Colonel's brow furrows with concern. Roger's mouth forms a small O of surprise. Before they can say anything, the technicians at the terminals punch in the new figures. *Invalid code.*

The Colonel delivers a barrage of furious Mandarin at the technicians, who stand and back away from their keyboards as though they had transformed into venomous snakes. He reaches inside his suit jacket and pulls out his familiar pistol. Training it at your forehead, he stalks toward you.

"Think you're funny, eh?" He moves toward you, until the cold steel of the barrel presses against your forehead, a small circle of death. Out of the corner of your eye you note the header on CNN is now simply a one-word question: *ALIENS?*

"You know, Colonel, I'm starting to recall a few key items left out of Aurora's notes. One of them being that three false code entries leaves the system locked in its current constellation. We just managed two. Pull that trigger and you've got three choices after that: Tokyo, Riyadh or war with China."

The Colonel's eyes don't leave yours. "Hal, is there a code related to Shanghai in those papers?"

"Now, there's a thought, Colonel. Bit late in the game, but ... ah ha! There she be, indeed. Eleven, sixteen, oh five."

The Colonel barks at the technicians who immediately scurry back to their keyboards. Hal seems lost in thought, whispering to himself. As the technicians punch in the codes, he starts to life and shouts, "No, wait…"

Too late. *Code accepted*, the screen flashes. The Colonel looks at Hal curiously. "What's the problem, big man? It worked."

Hal snorts. "Worked? I bet it worked. Sixteen, five, eleven, P-E-K. Peking is the old name for Beijing, afore the commies done got hold of everything. Mark mah words, in about an hour CNN gonna start this same broadcast from Tiananmen Square isself."

Indeed, the mysterious spectral illumination of Shanghai's main square has vanished as suddenly as it initially appeared. The reporter jabbers inanely about what this might or might not mean, while the crowd slowly, perhaps disappointedly, disperses. The screens in the control panel go dark. Gunnar's robots are presumably mindlessly clambering over one another in the airless, radioactive lunar void to create a new ellipsoid of destruction, focused on a new target.

Lee emerges from the entryway, looking haggard and wan. "Well, apparently the Chinese government is not wasting much time coming to conclusions. They claim they know we are responsible, and if the system is not stood down immediately they will invade the island with overwhelming force."

Hal chimes in. "Well, Mr. Shan sir, good news is we got things off air in Shanghai. Ain't nothin shinin there now."

Roger glares at him with contempt. "There is bad news as well, I'm afraid, Uncle Lee. We have only succeeded in shifting the target. We believe Beijing will be illuminated in a matter of hours. We don't know how long."

Lee staggers as though he has suffered a physical blow. "*Beijing...*" he whispers, as if to himself. Roger continues in Mandarin, gesticulating at you and Hal. They have a few moments of animated discussion. Lee cradles his head in his hands. After a few seconds he regains his composure. Straightening himself, he brushes away imaginary dust from his sleeves.

"Gentlemen," he addresses you and Hal. "I will need to confer with my colleagues from our consortium. This is an unexpected development. One which perhaps can still be turned to our advantage, however. I will have you escorted to a secure location in the meantime." As if on cue, the elevator door opens and two bulky, formidable figures waddle out into the control room.

They lead you and Hal to the elevator and subsequently to different floors. You are shown into a nondescript studio apartment. It looks more like a cheap motel room than anything else. Couch, TV, bed, small table, bathroom, anonymous wall-to-wall gray carpeting. You open up the blinds of the window, revealing that you are a good twenty stories up in the air. The windows do not open, not an uncommon feature in office buildings in large cities.

You pour yourself a glass of water and turn on the television, flipping past the incomprehensible local channels to CNN. The mayor of Shanghai, a squat, bespectacled man, is giving an impromptu press conference. Understandably, at this point his answers mostly consist of rambling variations of "we don't know what happened, we need to investigate further, it does not seem to have had any health effects on anyone…" After this meandering performance, they fill in time by taking in reactions from around the world. Sizeable contingents of UFO believers are turning out in cities across the United States and western Europe. A young student with a nose ring and dyed pink hair in Salt Lake City holds aloft a sign reading "TAKE ME! Get me off this crummy planet!" Televangelists are beginning to rant about how it was a ray of angelic light sent by the Divine as a warning to the godless Chinese communists to mend their evil ways. The US government has thus far refrained from comment, though of course it is only 3 AM in Washington DC.

You flip around the other channels; with a few exceptions for the hideously violent movies typical of the region, mostly every channel is carrying some kind of live coverage of the weird phenomenon in Shanghai, though after about an hour of darkness a few are starting to migrate back toward regular programming. Even CNN, perennial inflator of any news to crisis proportions, begins to drift away. This has provided a welcome break from the interminable standoff in Kuwait, but it's hard to make news out of a momentary flash of grayish light. You flip to CNBC, where their new late-night host is busy with a weirdly self-deprecating monologue. That he seems to be able to get on television in spite of his goofy, elongated form and unmanageable shock of red hair provides you with some comfort.

You begin to doze off when another "breaking news alert" shocks you into wakefulness. As anticipated, another distressed looking reporter with Tiananmen Square as a backdrop, a weird, dirty light flooding down, turning the night into an ungodly bluish dawn. They are equipped with visuals now, showing a map of Beijing and the extent of The Shining, as they seem determined to christen it.

While it's now nearly ten in the evening, more senior officials from the Chinese government are beginning to appear to make statements. *While this does not appear dangerous, obviously it is an intolerable infringement of our sovereignty, yes we have suspicions who is behind it, no we do not believe it is aliens…* The main point of the conference seems to be to announce that they are moving their military forces to a high stage of alert, and particularly into positions "designed to prevent imperialist efforts to destabilize the Premier's One China policy," - presumably a reference to Hong Kong and Taiwan. The British, American and Australian navies have moved to a higher alert in response.

They move onto a story about a surge in panic buying beginning to occur across Asia, from Karachi to Manila. Hordes of people emptying stores of bottled water, batteries, flashlights. The Moonies in Korea have called a mass rally on the basis that The Shining is a sign from God that the Rapture approaches. There seem to be some rapidly snowballing side effects to this project appearing that you wonder if Lee has fully thought through.

There is a knock on the door. You open it. Roger is there, with a Styrofoam container. "Thought you might be hungry."

"Starving. Thanks." You sit on the couch and dig into the fried rice inefficiently with the provided chopsticks.

"Looks like we've started quite a ruckus," he comments.

You nod, your mouth full of rice. "Seems that the urban climate isn't the only precarious equilibrium out there." On CNN you note that a curfew has been declared in Beijing. Apparently, no one has told the vast crowds who have appeared on the streets, craning their necks toward the sky.

"Yes, this is what we were counting on. Uncle Lee has decided to take advantage of this unexpected turn of events and roll the dice, as it were. Those who own casinos are typically not gamblers at heart. But he and his friends have decided it's now or never. In time, China will only become stronger and more determined, the UK less resolute."

"So what happens now?"

"Well, the Chinese have delivered a new ultimatum to the governor of Hong Kong that someone on its territory is responsible and they have twenty-four hours to turn off the system and deliver those responsible to China for trial."

"I can think of more pleasant ways to spend the rest of my days."

Roger grimaces. "So can I. We delivered data to the Governor's office that supports the idea that this is a false flag attack, designed to provide a pretext for the Chinese to demand an early handover of Hong Kong. Hopefully they'll buy it. The rocket did emerge from China. This makes it hard for them to dispute, of course."

You munch on more rice, suddenly tasteless in your mouth. "So now what?"

"Now? We wait. The Chinese are starting to move their forces into a threatening posture. A US carrier battle group is steaming through the Straits of Malacca as we speak in response. The British are mobilizing from Diego Garcia."

"Jesus Christ."

"Exciting, isn't it? The US seems determined to show they're not so bogged down in Saudi and Kuwait that they can't still project power elsewhere."

"That's one word for it."

Roger gives a leonine yawn and stretches. "Well, we won't solve it tonight. Get some sleep. Sorry about the accommodation, but we'd all best stay on site." He exits with a bright smile.

Though not really hungry anymore, you finish the rice for lack of anything better to do. Flipping to CNN, you see troops have started to move into the ghostly streets of Beijing to enforce the curfew. Reaching for a last mouthful, you instead pick up a neatly folded piece of paper, oily grains of rice and bits of egg and onion stuck to its surface. You open it to reveal a short note, in neatly typed font.

Sit tight. Play dumb. Should be easy for you. We're coming.

You sit and stare at the note for a long time, turning it over in your hands, wondering what it might mean: a promise, a trap, or something else? You collapse onto the hard, lumpy mattress, tossing restlessly under thin sheets that do little to protect you from the relentless chill of the air conditioning.

Oblivion on an empty stomach

Early the next morning they escort you once again to the subterranean war room. Fortunately, there is a breakfast buffet set up. You sidle over to the creamy Danish pastries and buttery mini-croissants, topping things up with a healthy pile of herb-encrusted salmon gravlax and dragon fruit.

The Colonel nurses a cup of coffee reflectively, watching you with a calm, predatory glare. "Good appetite still. At least someone does. Nice to see."

"No reason to be bombed into oblivion on an empty stomach."

"Fair enough."

Munching on the croissant, you peruse the screens. Even in the daylight, the installations shine from the lunar surface like the North Star. CNN reporters on site in Beijing are wearing sunglasses at 8:30 AM. It does seem very bright for an October morning that far north.

"We should get a photometer there and start measuring," murmurs the Colonel.

Roger emits a tepid laugh. You had not noticed him slouched in a corner of the room. He wears the same clothes as yesterday. "We've had someone measuring since last night. We're not fools, Colonel. But we have no baseline. We're searching for any public records."

The Colonel nods sagely. "OK, but it's bright there, for sure."

"Yes. It's bright out there."

One of the technicians chimes in, clearly uncomfortable with his English. "Visual light understate effect. Infrared, ultraviolet, penetrate cloud cover with more effect. Heating impact more big than visual may indicate." He nods in relief.

The elevator doors slide open. Lee enters, flanked by two black-suited bodyguards. He settles into one of the office chairs. "Good morning, gentlemen. What's the situation?"

The Colonel gives a brief overview of the geopolitical situation, a summary of news reports, and a number of graphs you do not entirely understand, which apparently model the various amounts of excess sunlight projecting onto Beijing and the potential impacts on the microclimate. Even to your inexperienced eye, the projections seem to have alarmingly yawing variances even weeks into the future, let alone months.

Lee steeples his fingers, pursing his lips, and listens patiently. Once the Colonel concludes, he thanks him. "What about retaliatory capabilities? Can they knock out our installations?"

"Well, given time, certainly. The delivery technology is not complex, as we have shown ourselves. However, they will need to engineer a rocket capable of delivering a nuclear payload or massive EMP device to the moon, and make all the necessary calculations, build two of them, and successfully launch them, of course. They will need to proceed cautiously. A failed launch with a nuclear payload ... well."

Roger interjects. "Then there is the question of legality. The 1967 Outer Space Treaty would probably forbid any such strike. However, China is not a signatory, officially at any rate. It was signed by the Kuomintang government in Taiwan. China can plausibly claim not to be bound by this."

Lee waves his hand dismissively. "It's a matter of self-defense. No one will be interested in what some thirty-year-old treaty says."

"The Americans or Russians could use it as an excuse to shoot down any attempted counterstrike. Neither has any reason to make life easy for our friends in Beijing right now."

"Hmm."

"Our sources say the Chinese realize the nature of the threat. The heating won't be noticeable for a week or two, but according to all our projections the city will be uncomfortable by the end of November, and the center virtually uninhabitable by Christmas. Civil unrest will become a significant issue long before then of course as the population realizes what's happening, and begins to panic."

"They could ask the Americans to remove it," Lee observes.

"Yes, but why would they? From Washington's point of view, this is a rash military experiment gone wrong. Then there is the matter of national pride. The CCP will look like some of the greatest fools in history if they do not deal with this themselves."

"So, what are their options?"

"There are three. Absorb the pain until they have a countermeasure prepared, which they know may or may not work as they intend. Invade Hong Kong, and precipitate a war. They can take the island in hours or days, of course. But the retribution could be fearsome. Or... they can give in to our demands."

"Do they *know* our demands?"

"A regional governor got himself into a, shall we say, extremely compromising situation in one of our hotels in Macao. We made an arrangement with the Party to send him back quietly, on a private plane. He is in the air as we speak. He has been given a message to relay upon arrival, before his execution."

"Excellent."

"It would be extremely embarrassing for them to trace this message back to us, given the Governor's well-known ah, esoteric preferences. And equally well-documented, by the way."

"Obviously." He pauses, lost in thought, then adds as an afterthought, "This is good work, Roger. Really, very good work."

Roger nods his head slightly in acknowledgment.

Lee slaps his hands together and stands. "Well, gentlemen, it seems there is nothing to do but wait and see how things develop. I have a board meeting to attend. I am sticking to my regular schedule as much as possible to allay any suspicions here in Hong Kong that we are involved."

You spend the rest of the morning flipping around news channels. Crowds of people in Beijing in sunglasses, looking skyward in a vain attempt to catch a glimpse of the mysterious source of summery light in late October. Astronomers, military analysts, politicians. The Chinese government thus far refrains from any public accusations, but continues to shift military assets into striking distance of both Hong Kong and Taiwan. The US State Department speaks sternly against any unilateral action, delivering a particularly bald warning about the possible deployment of weapons of mass destruction into space. By this point the locations of the facilities on the moon have been pinpointed precisely, but there are no better visuals available than what you already have at your disposal. There are unconfirmed reports of a rocket launch out of earth orbit several months ago from Chinese soil.

Hal chuckles at this last. "Now *that's* a leak from our people. They saw that rocket and knew plum well where she were heading. Musta thought at the time it was a failed probe, whichus why no announcement bout it. Setting things up to make it look what the Chinese done gone an shot they own feet."

The breakfast buffet is replaced with sandwiches and snacks. Roger and the Colonel are called out by functionaries several times, bearing communications from Lee, his partners and other, unclear factions. The Chinese government apparently is negotiating a fine line with the US and UK embassies, at once vigorously trying to convince them they are victims of a foreign attack, but without delivering the proof that would demonstrate the source took place under their very noses.

"They naming names, ah wonder?" asks Hal.

Roger rubs his temples. "Well, not in so many words. But they have pointed the finger at Hong Kong, notwithstanding if it is a state-sponsored operation or private enterprise. The UK government knows it is not involved. The private concerns on the latter list who are capable of this is very, very short of course."

Another soft knock on the door. A slight girl delivers a thick manilla envelope, giving a slight bob of her head as she does so. She speaks briefly, softly to Roger. His eyebrows lift in surprise. Taking his seat, he murmurs to himself and rips open the envelope. Inside is a single CD in a clear plastic case. Roger holds it up to the light appraisingly.

"Hmm, better run this on a separate laptop or something. I wouldn't put it into the mainframe. Could have a virus." He speaks softly into his watch. Several minutes later, the same girl appears with a nylon computer bag. Roger plugs in the laptop and inserts the disk. There is one video file on it. He pushes play.

A man's bruised and swollen face fills the screen. He has been badly beaten. He begins to speak in Mandarin. Several of his teeth are missing or broken. A few splinters of enamel are still stuck to his lips.

Roger whistles. "Well, that's the regional governor we packed up for them in Macao. That didn't take long."

"What's he saying?"

"Uh…" he listens for a few moments. "Well, that there is only one fate for enemies of a unified, One China and the eternal Communist Party, their usual tripe…" The man is suddenly pulled away from the camera. A single gunshot rings out, startlingly loud. Everyone jumps in their seats. The man slumps over to the side slowly, until his head and torso disappear from the screen. The screen goes blank.

There is a moment of stunned silence. Hal chuckles softly. "Look like we gots our answer. Yes we do indeed."

"At least he got out of a trip to the organ farm," you comment.

The Colonel gives you an irate glance. "This isn't funny, Robert."

"Come on, it's a little funny. You know, sometimes I think you guys might have bitten off a bit more than you can chew."

Roger stands up and begins to pace back and forth. "This is just their opening negotiation tactic. Show strength. Frighten us. If they really intended to do anything, they wouldn't send a warning. They are just upping the ante, hoping we will panic and fold." His features are illuminated starkly by the huge, flashing screens of the control panel. You see that an urban climatology specialist is being interviewed on CNN, discussing the mechanics of urban heating, the efficiency of various visible and invisible bandwidths, and so forth. It hasn't taken long for others to catch on to the purpose of these installations, you note.

As Roger talks, there is a sudden dull boom from outside the building, then another, and another a few seconds later. You can even feel a slight tremor in the floor and desks. His face pales. Alarmed, he whispers into his watch. A voice crackles back. After a couple of exchanges, his shoulders slump.

"What is it?" you ask. "Sounded like bombs."

"That was what I was afraid of. Fortunately, those were only sonic booms. A flight of Chinese jets just buzzed the city."

"Hmm. That's all?"

The Colonel chimes in. "This is very serious, Robert. They penetrated the British air defenses. Basically dared us to shoot them down. Hopefully no one took the bait. One flight was obviously not a military threat. It's a warning that they mean business."

CRISIS IN HONG KONG appears on CNN in another breaking news report. The press appears to be starting to put two and two together regarding the strange events in China and the emerging military standoff in Hong Kong. The Governor of Hong Kong appears to make a brief statement to the effect that he knows nothing of the phenomenon affecting Chinese cities, that the city has neither the capability nor the motivation to execute such an attack, and suggests bluntly that this is either a botched initiative from the Chinese themselves, or a false flag attack. He makes a lengthy reference to the German invasion of Poland in 1939 under the pretense of a staged raid on a radio station as a similar example, which causes Hal to whistle in amusement. "Feller ain't pullin no punches, is he?" The UK and US release increasingly intransigent statements about Hong Kong's status as sovereign British territory, and making no mistake about their will and capability to deal with Saddam Hussein in the Gulf concurrently with any unlawful, irredentist activity in Asia.

Time passes quickly in the windowless, underground chamber. Lee drops by in the evening to confer quietly about strategy with Roger and the Colonel. After a few minutes, he leaves, considerably calmer than in previous meetings.

Roger shakes his head in amazement. "Lee never ceases to surprise, you know. What a gamble this has been! You know, they tried to convince Thatcher to take this step, back in '84 or '85. She wouldn't do it. Of course, if the Iron Lady wasn't willing to take on this fight, surely none of the weak-chinned clerks who succeeded her would have the stones for it. They needed to be forced to take a stand, and by god we might have done it!"

"What? Is there any news?"

"We intercepted some communications from the Governor's office to Whitehall. The Chinese have reached out. They are willing to explore 'amendments' to the 1985 Sino-British joint declaration if the system is shut off within days. Otherwise, they threaten some er, unspecified consequences."

"Deng told Thatcher to her face a few years ago he could take Hong Kong in an afternoon if he wanted to," remarks the Colonel, casually peeling the skin from a stubby, purplish banana. "They don't need to specify the consequences. They're pretty damn obvious." He chews delightedly on the banana, eyes closed reverently. "Why we don't import these Asian bananas to the US has always escaped me. Did you know, Robert, there are over a hundred distinct breeds of banana grown in the Philippines alone? Those ridiculous things you buy at home get fed to the pigs in Asia."

Hal stretches his vast arms. "Well, mebbe we should git some shuteye in that case, fellers. If the Chinese done be negotiatin wit the Limeys, hain't likely to start dropping bombs overnight."

The logic is incontrovertible. You decide to retire for the night, escorted by your lumpy, ill-suited guard. You lie on the couch for a couple of hours watching the rapidly gathering military and political storm on CNN before you go to bed, wondering what you have wrought.

Deeper, deeper

Another series of booms shake you awake. These are not jets miles away, you realize instantly, but concussive detonations close by. Very close by. You turn on the light. A bit of plaster dust floats down from the ceiling. There is a sharp rap on the door. You open it slightly. The Colonel, wild-eyed, pushes his way in. As he does, the lights snap off both in your room and the hallway. Greenish emergency floor lighting flickers into life in the hallway. You notice the Colonel steps across the prone form of the man guarding your room to enter. It is unclear if the guard is dead or unconscious. He shuts the door and grabs a chair, setting it under the handle to block entry.

"What's going on?"

"What's it look like? Visitors. Not friendlies." He has traded in his pistol for an ugly, snub-nosed assault rifle. He flicks on a flashlight mounted on the barrel. Opening a knapsack, he pulls out two gas masks. "Here, put one of these on and let's go. Upstairs they're using tear gas and stun grenades."

"Go? Where the hell do you want to go?"

"Control room. They've cut the power, but there are a couple of backup diesel generators. We need to get there before they do." He slides on his own mask, and pulls the chair from the door handle. Carefully sticking his head outside, he scouts the hallway, then looks back at you. "Come on! We'll have to take the emergency stairwell, the power's cut."

You make your way into the stairwell and begin to descend. You can hear clattering steps many floors above. There is a tinge of acrid smoke in the air, detectable even through the mask. "What do you want to do in the control room?" you shout. In the mask it feels as though this must be barely audible. The Colonel stops and looks back at you.

"Just punch in one more nonsense code. Like you said, that locks the arrays in place. At least we can make life difficult for them. They'll still need help from the US; maybe they'll take the chance to assure Hong Kong's independence."

"I made that up. That's not the way to freeze it," you say. The Colonel blinks at you slowly, the muzzle of his rifle rising to your sternum. You see a bright halo of light from his flashlight covering your breast.

"Excuse me? Now why would you do that, Robert?"

You reach out and tap the barrel of his gun. "This is why. I figured the more you knew the more likely it is I start to become a liability instead of an asset."

The Colonel glares at you. You hear from above a *dink – dink – dink* of metal bouncing on metal. "Get down!" he shouts, diving toward the floor himself. A floor or two above you, an impossibly loud explosion goes off. The shock of it reverberates through your bones. There is a strong taste of blood in your mouth, and you can feel claret dribbling from your nose. The world swims in front of your eyes. The Colonel fires a couple of brief bursts up the stairwell in response, the shots reverberating between concrete walls.

"Come on, let's go!" You continue down the seemingly interminable stairwell. Another projectile rattles down past you. You cower against the wall, but this one only emits a sharp *poof* as gas begins to billow forth. Waving your way through the smoke, you come to the entrance to the control room. You hear feet stomping down toward you. The Colonel releases another staccato burst of gunfire up the stairwell. A high-pitched scream echoes back toward you. He levels the gun at your chest again.

"Now Robert, convince me you know that code."

"Why? You'll shoot me if I give it to you."

"Two of us need to enter the coordinates simultaneously. Look, there's a passage from here to the harbor. I can get us both out of here. Or I can leave you here to the tender mercies of Chinese commandos. Decide now. We don't have much time."

The crashing din of approaching feet and shouting of approaching soldiers on the stairwell intensifies as you watch one another in silence. "All right. It's the same six base numbers, plus three zeroes. That's it. That locks it."

You stare at one another through the gas masks, condensation forming on the inside of both from your rapid, labored breathing. The incoming troops can only be two or three floors away. Finally, he nods curtly at you and stabs his finger at the keypad by the door. It opens and you move quickly in. Turning, the Colonel spatters the keypad on the inside with a few rounds from his gun. It explodes in a flash of sparks and smoke.

He rips off his mask. You follow suit. "That won't hold them for long. They'll have C4 charges with them. And I don't think they'll be too interested if there are any survivors left in here or not." He darts toward a terminal. You move to the second. The Colonel initializes the system and inputs his coordinates. You do the same. *Code accepted*, it notes calmly.

"OK, Robert, stand back." You move away from the terminal. The Colonel empties the remainder of his magazine into the terminals and screens, which erupt in a satisfying array of smoke and sizzling wires and electrical components. Kicking open one of the cabinets under a desk, he yanks out a dull gray module about the size of a shoebox, multicolored wires dangling from every side. He stuffs it in his backpack.

"Brains of the system. Don't know if that's of any use, but no point leaving it behind for these assholes," mutters the Colonel. Standing on a chair, he begins feeling around the joint between the far wall and the ceiling. Acrid smoke from the destroyed electronics makes you cough violently. You refasten your mask. Eventually the Colonel finds some hidden latch and with a barely audible click a door swings open. A narrow, dimly lit passage waits beyond.

"This way." You follow him through the door. He slaps a button on the wall and the door eases shut behind you. Replacing the clip in his gun, he shines the light down the hall. He notes your apprehensive glance at his weapon.

"Don't worry, Robert. Lee gave me instructions not to leave you – or your body – here for our Chinese friends to find under any circumstances. Too easy to identify. Too many difficult questions subsequently."

"Good to know. What's the plan?" You begin to jog down the hallway, your feet echoing off of dimly lit concrete.

"We'll grab one of those cigarette boats from the harbor. We'll regroup with Lee and his people in Macao."

"How far is that?"

"Forty miles, give or take."

You grimace at the memory of that endless, bile-sprayed journey from the mainland to Hong Kong. *Hopefully the sea will be calmer*, you think.

You don't know how far you jog until reaching the end of this dimly lit concrete corridor. A nondescript steel door marks its conclusion. The Colonel punches in a series of digits into the ubiquitous keypad. The door slides open without complaint, releasing an influx of cool salt air into the stale atmosphere of the tunnel. He flashes his light around through the door cautiously. There is no sound, save for the gentle whoosh of waves breaking steadily against the stone and sand of shore.

You creep through the exit onto a moonlit parking lot. You seem to have exited a false entrance to one of the hundreds of warehouses at the harbor. Cautious at first, but with increasing confidence, the Colonel moves catlike between the long buildings, making virtually no sound as he flits from shadow to shadow. After a few hundred yards, he halts by a dumpster that reeks of decaying fish. He peers carefully around the corner. You crane your neck, attempting to follow his gaze. A number of small boats bob gently in the waves.

"That's our ride," whispers the Colonel, pointing with his flashlight briefly at an elongated, low slung craft about fifty meters away. "Why don't you go out there to the boat. If they're going to ambush us, it'll be here."

"How about you take the lead? You have more training than I do."

"I'll keep you covered from here."

"Great idea. Thanks."

You gingerly creep across the uneven ground, strewn with empty cigarette packets and crushed bottles, and desiccated mollusk shells lying amidst the gravel that crunch loudly with each step. Every creak of the docks from the pressure of incoming waves makes you start; every splash of a buoy in the incoming tide seems like an enemy.

Eventually, you reach the dock and pad down to the familiar, elongated silhouette of the speedboat that ferried you from the mainland. Every moment, you expect the crack of incoming gunfire, which miraculously fails to materialize. Once you stand at the prow of the boat, the Colonel begins to make his cautious way among the shadows toward your position. As he arrives, he cautiously unties the ropes binding the boat to the dock, tossing the rope into the hull. He checks the fuel reservoirs.

"Excellent. Nearly full. Let's go."

The boat trundles quietly out of the harbor, the Colonel standing at the helm, peering left and right continuously as you slowly pass boat and buoy. Once you pass the end of the jetty, he accelerates, shifting gear after gear as the boat carves an ever-larger wake into the darkened surface of the bay. Once out of the bay, the Colonel allows himself a small smile and pushes the engine into high gear, skipping along the waves with the evil buzz of a giant aquatic hornet. Remembering the horror of the previous trip, you struggle toward the bow where the Colonel holds the wheel, gaze fixed on the horizon.

"You know where we're going?" you scream over the roar of the motor. The Colonel shrugs. "246 degrees south by southwest. It's a well-known heading for smugglers, thieves, and assorted misfits. We aren't the first people to flee Hong Kong for Macao in a motorboat, that's for sure." He glances at you. "This'll take about an hour. Why don't you have a seat. It'll be a bit bumpy. Not like last time, but it won't be smooth either."

You retreat to the back of the boat by the twin outboard engines. The smell is awful, but the swell seems to have somewhat less impact than up in front. You hang on to the handholds, swaying back and forth as the boat skips over the surface of the darkening sea.

After twenty minutes, the boat begins to slow. The engine nearly cuts out, and the bow noses back toward the surface of the sea.

You stand, unsteadily. "What's going on?" you shout at the Colonel.

For a moment he keeps his gaze fixed on the horizon, then wheels toward you. The snub nose of his gun points toward your abdomen. He gazes at you implacably, eyes hidden in the shadows, silver hair illuminated by star and moon.

"Like I said, Lee only instructed me not to let the Chinese find your body. We're far enough offshore. The sharks will find you before the coast guard does." He pauses. "I'm sorry, Robert. You didn't do anything to deserve this. Any of this."

Now that the engine has cut out, something else is audible. The unmistakable *thump thump thump* of an approaching helicopter, not far away. The Colonel curses, pointing his gun toward this incoming threat. He turns on the flashlight. In response, an overwhelming halogen flood illuminates him at the con. Instinctively, he raises the gun to shield his eyes from the overpowering beam.

Without thinking, you dive from the stern of the boat into the choppy seas, struggling to push yourself further and further down into the depths. You feel the impact of bullets slamming into the water by your feet.

Deeper, deeper. There had not been time to take a deep breath. Your lungs scream in agony.

Deeper.

Stop, your lungs command pitilessly. You struggle toward the surface, breaking through with a desperate gasp. You wipe the seawater from your eyes so you can see.

To your left you hear the rattle of automatic gunfire. The Colonel stands at the boat's gunwale, half kneeling, weapon trained at adversaries above. The flashlight on his rifle half illuminates a helicopter hovering seventy or eighty meters off the stern of the boat. Rounds from his gun cause sparks to fly from the fuselage of the craft. After a few seconds, a much heavier caliber weapon opens fire in response. Dozens of geysers spout into the air from the water around the boat. Holes the size of softballs begin to dot the hull. The Colonel disappears in a sudden mist of flesh and bone, dead before he even has time to scream.

A searchlight appears in the fuselage of the helicopter, probing the smoking wreckage of the boat and its environs. The light, impossibly bright, begins to make rapidly expanding concentric circles around the craft. After a few seconds it captures you taking an involuntary gulp of seawater. You spit out the metallic, salty taste. It remains trained on you; you sense the helicopter shift its position toward yours. You swim away, wildly, hopelessly; after a few seconds the thumping pressure of rotor blades is directly above you. You continue to swim away with all your might.

A few meters away, you hear a splash in the water. Instinctively, you dive back into the darkened depths. After a few seconds, your lungs failing, you resurface. A hand grasps your shoulder. You flail wildly against this unexpected opponent. In seconds, heels deftly find their way around your waist, serpentine arms encircle your shoulder and neck, pushing you beneath the waves. Helpless, you bob beneath the surface, chest screaming futilely for air. Your mind is oddly calm, reconciled to the fact that, after all this, the end has finally arrived.

Your captor releases your legs and allows you to surface, You take a great, ragged gasp of air. The figure bobs next to you, insectoid like mask regarding you unforgivingly. You begin to aspirate in panic. A gloved hand emerges from the black waves and pulls away the mask. You recognize the angular cheekbones and alarming blue eyes of the girl who was with Aurora in the club in Hong Kong, seemingly an eon ago.

"God, you're even dumber than she said you are. Relax. Stop trying to drown yourself. Who did you think this was? Come on. We're going home."

The future is bright

The girl's name is Inese, she shouts at you over the din of the helicopter engine. She claims to work for the NSA. The Special Collections Service, she informs you seriously.

"What do you collect that's so special?"

"Sigint, usually. Today, you."

"Well, thanks for that. Where are we going?"

"Home base. The USS *Bunker Hill*."

She leans back into her seat and closes her eyes. You shift your bedraggled body around the uncomfortable plastic seat. Someone gave you a blanket after winching you on board, but you still shiver uncontrollably, nevertheless. Out the window you see the moonlit waves, uncomfortably close, seemingly only a few meters beneath your craft.

Fortunately, the frigid, nerve-wracking trip is mercifully short. In several minutes you land on the upper deck of what seems to be a formidably sized navy ship. You begin to believe there is a chance the girl has not been lying to you. Faking a uniform and insignia is one thing. Faking a functional warship is something else entirely.

A small crowd of people awaits, shielding their eyes from the gale of the approaching aircraft. As you disembark, a small, familiar figure darts toward you. "Robbie!" Aurora leaps at you and embraces you fiercely, laughing hysterically, hanging onto your neck like a small child.

You are taken aback by the sudden, unexpected encounter. You return the embrace gingerly. "Oh, hey, uh, good to uh … so, what's so funny, anyway? Do I look that bad?"

Aurora buries her face in your chest and shakes her head. In between howls of laughter, she struggles to get words out. "Just a coping mechanism … sorry … beats crying. I figured that out… a long time ago." In spite of yourself you begin to laugh as well.

"Not the worst idea you ever had." This causes you both to explode with gales of hilarity for some reason, leaving you gasping for breath. The remainder of the party has approached cautiously, unsure what to make of the frantic mirth of this strange reunion.

"Ah hem, excuse me, folks…" A man, early forties, in a navy uniform addresses you. "Commander Carl Williams. Welcome aboard, Robert. Let me be the first to say, you've been a credit to your family, and to your country." He offers his hand. Extricating yourself from Aurora's manic hug, you shake the proffered hand. A considerably taller, lanky man with longish, curly blonde hair and an impish smile, dressed in civilian clothes, offers his hand as well.

"Robert. I am Sergejs. A friend of your uncle's." He speaks with a slight accent.

"I remember the name."

"You have already met my daughter." The fierce-eyed blonde, still in her wetsuit, stands behind you. She nods coolly.

"Yes, she was nice enough to fish me out of the water."

He laughs. "She is quite the fisher of men. I represent the United States National Security Agency in this matter."

"I thought you were the No Such Agency? All of a sudden I can't swing a dead cat without hitting one of you guys."

Sergejs' eyes light up with delight. "Ah, shades of the uncle. It warms my heart. Come, let's go inside. You surely have many questions."

The Commander speaks. "Go ahead and use my quarters, Sergejs. I'll have some food and dry clothes sent up. I have some matters to attend to on the bridge."

A brisk walk through a series of mazelike corridors and the occasional sailor eyeing you with curiosity leads to the Commander's private rooms. Unsurprisingly, on a boat designed to be lean and lethal, they are not exactly luxurious. A cramped room with a dining table for six people, a small television, and a door leading to a tiny bedroom. There are windows through which you see the moon hovering dutifully above the sea, possessed of a dull, angry orange color.

You start to take a seat but Aurora marches up to you, looking you squarely in the eye. She wears a pair of ragged jeans and an impossibly oversized, green sweater. "Give me another hug, dummy." Awkwardly, you put your arms around her. She starts to giggle uncontrollably. You feel her hot breath in your ear. "I'm sorry I was such a dick to you, man."

You push her away. "You were. Why?"

Aurora wipes her eyes carefully with the sleeve of her sweater. "You have this habit of talking before you think. Which in most situations is kinda charming. But in this case, we needed deception. The idea you were gonna lie with a straight face to these people for months was a bit of a stretch, to be honest."

A momentary flash of offense is extinguished by Aurora's lupine grin. "Well ... OK, I gotta admit, that's kinda hard to argue with."

Sergejs pulls a bottle from his backpack and finds a few glasses in a cupboard on the wall. "Let us celebrate your safe return, and successful completion of your mission. A small drink. This is from my homeland. We call it *slivovitz*. It's a kind of, ah, plum brandy, I guess you would say."

You take a seat, settling into the padded chair with relief. "I heard the accent. You on an NSA exchange program with Ukraine, or what?"

Sergejs chuckles. "I am from Riga. My family is Latvian. We fled the Soviets when I was a boy. I became a codebreaker for the NSA. That is where I met your uncle, many years ago."

"He said the NSA would turn him into an unfortunate statistic if they ever found out about his work."

Sergejs laughs as he pours out three robust glasses of a clear liquor from his unmarked bottle. "Your uncle always did love his four-dimensional chess. No, he worked for us in Alaska. We recruited him when he was in the Coast Guard. Everyone thought he had a harmless side business in diving to poach sea urchins for their roe; he was actually planting NSA underwater listening stations in Soviet territorial waters from a little inflatable Zodiac he had hidden on his patrol boat. *Priekā!*" He downs his glass. You take a sip from yours. The liquid is a fiery, fragrant, fruity liquor that nearly makes you gasp.

"He actually made quite a bit of money on those sea urchins, by the way. Anyway, I actually met him on a meteorological modeling project. We wanted to see what the impact of global warming would be on opening up Arctic shipping lanes for deployment of naval forces. We stayed in touch after he retired."

There is a knock on the door. A sailor, an African American man hardly older than you, carries a tray of food and a bag of clothes. With a smile, he places the tray on the table and the bag on one of the chairs. You take the bag and retreat into the captain's quarters. You strip off your soggy clothing with relief. The replacement is a beige tracksuit and gym shorts and shoes. The feeling of dry clothes on your chilled body is heavenly.

Aurora and Sergejs have spooned out food onto three plates. Overdone pork chops, mashed potatoes and peas. While something of a step down from what Lee's coterie of executive chefs regularly produced for you, it is a relief to have such humble fare after months of exotic meals. You are ravenous, you realize. You have no idea what time it is.

"OK, so what happened?" you manage to enunciate through a mouthful of pork.

Sergejs looks at Aurora. She shrugs. "Right, I'll begin. Your uncle kept in touch with us and gave us periodic updates on his work. He wanted funding, actually, but none of the higher-ups believed in his project. About two years ago, he started to get awfully paranoid that he was being watched. I mean, it wasn't implausible. The Soviets did watch a lot of people like him. The Chinese, and Israelis to some extent, have begun to fill the void they left when they collapsed.

"So, he sets up this system, part of which you saw. He gave a few people he trusted access to some monitoring systems. His biometric watch. The GPS on his car."

Aurora interjects, poking disconsolately at a pile of potatoes with her knife. "That's how he found me. I was motoring along the I90 outside Utica when this black helicopter forced me off the road. Thought I was done for. Then this goofball…" she nods at Sergejs, who juts out his tongue at her saucily. Aurora catapults a pea at him from her fork. "This goofball jumps out of the helicopter, gets in the car with me and is like, OK, let's drive and you tell me your story."

Sergejs continues. "It was a big risk, but the bosses let me commandeer a copter and run with it. There was obviously a strong Asian connection. Hal is ex-CIA. He was undercover in the cargo ship industry in the 1970s. His job was to recruit people like Lee to feed us information. Hong Kong, Indonesia, Malaysia, India, all over. Apparently, Lee and his people were desperate enough about the impending handover to do some reverse recruitment, looking for something, anything, that might stop it. It seems that something leaked from my organization to someone in the CIA. Similarly, to your uncle; Hal had kept up his contacts with friends in the Agency. He got wind of the project, and started renting the place across the street to see if your uncle's ideas had legs. Once he realized what it was, he sold the idea to Lee."

"Who already had a sort of organization ready to act on this with his weapons research facility in China," you muse.

"Yes, Lee's not dumb. He has his Plan A, but he also has Plan B, C, D, etcetera. Plan C was 'if you can't beat them, join them', delivering non-lethal crowd control tech to the Chinese as part of the takeover."

"I wonder what Plan D is?"

"Whatever it is, he's seething in one of his casinos in Macao right now and starting to work on it."

"What happened to Hal, by the way?"

"The Chinese have him. They will trade him for a couple of their spies at some point. Then we'll figure out what to do with him."

Sergejs pours another round of his Baltic firewater. The second goes down markedly easier than the first.

"At any rate, the shit really hit the fan once we pieced together what was happening. Aurora and I worked up a set of fake notes, and I exited, assuming Hal and his people would grab her eventually. This was on my own recognizance. Making a unilateral decision to leave two minors in the hands of an international terrorist organization was not, ah, universally applauded, let's say. But at that point, the brass couldn't do much except say ok, let's see how it all plays out. They still didn't believe a rocket carrying anything workable was ever going to leave the atmosphere."

"But then it did."

Sergejs breaks into a wide smile. "Yes, it did, and by god the old man's mad idea actually worked. Which changed the situation drastically. Instead of my supervisor laughing at me, suddenly I was on conference calls with the Secretaries of State and Defense, the British ambassador and the NATO emissary." He gives a loud hoot of laughter.

"So, we realized we were probably putting the Chinese in a tight spot in terms of how we switched the codes. The speed of their reaction surprised us, though. They were really ready to invade Hong Kong in a matter of hours. They knew perfectly well who was behind it. So we made them a deal. We'll get the system off one way or another, they make significant compromises to the Basic Law after the handover, and we never publicize proof that the initial rocket left Chinese soil. The only question was when we executed our operation, what would you do?"

Aurora intervenes. "We decided to give the Colonel enough time to get you to the control room. But we didn't know if you'd lock down the system, or move the targeting to the geosynchronous orbit. Thank god you did the second."

"We?" you ask. "I thought you were in the same situation as I was, stuck in school with bodyguards watching you every time you went to take a crap."

"I was. But I had a friend who helped me escape."

Sergejs chimes in. "We had the Latvian ambassador enroll Inese into the school where Aurora was, claiming it was his goddaughter. She managed the extraction when the time was right. The Latvians are keen to get into NATO, you know. They'll do more or less anything at this moment, while the bear still sleeps."

"So how did you know what I did?"

"We could intercept and decipher the commands, but not influence them," explains Sergejs. "We were hoping you'd be smart enough not to lock the beam on Beijing. We were ready to take out the installations with EMP missiles if need be, but that's difficult, obvious, and of course renders the whole installation useless for the future. We're not at all sure we can replicate it."

You stop chewing a mouthful of potatoes and peas. "The future? What do you mean?"

Sergejs laughs. "Oh yes, the future is bright, my boy. Very bright. Look, why don't you get some sleep. You've had a hell of a day. We'll fly you to Los Angeles tomorrow. Your mother is already en route and dying to see you. But there are other people who want to meet you as well. You've got a busy couple weeks ahead of you."

"Super busy, dummy." Aurora flicks a pea at you, which bounces off of your forehead and back onto your plate. You look out the window. Dawn's first fingers are slowly beginning to peel apart the darkness of the horizon like an orange. A wave of exhaustion washes over you.

"You know, I think … I could actually use some sleep." Aurora and Sergejs half support you, half drag you to another compartment and lay you down in a bunk where darkness overcomes you in moments, the sea rocking you to sleep with its crashing lullaby.

Epilogue

The plane descends from sunny skies to a small airport, a rectangular nugget of concrete nestled in an unending sea of yellowing, long-since harvested cornfields. Peering out the window, there is really nothing except this unending sea of brown, interspersed with a few patches of white snow. You settle back into plush leather seats. A hostess walks the few steps toward you. She speaks with an incredible midwestern twang. "We'll be landing shortly, hon. Could you put your seatbelts on for me? Thank *you*." These last vowels are drawn out interminably.

"This sure beats commercial," comments Aurora. She looks stunning, as usual, in her torn jeans and leather biker jacket over a pink blouse. In a fit of nervousness you'd bought a cheap suit in Los Angeles, a far cry from the Brionis to which you'd become accustomed back in Hong Kong.

"Not to mention the rickety Chinese military cargo planes." You tug at your collar. "This was a stupid idea."

"Don't worry, you look great." She bursts into laughter. "Actually, you look like a waiter at a cheap restaurant. But relax. Attitude's half the battle. Come on, thumb war." She holds out her coffee-colored fist, thumb extending toward the ceiling. You grasp her hand. She beats you easily, twice, black lacquered fingertips pinning you firmly.

"Cheater."

The aircraft taxis to a halt. You stand up and stretch your arms. The hostess approaches you with a wide smile. As the only two passengers, she doesn't have much else to do. "I hope you two had a nice flight. We're just moving the stairs up so you can get off. Give us a sec. Your ride is waiting for you on the tarmac."

After a few moments, you disembark, bags clutched in your hands. An unexpectedly frigid wind whips across the barren landscape. The collar of your coat leaps up and smacks you on the cheek. You hurriedly trot down the mobile staircase that has been driven up to your plane. At the base waits a long Lincoln Town car with tinted windows, its engine humming audibly, a plume of exhaust rising in the frigid air. A tall, thin man in a gray suit, wearing sunglasses in spite of the low light, greets you at the base of the stairwell.

"Good afternoon. Welcome to Omaha. Can I take your bags, folks?" Without waiting for an answer, he grasps them and places them carefully in the trunk of the car. He opens the back door of the limousine. You slide in next to Aurora.

Inside waits a gnomish-looking old man, well into his sixties, in a navy blazer, with accompanying blue dress shirt and red tie. His bulbous features and wisps of snowy white hair spouting at odd angles reminds you a great deal of Gunnar. He smiles at you genially, breaking into the same midwestern dialect as the stewardess.

"Robert and Aurora, if I'm not mistaken? Aurora. Such a lovely name. So nice to meet you." He extends his hand. You each shake it in turn. The car slides into gentle motion.

You clear your throat. "I've heard so much about you, sir. This is such an, er, honor…"

The man interrupts you with a wave of his hand. "I assure you, the honor is mine. I've been told what you've been through to get to this meeting. What a remarkable, even extraordinary, story! I know that it's been not without adventure, great danger, and…" He extends a hand and places it on your knee, looking you in the eye, twinkling blue eyes suddenly sad and serious. "…and, I am also aware, that you have sustained considerable personal loss on this journey. For which you have my deepest condolences."

Tears sting your eyes. This was not the conversation for which you had prepared.

Aurora thankfully interrupts. "That's very kind of you to say, sir. Thank you so much."

"Now, I don't suppose you're hungry? We have many, many things to discuss. If there's one thing I sure hate, it's doing business on an empty stomach. If you'd care for a bite to eat, there's an absolutely fantastic Dairy Queen just two exits from the airport that I can highly recommend…" He rummages around the pockets of his jacket. "You know, I might just have some coupons, somewhere in here…"

Aurora smiles brightly. You still do not trust yourself to speak. She glances at you, then back at your host. Her hand makes its way casually across the seat and finds yours, fingers interlocking with yours. She gives a tight squeeze. "That sounds absolutely perfect, sir," she announces. "Nothing would make us happier after all this than some good old fashioned Dairy Queen."

The man's face breaks into a worn, crinkly, kindly grin. "Well, that's settled then. Let me just tell the driver…" He raps on the window separating you from the front of the car, and dictates instructions. You lean back into the plush leather of the seat and exhale. You look at Aurora. Calm brown eyes gaze back into yours. She gives your hand another squeeze, and smiles.

"Gunnar would be proud," she mouths silently.

You nod. Yes, he would, you think. He would indeed.

© Colin Shea

Děčín, 2022

Manufactured by Amazon.ca
Acheson, AB